Devine Legacy Series, Book 2:

Army Rising

C.J. Peterson

Texas Sisters Press, LLC

ISBN: 978-1-952041-15-0

Published by Texas Sisters Press, LLC. Lufkin, TX U.S.A.

Texas Sisters Press, LLC.
2020

Second Edition

This book is dedicated to my loving husband and dear family who love and support me. You all mean more to me than you will ever know. Thank you! I love you!

A portion of the proceeds of this series will go to Airborne Angel Cadets of Texas – a non-profit group of hardworking volunteers who send care packages to our soldiers overseas. You can find them at: http://www.airborneangelcadets.com

To learn more about C.J. Peterson, you can find her online at:

http://cjpetersonwrites.com/

'While the stories are fiction, the journey is real!'

<u>Summary</u>

As the A.N.G.E.L.s gather their forces, so does the other side. Though they were dealt a blow at Black Rock, the Unnaturals are more determined than ever to exterminate the A.N.G.E.L.s, who have been a thorn in their flesh since the ascension of Christ.

Are the A.N.G.E.L.s ready for the battle or is the next generation in over their heads? Have all of the issues within their unit been fixed, or will they implode? Find out in *Army Rising*, the next adventure of the *Divine Legacy Series*.

Ephesians 6:12 – *"For we wrestle not against flesh and blood, but against principalities, against powers, against the rulers of the darkness of this world, against spiritual wickedness in high places."*

Table of Contents

Chapter 1
Plans to Give You a Hope and a Future

As the plane landed in Ireland, Mark English's words at the Safe Haven ran through Rachel's mind, "You were all called for a reason. You were called to fight the good fight for the Kingdom. This is not a position that will land you with fame and fortune. You'll never be on television, nor will you be a startling success in the eyes of the world. You will not lead a normal life in this job. You will operate in the shadows. But, you will receive blessings beyond measure for what you do. There's a new army rising up all over this world – The Lord's Army. You are all a part of this. Your job is to bring those into this to help others. The Spirit has given you an assignment. You are to free those who are bound in spiritual chains. You will help provide what is needed for those who are His. You will fight some literal battles, as well as spiritual ones. You will literally take on the gates of Hell. I will caution you in this, and I pray you heed my warning. Do *not* underestimate the other side. Don't think for a moment that Black Rock was a victory. You may have woken a sleeping giant when you attacked the den. They will be waiting around every corner. They will do their best to stop whatever it is that the Lord God Almighty wants you to do. This will be a race for lives, while trying to stay alive yourselves. The rewards will be great, but the cost will be tremendous. Amber and Terrik have already paid a portion of the price. There will be many people you will meet along the way. Sometimes you will get there in time to help.

Sometimes you will not. Know whatever you choose on this day, there will be no turning back. If you choose to go, you are potentially volunteering for your death. You *will* be marked. Satan would like nothing better than to take you out. He has had a lot of time to study you. He knows you better than you know yourself. Having said all of that, I feel each of you are here for a purpose. I feel you were each brought here for such a time as this. The Kingdom needs you. They need your training and expertise. You have been called. What is your answer?"

"Here am I. Send me," the group said in unison.

"Then, here are your tickets," he said handing Angel and Rachel their team's tickets, "The Lord reminds us in Luke 10:2 that, '*The harvest is plentiful, but the workers are few. Ask the Lord of the harvest, therefore, to send out workers into His harvest field.*' You are part of those workers. You leave in the morning. Get a good night's sleep. You're going to need it."

*   *   *

Knowing it was an encouragement, as much as a warning, Rachel held those words close to her heart as the tired and groggy team trudged over to claim their baggage at the airport in Cork, Ireland, before picking up the van they'd rented. Once everyone was loaded in the van, they headed to their hotel. Rachel, who was team lead, had chosen a hotel away from the airport. It was near a river on two main crossroads. Using those landmarks, she knew it would be easy to find the hotel, thanks to a warning from Mark. Before they left, he explained to Rachel that the streets and address numbers in Ireland were few and far between, so the best thing for Rachel to do was to find something on main roads, using landmarks to find their way around. How they were to find their next team members would be the issue. Three of their new members were in Cork. Finding Joe and Val were a piece of cake compared to how this would work.

Mark was Angel, Jon, and Jesse's father, and one of the few older A.N.G.E.L.s left. He and his wife, Casey, live in a house in Nevada that was nicknamed The Safe Haven. God set a hedge of protective angels to watch over the central housing of Rachel and Angel's teams, and the few members left from the American A.N.G.E.L.s in the English home. This gave them a singular place in the world they knew was protected for them - a place of rest. In Derek (another of the older A.N.G.E.L.s) and Mark's many years in the Air Force in Special Operations, they had many missions throughout the world, and often passed their wisdom and experience onto the new teams.

"Do we have an extra bed in the room?" Rachel asked the desk clerk when they checked into the hotel.

"Of course. It's up there as requested. You are a lovely group of young people. I don't expect t' have too much trouble with ya, yeah?" the older clerk asked, looking at them over her wire-rimmed glasses.

"No, ma'am," Rachel assured her.

"Just be quiet-like, yeah? There are others here as well."

"Yes, ma'am," Rachel said, accepting the key to the room. The spare twin-sized bed would be Rachel's. Since Jesse was so muscular, he would have one queen-sized bed, while Jacob and Joe would share the other one. It would be close quarters for a while. They had to go easy on the money in their travels.

"Well, this is *lovely*," Joe said, in a fake Irish brogue he'd been practicing since they'd landed.

"You forgot to add the 'like' or 'yeah' at the end of your sentence, Joe" Jacob pointed out, setting his bag on the dresser. "I feel like I'm in the eighties."

Chuckling, Jesse reminded him, "There'll be a lot we're going to have to figure out. Language quirks will be the least of them."

"So, where do we start?" Joe asked with his usual Texas drawl, as he sat on the bed. "I have to admit that I really like what I've seen so far, and am looking forward to seeing more of Cork."

"Cork has a lot of history. While we're here, I would like to look around a bit," Jesse said. With Jesse being a graphic artist, his eyes immediately went to the picturesque settings, and the thousands of years of history throughout the country. "I would hate to come to such a beautiful country, and miss checking out the cool structures. I'd like to do some drawings here."

Putting her bag at the end of her bed before she sat down on it, Rachel said, "Unfortunately, we're not here as tourists."

"Do you have a plan in finding them?" Joe asked.

"I have an idea. They're our age, right?"

Stretching out on his bed, Jacob yawned as he agreed, "Right."

"Well, if you are our age, and tend t' work with computers, where would you likely be?" Rachel asked the group.

"What kind of computers? Are we talking hackers?" Joe asked.

Rachel acknowledged, "That's a strong possibility. These are supposed to be our support team members. Unfortunately, we don't have a lot to go on."

"Seriously?" Jesse asked. "Dad sent us here without a plan?"

"He said God would lead us to who we need t' find," Rachel explained, her Australian accent still thick, even though she had been out of Australia for several months. "When I asked him about it, he said that God had a way of bringing those to us who we need to find.

"What about a cyber café or college?" Joe asked.

"Good start. There are a couple colleges in this area. The one I'm thinking of is in a section called Bishoptown. I reckon that's where we'll start…tomorrow. I don't know about you blokes, but I'm exhausted," she said, falling back onto her twin bed.

"Hate to pull a page out of my brother's playbook, but what about eating first?" Jesse asked, resting his hand on his stomach as it growled for the umpteenth time since mid-flight.

"Good idea," Jacob said, his stomach rumbling at the mention of food. "Plane food stinks."

After they freshened up, the group headed down to the desk to speak with the clerk again. "What can I do for you lot?" the older clerk asked. To Rachel, she reminded her of a grandmother type.

"Well, we're a hungry bunch," Jesse explained. "Is there somewhere around here that has good, hearty food? We'd like to have something that's more local than commercial if we could."

"Oh!" the lady exclaimed, pleased to have them seek her advice, "I know just the place." With a gentle, but excited smile on her face, she leaned forward, motioning for Jesse to lean closer. When he did, in a low voice, she said, "My son's best friend's step-mother's cousin has the best little pub in the area."

Chuckling, Jesse said, "I *think* I followed that. Care to share where this spectacular secret is hiding?"

"Ahhh, that, boy-o, is the beauty of it! Ya see, it's only a few blocks from here. It may look dark and scary, but it has the best food in town, and only the locals know about it."

Leaning on the counter as the lady stood taller, Jesse smiled and said, "Now *that* sounds like the perfect place for us."

Pulling out a map, the lady drew the way through the streets with a highlighter. When she finished, she explained, "Okay, it's right here. You can't miss it."

"Wonderful! Can we bring something back for you?"

"Oh, aren't ya a sweet one! A shepherd's pie would hit the spot on such a chilly night."

"Consider it done," Jesse said, picking up the map. "Since you shared your secret with us, it's the least we can do."

*   *   *

As they stepped into the pub from the drizzling rain, and Rachel's eyes adjusted, she immediately understood why it seemed so dark. The lights above the cherry wood tables and bar had stained glass shades with green Celtic symbols in a thick, white setting. The traditional Celtic music played quietly in the background, while the televisions were set to various sports going on in the area. As always, the team chose a table in the center, which allowed them to see all points within the tiny pub for safety purposes.

The heavenly scent of food cooking, mingled with the strong aroma of beer. The laughter and chatter of those seated throughout the little pub echoed from all corners. There was definitely an air of familiarity among those playing pool or sitting at the bar, while others were nestled in tables around the pub, talking and laughing.

Rachel cringed as she scanned the menu. There wasn't a low-carb meal to be seen. "I see the Irish like their potatoes," she commented with a sigh.

"Probably to put meat on their bones to keep them warm. That drizzle outside may be light, but it soaks ya to the bone," Joe said with a shudder.

"How do we order?" Jacob asked, looking around.

"Pretty sure we do it at the bar," Rachel explained.

"Okay. So, do we make a list and send a representative?" Jesse asked.

Pulling a piece of paper and a pen from her tiny purse, which had a strap that crossed her body, Rachel volunteered, "I've got it. What does everyone want?"

After everyone gave her their order, she went to the bar to order the food. She took a deep breath when a male waiter approached her. While she enjoyed hearing the Irish brogue spoken, she knew the moment she, or any of those with her opened their mouths, they would be labeled as outsiders. She didn't mind, though, the people seemed friendly enough. As she gave him their order, she prayed God would help them find the people they were looking for, knowing they didn't have much to go on.

Due to Rachel's spiritual gift of being able to see by the brightness or darkness of a person if they were Christians, seeking God, or from the other side, she took a good look around. From what she could tell, the people in the bar were split evenly between those who were the Lord's, and those who were not His. At least none were from the other side, meaning one of Satan's legions. Glancing toward her right, she noticed a young lady who was exceptionally bright, and wondered if she was one of those they were searching for. Filing it the back of her mind, she shoved her hands in her pockets as she made her way back to the table.

When their waiter brought their food to the table, Rachel's eyes just about popped out of her head. "That's a *lot* of food! Is this all mine?"

"A thin bird like you?" the waiter chuckled. "Yeah. You need to put some meat on your bones, lass. It gets cold-like in these parts."

"Well, it *is* chilly," Rachel said, slightly blushing. "Thank you."

"Have t' ask. Where ya from?" The waiter asked. "I hear a couple different accents, yeah?"

"I'm from Texas," Joe said proudly.

"I'm from Nevada in the States," Jesse said before taking a bite of the fresh bread.

After clearing his mouth from the shepherd's pie, Jacob added, "Me too. Nevada."

"And I'm from Australia," Rachel finished.

"Brilliant! What a diverse group. Are you here for uni-like reasons?"

"No, sir." Rachel shook her head. "We're looking for some friends of ours."

"Really? Who?"

"The Claire, Callahan, and Kearney families."

"Hmm," the waiter looked deep in thought, "that's quite a challenge. Are there first names for those?"

Biting her bottom lip, Rachel shook her head. "Our parents only gave us the last names. It's…complicated."

The waiter shook his head. "Not sure how to help ya there."

"That's okay. Neither do we," Jacob said under his breath.

"Well, I have food for another table ready. Enjoy your time here in Cork. Just go to the bar to refill your drinks, and they'll put it on your bill. Feel free to flag me if you need anything else," the waiter said, and then disappeared into the kitchen.

Once he was out of earshot, Rachel turned to Joe, knowing he had the spiritual gift of visions, and asked, "Do you have any information for us? Any visions? Any hints? *Anything?*"

"Sorry," Joe apologized. "Wish I had something. Been a bit dry lately. Hoping maybe the Spirit'll let me know something soon."

"What if I told you that *I* know?" Jacob said quietly, nodding toward the young lady at the bar Rachel was curious about.

Raising an eyebrow, Rachel asked, "How?"

"I can draw the future. No one believes me when I tell them, so I don't share it often, but I do," he said in one breath, searching their faces for a hint of what they were thinking. Then he added, "I draw things, and they happen later. There's no time limit as to how far out the drawings go."

"I understand you not sharing that with us, being that you're still trying to figure your way around the group, but if it makes you feel any better, my mum has that gift as well," Rachel said. "I don't doubt that others would have it too. Having said that, if anyone else has any other gifts they haven't mentioned, please share. We're a team, and we need to know *all* of our assets."

"Um," Joe jumped in, "If you don't know the time limit, then how do ya know it's here?"

"Because I see one of the girls I drew about three weeks ago over there at the bar," he said, nodding toward the young lady with dark skin that Rachel was wondering about. Sitting on a bar stool, she sipped her coffee, while working on her computer.

"Seriously?" Jesse asked, stunned. "Why didn't you tell us this before?"

"Because I had to get a feel for you guys. Normally when I tell people, they look at me funny."

"Have you had any more of these since joining us?" Rachel asked.

"Yes," he admitted. "I usually draw landscapes, but in one I drew three weeks ago, that girl was in it, with two other people."

"Girls or boys?"

"One of each."

"What did they look like?" Jesse pressed.

"The other girl was shorter. She couldn't be more than about five foot two or three, with a stocky build. Her hair is long, red, and curly, and she has blue eyes. The guy is a little taller than the girl at the bar, about six foot, and has medium-brown hair in a skater-type cut, where his hair goes down over his eyes and to the side, and brown eyes. All three are sturdy in their body structure, but not plump."

"Interesting," Rachel said, sitting back in her seat. "Do ya have your sketchbook with you?"

"Yes. It's in the room in my bag. I can show you when we get back to the hotel."

"Good. For now, I guess I should go talk to her, but I'm not exactly sure how t' start this one. She *is* bright, but there are a lot of bright people in here."

"So, how does your gift work?" Jesse asked Rachel.

"Everyone has a certain amount of light and dark, depending on where they are in their walk, or if they are even one of God's. For example, our waiter has some light, meaning he's not a Christian, but he's seeking. That guy at the corner table is just plain dark, meaning he's is not a Christian, and wants absolutely nothing to do with God."

"Like, from the other side dark?" Jesse asked.

"No. That's even darker. There is no mistaking the darker ones. And the Unnaturals," she shuddered, "are something else entirely."

"Well, I could go talk to her," Joe offered, with a smile, showing his dimples. "Put on a little southern charm."

"She'll think you're hitting on her," Jacob pointed out.

"Right. And in doing so, I should at least get a first name out of her."

"Go for it. If that doesn't work, I'll give it a shot," Rachel said.

Joe made his way to the girl at the bar. "Hi," he said, taking a seat beside her.

"Hi," she said cautiously, closing her computer.

"My name's Joe, and you are?"

"Delaney," she said with a thick Irish accent, while she shook his hand.

"How are ya doing this evening?"

"Not too bad. That's not an Irish accent I hear."

"No, ma'am." He smiled. "I'm from Texas."

"The States?" she asked. He nodded in response.

After an awkward moment, Joe asked, "Mind if I sit here and have a drink? I'm new to the area and I'd like t' pick your brain on what's here."

"Go ahead. I'm almost done," she said, just as the bartender set her dinner in front of her. Delaney cringed. "Or, just eating," she corrected herself.

"May I have a water with lemon?" Joe asked the bartender, who nodded before making his water, with a lemon on the rim. Once the bartender took off for another patron, Joe turned back to Delaney, "I'm going to ask you a weird question."

"Okay," she said hesitantly. "I'm going to warn ya that there are any number of people in here who will come to my defense in a moment's notice."

He raised his hands. "I promise not to do anything inappropriate. That wouldn't be gentlemanly of me, which goes against my upbringing."

Rachel suddenly appeared at his side. "G'day!" Rachel said, shaking Delaney's hand. "How ya going? I'm Rachel. We're looking for a couple different people, and hoping you can help."

"I'm confused," Delaney said, as she looked at the pair with her big brown eyes. She had a thin build, with straight hair that hung just below her shoulders.

"Rachel, this is Delaney," Joe introduced them.

"We're looking for some people. We know their last names, but not their first names," Rachel explained.

"What is the last name of the people you're looking for? We'll start with that, yeah?" Delaney asked.

"There's Callahan, Kearney, and Claire," Rachel said. As soon as she said 'Claire,' Delaney stiffened. "You wouldn't happen to be Delaney Claire, would you?"

"I'm not sure who you are or what you want, but I don't know you so I'm going to take my dinner and go home now," she said, flagging the bartender.

"Joe, why don't you go back with the others," Rachel said, sending him away. As he left, she asked, "Delaney, do you believe in angels?"

"I do."

Sitting in Joe's seat, Rachel continued, "I know things seem a bit off, but this is a public place. Do you mind if we talk for a few? You can always call for help if you feel the need to."

"I guess," Delaney said, as the bartender came over. When she did, Delaney asked her to get Rachel another drink of whatever she was having. "Okay. Who are you, and who are *they*?" she asked, suddenly noticing the trio still at the table.

"Well, the big one is Jesse, the one you already met is Joe, and the other one is Jacob," Rachel explained, as the bartender set a soda in front of her before he left for another patron down the bar. "If you want to, we can sit over there?"

"No. While they may be good looking, I don't know you. I want to know who you are and why you're looking for me."

"So, you *are* Delaney Claire?"

"Yes. How did you know?"

Tucking a portion of her hair behind her ear, Rachel nervously cleared her throat. "This may sound weird."

"Go ahead. I've seen a lot of weird in my life."

"While I don't doubt that, I've seen some pretty weird stuff myself."

"Really?" she asked, intrigued.

"This is going to sound *really* weird," Rachel started.

"You have already said that. Go ahead."

"Well," Rachel said, taking a deep breath, "Ever see a real angel or demon?"

Sitting up, Delaney pushed her dinner forward. "You know, they have medication for that."

Chuckling, Rachel explained, "There are days I wonder if I need to be on it. But seriously, I'm going to tell you that you're a Christian. When you ask me how I know, I'll respond with the fact that it's a gift from the Spirit. I know who in this place is a Christian and who isn't."

"Well, I am. And, while I *do* believe in gifts of the Spirit, I have to say that's a new one."

"Do *you* have any gifts of the Spirit?"

"I do."

"Really? What?"

"Not sure if I'm ready to share that with you yet."

"Try me."

"Well, one of mine is discernment, and it's telling me to trust you. Having said that, I don't know you well enough to follow that yet."

"Life is full of twists and turns. We meet new people every day. During those meetings, there are times where we feel we need to trust some, and not trust others."

"Sounds like you're trying to convince me to trust you."

"I'm trying to make you comfortable enough for us to chat."

"Not sure if I'm there yet."

"What if I continue to share about myself first?"

"Sounds fair," Delaney agreed.

"Well, I grew up in the Outback of Australia on a station. We raised cattle and sheep."

"Sounds relaxing."

"It had its ups and downs. But one thing was always certain, we could count on family and God." When Delaney just nodded in response, Rachel continued, "While growing up, I was trained by a group called A.N.G.E.L.s, which stands for Available to Nurture God's Eternal Love. They often went around the world, on missions from an archangel. Sometimes they were given to them directly from the archangel, and sometimes the missions were given through other spiritual gifts. Joe, for example, has visions. One of his visions led us to help a young lady named Amber."

"I see."

"As I mentioned, one of my spiritual gifts allows me to see who is a Christian and who is not."

"How does that help you?"

"Because where there is good, there is evil. Wile there are angels, there are also demons. My gift allows me to see those who are on Satan's side. This sometimes gives me an idea of who or what we're fighting."

"I can see that."

"Well, since I've shared some. What about you?"

"Well, it may sound weird."

"Try me."

"I can speak languages I've never heard before. For example, I met a girl from China in college. Her brother came to her and said something at lunch in their native tongue. When he did, I responded in Chinese in the same dialect he used. I swear to you that I have never taken a single class in Chinese."

"I'm sure. My brother has that gift as well. My mum, brother, and I are the only ones in our family with these unique gifts."

"Talented family. Is that him at the table?"

"No, he's with another group."

"Another group of what?"

"Well, remember those A.N.G.E.L.s I told you about earlier?"

"Yes."

"Well, I'm part of team of them as well. We basically work directly for God. He has an archangel over us who gives us assignments either directly or through those who have the gift of prophecy, dreams, or visions, like our friend Joe over there. Meanwhile, Jacob, the shorter one, draws the future. He drew you, along with two other people about three weeks ago."

"That medication is looking better and better by the minute, yeah?"

Chuckling, Rachel continued, "Some days I wonder. Seriously, though, I'm being honest with you."

"Okay. So, if you all have gifts, what does the big guy do?"

"He can feel those from the other side. He can tell how close they are to us. He senses, for example, those demons I mentioned earlier."

"Are you telling me they're real-like?"

"Hate t' break it to you, but yes."

"Hmm."

"I'll tell ya what, we have two other people to look for –"

"That's my other question," Delaney said, cutting Rachel off. "You said you were looking for me. What do you mean by that? Why would you look for *me*?"

Taking a deep breath, Rachel thought through her response for a moment before she explained, "As I said, we're sent on missions by the archangel. We're also given a list from God on who to look for – those who are called to be A.N.G.E.L.s. Now, you can say no at any time. We still have the free will to do that, but before you do, I ask you to pray about it."

"Pray about what? What do you need *me* for?"

"Well, that's what I don't know yet. We're looking for our support team for the Haven, and your names are on the list as being part of the team."

"What's the Haven?"

"It's the big guy's parent's house. They call it The Safe Haven, or Haven for short. It's my understanding that you have some skill in computers?"

"I do, but I have another skill I think you may potentially utilize more."

"Which is?"

Considering it for a moment, she decided against it. "Not sure you're ready to hear that yet."

"Fair enough. When you're ready, we're willing to listen."

"Good to know. In the meantime, I'd like to get to know you more before I share my deepest, darkest secrets, if you know what I mean."

"I do. I know I'm asking a lot of you for a stranger. I'm sure we have time to get to know each other for a few days. In doing so, you may come to actually trust us."

"Trust for me is hard."

"Trust for a lot of people is difficult. We'll be here for a bit. We still have two more people to find."

"Pretty sure I may be able to help you there."

"What do you mean?"

"You're looking for computer people. I know two hackers. One has the last name of Callahan, and the other is Kearney."

"I see."

"Let me contact them and I'll get back with you."

"Okay," Rachel said. She wrote her name, along with their hotel and room number, on a napkin before handing it to Delaney. "We'll be there for the most part. You can either leave a message or come over. In the meantime, we'll probably be looking for the other two as well. It's not that I don't trust you, it's that it's our job to find these people."

Delaney chuckled. "Pretty sure there's one you'll *never* find on your own. The other one you *may* have a shot at if you're around long enough, but he's pretty scarce as well. I think you were led to me first for a reason."

"Why is that?"

"Well, the one's blind, and the other knows how to hide very well…especially if he knows someone's looking for him. In our line of work, you know how to be a ghost when needed."

"I see. Wait," Rachel said, shaking her head. "Did ya just say one of the hackers is blind?"

"Yep. That would be Cori Callahan. She's a short spitfire with long red, curly hair, and really cool blue eyes, but she can't see a thing."

"Then," Rachel furrowed her brow, "how does she work with computers?"

Delaney laughed. "She's unique, but it's her uniqueness that allows her to hear a lot more than the average person. She can hear a recording of an event and pick out the tiniest of sounds. She also has a braille keyboard, and has a program where she runs her mouse over the words on the screen, and it reads it for her. Don't let her blindness deceive you, she's one of the top hackers in Ireland, if not all of Europe. You won't see her around much, because she's well protected. Now, you *may* run into Kai Kearney. He hides, but comes out into the real world every once and a while. They're in one of my circles as a resource. Very few know how to get in touch with them."

"I see."

"I don't think you do. The *only* way to find these two is through another contact. They don't trust *anyone.*"

"Okay. So, where do we go from here?" Rachel asked.

"If you want me to trust you, you have to trust me."

Studying her for a moment, Rachel felt at peace before she agreed. "Okay. I trust you. What do ya need from me?"

"If you are who you say you are, I should be able to find some kind of record of you."

"Not necessarily."

Delaney furrowed her brow. "What do you mean?"

"I mean, we're ghosts too. Our records have been erased. There is no online presence of us…at all."

"Seriously?"

"Seriously."

"Then how am I supposed to check your story?"

"You're going to have to trust God on this one. You said you have the spirit of discernment, right?"

"Right," Delaney said hesitantly.

"If trust is your hang up, as it is with most of us, then trust in the Lord. He won't steer you wrong. He gave you that gift for a reason. Use it. Pray and talk to Him about us. See what He says."

"All right," she agreed. Turning back to the table, she asked, "Is that offer to meet those other three still out there?"

"Of course."

"Are any of them spoken for?"

Taken aback for a moment, Rachel gulped. Taking a deep breath, she said, "That would be up to them."

"Are they at this point?"

"No."

"So, they're all three available?"

"We've been more concerned with the lives of those we were sent to protect then in forming relationships. The big one, Jesse, and I have talked, though."

"I see. He wasn't the one I was asking about."

"Joe or Jacob?"

"Not sure. I may have to go talk to them to check this out. It sounds very intriguing," she admitted.

"Then," Rachel said with a smile, "let's go meet them."

*   *   *

The next morning, the sun breaking into the darkness of the room woke the group, piercing through a crack in the curtains. Rachel groaned as she covered her head with the pillow.

Jesse rolled toward her with a chuckle. "Kinda thought you'd be used to getting up early after living on a ranch all your life." Even early in the morning, to him, she looked beautiful. Though she looked at her worst, the beauty of her spirit and heart was the only thing he saw.

"I am *not* a morning person," she grumbled from under the pillow.

"I'm sure we all have our idiosyncrasies. We'll figure them out along the way."

Pulling her head out from under the pillow, Rachel glared at him. "It's a good thing you're cute. Otherwise, with you being a morning person, things could seriously go sideways real fast. Remember, I'm good with knives *and* a gun."

"Oh, I remember," Jesse chuckled, braced on his arm. "I've seen you in action. I wouldn't mess with you on a *good* day."

"Me neither," Jacob mumbled. "I've already had the unfortunate occurrence of having to fight her more than once."

"You did well," Rachel reminded him.

"Your encouragement isn't very convincing in the morning," Jacob said, rolling away from her. "Neither is the sun."

"Is anyone else in here a morning person, or am I it?" Jesse asked.

"I am," Joe announced.

"I'm kicking you out of this bed!" Jacob grumbled, shoving Joe out of the bed with his hands and feet, and onto the floor.

Laughing, Joe peeked up and over the bed. "You can be dealt with," he teased.

"And you can be blown up."

Putting his hands up in surrender, Joe asked, "Do ya want to go get some breakfast? Or do you want it brought to you?"

"Bringing it to the room is an option?" Rachel asked, excitement evident in her voice.

"Tell you what," getting up, wanting to please Rachel, Jesse offered, "Joe and I will go get breakfast, dragging Jacob with us, while you get a shower and get ready. We take less time to get ready."

"Ya know what? I'm not even gonna argue with that one," Rachel said, getting up in her pajama pants and tank top. The others had shorts and t-shirts on.

As the guys got dressed and left, Rachel went into the bathroom. Letting the warm water run down her cold body, she shuddered as a chill ran down her spine. She really didn't want to get out of bed, but they had a job to do. They had to find the last two in Ireland before they could move on to Jordan or Egypt, whichever God led them to first. She had a feeling, though, that with one of them being blind, the better idea would be to get the two hackers from Ireland back to the Haven before moving on, keeping Delaney in the field since she knew languages. Not only would there be less to house in the field by taking the two back, but there would also be fewer people to have to keep track of, and out of trouble.

* * *

That morning after breakfast, the team went down to the college in Bishoptown. Choosing a spot in the middle of a grassy circular area near the administration building, they pulled out a map of Cork to study it.

"Are you looking for somewhere in particular-like?" their waiter from the previous night asked. They jumped. "Sorry to scare you," he apologized, "Just know you were looking for people yesterday, and now you have a map out. Did you find them?"

"Actually, we got some leads," Rachel admitted. "We found one last night, but we're still looking for the other two."

"Who are they again?"

"We found out all of their names. They are Cori Callahan and Kai Kearney."

"Cori Callahan and Kai Kearney? Hmmm. Cori used to go here, but she dropped out last year. Last time I saw Kai was a couple days ago. He's usually over there in the student center if you're going to find him anywhere," he said, gesturing toward the student center on the other side of the grassy area, just as a drizzle started once again.

The lush green of Ireland in September thrilled Rachel, but the rain and drizzle messed with her hair in a bad way. She sighed as she braided it. "I don't even know why I bother doing my hair here."

"I wouldn't," the waiter chuckled. "The name's Owen Quinn. And yours?" he asked Rachel.

Standing, Rachel put a hair tie in to hold her braid, then shook his hand, "My name's Rachel Sullivan, and this is Jesse English, Jacob Armstrong, and Joe Mason. Do you know Kai?"

"Kai goes here. Cori used to go here, but doesn't anymore, and Delaney graduated last year, but still takes a class here or there. Otherwise, the only time I see Delaney is in the pub."

"Kai is usually in the student center, though?" Joe verified, as the three guys stood to shake Owen's hand.

Owen stood to six foot, with ginger hair, and freckles across his nose. His sharp features allowed his blue eyes to stand out on his stocky build. If Rachel had to guess, he probably played a sport like rugby.

"Let's head over to the student center. I have class in about an hour. I was just on my way to study when I saw ya sitting here and remembered you from last night. You're kind of unforgettable," he said, looking at Rachel.

Jesse stiffened, noticing how Owen looked at Rachel. He would keep an eye on him, but since he knew Kai, they would have to trust him for a bit in order to have another outlet to get to him in case Delaney fell through.

Heading over to the student center, the group got to know Owen a bit more. He was in his second year at the college, but was a life-long Cork resident. He had hopes of getting on the Irish Rugby Union team after university. Growing up in the area, he knew of the three they were looking for, and was curious as to how they knew them.

"They are friends of our family," Rachel mentioned as they entered the student center.

"And, they didn't tell you their first names?"

"As I said last night, it's…complicated."

"I'm sure. It sounds it."

"Owen!" a young man called from the bistro in the student center. Jogging over to Owen, he asked, "Who is *this* young lady? And, you," he said to Jesse, "Ever play rugby?" When Jesse shook his head no, the man turned back to Owen, "Is this a group of new transfers?"

"No. They're visitors. They're looking for Kai. Have you seen him this morning?"

"Not this morning, but I'll see him tonight at the pub. He's supposed to meet us up there for pool and to watch the game."

"Brilliant!" Owen smiled. "See, that'll be two. Thanks," he said, and the guy left with a group of his friends. When he was out of earshot, Owen offered, "Do you want to have lunch? I have class in an hour, but I can stay until then."

"Actually, that sounds like a great idea," Joe agreed. "We can pick your brain about the area."

After they got their lunch and sat down at a table, Owen quietly said, "I know you want to go to the pub tonight, and I know you just came in last night, but you are not exactly in the best area here at night." Turning to the guys, he warned, "Keep an eye on her, yeah?" As the three guys burst out in laughter, Owen asked, "What's so funny? I'm trying to warn you. That place is not exactly the safest at night."

Finishing the bite in his mouth, Jesse then explained, "We know what she can do. We're not worried about her. She may *look* fragile, but she is *far* from it."

Confused, he said, "I don't understand."

"And I pray you never have to find out," Jacob said, rubbing his jaw.

"Meaning?"

"I've fought her. She doesn't believe in mercy."

"I see."

"I hope you don't have to."

"Me neither," he said, studying her a bit more. He may have underestimated this little band. His uncle was with the group up in Derry who searched for strong warriors to fight for Ireland. He helped his uncle with recruitment in the college, and half-wondered if this group would be a good addition.

C.J. Peterson

38

Chapter 2
To Give One's Life

Landing at Heathrow Airport in London, England, Angel and her crew were beyond fatigued. After weeks of training and working out the kinks, out of pure exhaustion they decided to skip dinner before going to bed in their hotel room near the airport.

"The name's Aden," the driver said as the crew got in. "How was your flight?"

"Long and…just long," Angel mumbled, while the guys loaded the luggage. She let Jon take the front seat, while she and Josh took the middle and Val jumped in the back seat.

After Jon gave Aden the address of the hotel, Aden asked, "So, what brings you to our lovely part of the world? Listening to your accents, you sound like an Aussie, a Frenchman, and two Americans. Is that accurate?"

"I'm Creole, from New Orleans, Louisiana in the States," Val clarified.

"I see. What about the Australian?" he asked, glancing at Josh.

"Yes, sir. I'm an Aussie, born an' bread."

"And, we're from Nevada, in America," Angel explained. "Jon's my brother."

"Well, if you're going to travel with such a lovely young lady, I can see the need for a couple large men to help guard her," Aden pointed out. "Are you here for a specific reason?"

"We're looking for someone," Angel explained. "Don't suppose you know someone with the last name of Knight, do you?"

"I know a lot of people with the last name of Knight. Anyone in particular?" Aden asked, suddenly visibly on edge.

"We're not one hundred percent sure, but it could be…you," Jon said, noticing the name on his posted license that said, '*Aden J. Knight.*'

"Why would you be looking for me?"

"Is your last name…? It is!" Angel said, excited, as she leaned forward, looking over the seat to see his license. "God is good."

Without thinking, Aden replied, "All the time."

"Aden, do you believe in angels?"

"I do," he said cautiously.

"Do you believe in demons?" Val asked.

"Yes. Where you have light, you have dark."

Angel nervously cleared her throat. These conversations were much easier with Val and Joe. She wished this one were just as easy. "Have you…have you ever *seen* a demon?"

Eyes wide for a moment, Aden just shook his head. "Never seen an angel either."

Pulling into the hotel parking lot, Angel asked, "Mind if we continue this conversation over dinner tonight?"

"Can't. Having dinner with my sister." Aden shook his head. "I can do lunch tomorrow."

"Perfect. Can you pick us up here at noon tomorrow?"

"That I can do. Have to admit, you've got me curious. It's not every day you get asked the questions you asked me by complete strangers."

"Well, you may not be a stranger for long," Angel said as she paid him, while the guys grabbed the luggage.

"I look forward to lunch tomorrow," Aden said before he pulled away.

"Well, that was easier than I thought. Let's hope the others are having the same luck," Jon mentioned as they went into the hotel.

Angel had a queen-sized bed, while Val and Josh took the other, and Jon took the twin bed. Praying for direction in the conversation the next afternoon, Angel dropped to the bed, exhausted. Knowing God gave her the gift of dreams, she prayed specifically for a dream from Him that night on how to navigate the conversation the next day as she drifted off to sleep.

*   *   *

The sun had just set behind the little chalet bungalow where the Knight family lived. The two children, Aden, nineteen, and Lauren, eleven, were often left home alone with Lauren's nanny. Their parents worked in the city.

There were two homes on the property. They lived in one, while their nanny lived in the smaller of the two. Truth be told, their nanny had raised Aden and Lauren since Aden was three years old. She was like a second mother to the pair, and they cherished her dearly for all she did for them.

"Can we please eat outside tonight at the picnic table?" the long, brown-haired, blue-eyed, Lauren asked their nanny, as Aden walked into the kitchen from the garage.

"Sure, love," she replied, before turning her attention back to the dinner she was cooking.

"How long before dinner?" Aden asked.

"About two hours."

"Can Lauren and I go to the park?"

"Which one?"

"Colne Valley. I want to show her the place I met Kara."

Chuckling at the young love she saw in Aden's eyes, the nanny replied, "Sure. Just be back in two hours..." then she glanced up at him and warned, "or you're dealing with me."

"Yes, ma'am," Aden said with a grin. "Come on, Lauren." Grabbing her wrist, they ran to the car, and then Aden drove them to the park.

"This is pretty," Lauren mentioned as they wandered into a meadow full of wildflowers and long waving grass that gently swayed in the breeze. The leaves had begun to change, setting off an abstract pattern of yellows, reds, and browns all through the landscape.

"See that place over there?" he asked after they'd walked for a half hour.

"Yeah," she said dreamily, watching the weeping willow that hugged the banks of the stream near the stone bridge. The water flowed under the bridge as the butterflies danced around the open meadow. All of the elements collaborated, creating a setting of romance.

"*That* is where I'm going to ask Kara to marry me – the exact place where we met."

"Seriously? When?" Lauren asked, excitement in her eyes at the idea of Kara being part of the family permanently.

"I'm going to ask her next weekend. That'll give us two years to finish uni before the wedding. She wants a September wedding, so this will give plenty of time for her to have the wedding she's always dreamed of. So, you approve?"

"Yeah. But, um, Aden?" Lauren asked nervously. "What are *those*?" she asked, pointing to the most terrifying creatures she had ever seen. They were bat-like creatures, whose scales were blackish-red in color. Their yellow eyes zeroed in on the pair as wings fanned out behind them, and their talons reflected in the dwindling sunlight.

Looking toward where she pointed, his heart took off at full tilt as fear surged through his body. Grabbing her wrist, they sprinted away from them. Glancing over his shoulder after a moment, he saw them still following. Suddenly, bursts of light stopped the creatures in their tracks. "Run faster, Lauren!" he shouted. "They're distracted! Here's our chance!"

Bolting for the woods, he hoped the streaks of light would slow the creatures enough for the two of them to lose the terrifying-looking beasts in the trees.

"Aden! I don't know if I can!" she yelled back as he practically dragged her.

Stopping momentarily, the young man of six foot, with brown hair and brown eyes, rested his hands on her shoulders. "Look," he said, breathing heavily, "I don't know who or *what* those were. I need you to climb that tree as fast as you can while I run. I'm going to distract them from you. I need you to be safe."

"I-I can't leave you."

"Yes, you can, and you *will*," he insisted. "Stay there until I come back for you. Do you hear me?"

Terrified beyond words, the little girl only nodded in response.

Giving her a kiss on her head, he said, "Know that I will always love you."

Lauren gave him a quick kiss on the cheek before she scampered up the tree as fast as she could. Looking back down at him for a moment, she saw him turn to look toward the creatures. They were headed right for them.

Knowing his sister was safe, Aden turned and bolted deeper into the woods. The branches cut at his arms where his white short-sleeve t-shirt didn't cover them. The vines grabbed at his ankles trying to trip him, but he pushed on, knowing it was him or his little sister. Letting them take out an eleven-year-old, to him, was *not* an option. "Lord," he looked up, "please protect Lauren. If it's Your will, please protect me as well."

Looking over his shoulder once again, he saw three of the creatures closing in. Pushing harder, he gave everything he had. Suddenly, talons wrapped around his ankle and Aden hit the ground with a hard thud, smacking his chin on a rock, immediately producing blood in his mouth. Rolling over to look at them, Aden let out a scream of terror at the creature hovering over him. Feeling its talons slice into him, he screeched in agony. The last thing he saw was the yellow of their eyes as the remaining creatures descended, mauling him to death.

"All hail Calliope!" they cheered, tearing his body apart. "Cal-li-ope! Cal-li-ope! Cal-li-ope!"

Bolting upright in bed with a scream, Angel sat there breathing heavily. Tears and sweat poured down her face as she shook in fear. Goose bumps covered her body.

Val flipped the light on as Jon and Josh ran to Angel's side.

"Calliope. Something about…Calliope," Angel said in between breaths.

"Who's Calliope?" Val asked.

"I don't know, but she's terrified," Jon said, climbing onto the bed to hold his sister until she calmed down.

"It was Aden Knight," she finally got out after a few moments. Getting her body under control, she took a few deep, cleansing breaths. "Aden Knight. Our driver. He was the A.N.G.E.L. from here, but…but he was attacked. How did they know? How did they find him?"

"They have a list too," Jon reminded her.

"But, how did they know?"

"Remember what Dad said about Ephesians 6:12?"

Angel nodded. "'*For we do not wrestle against flesh and blood…*'" Taking a few deep breaths, she continued, "'…*but against the principalities…against powers…against the rulers of the darkness of this world…*'" Slowing her breathing before she hyperventilated, she then finished, "'…*against spiritual wickedness…in high places.*'"

"Exactly. He's got this place wired," Jon said. "This is his playground. Just remember that God is stronger. Aden was to be one of us, but the other side got him. We'll verify this in the morning. Maybe it was a warning, or maybe he's gone. We need to make sure. If it's a warning, we need to tell him quickly. Unfortunately, we'll have to wait until lunch."

"It was from earlier tonight," Angel explained. Shuddering, she took a moment. "You don't understand. I saw his home, his car, and his sister. Last I saw of her in the dream, she was up in a tree. He sent her up the tree to keep them from getting to her. He sacrificed himself for her."

"Then let's not sit around," Josh said, getting off the bed. "We need to find them both…and fast!"

*   *   *

In order to go in with a plan, the group did some research on Colne Valley Regional Park on the computer before they left. They also picked up a map of the park from the hotel lobby. Angel studied it in the back seat with Val on the way, hoping to get a sense of direction while Josh drove. Jon was in the passenger seat of the rental car that was dropped off for them at the hotel earlier that evening, directing Josh.

"Here," Angel said, "or maybe there. It's near a stone bridge with a willow tree, and a large open meadow."

"What about here?" Val pointed to another one.

"Ugh! This'll be like looking for a needle in a haystack!"

"That is, *if* they're here," Josh said. "Remember, we don't know if this is to come, or has happened already."

Angel growled. "Why can't these dreams be more clear?"

"I wish we had a time so we knew whether we could eat or not," Jon pointed out. "At least drive-thru, huh?"

"Fine," Josh said, pulling into a fast-food restaurant on the way to the park.

When they finally reached the park, in the rearview mirror Josh saw the color drain from Angel's face. Seeing police lights in another parking lot next to a lone car, he pulled into a different parking lot. Turning the car off, Josh asked Angel, "What is it?"

"Th-that's his car," Angel's voice barely a whisper. "Oh, God, please don't let it be true yet. Please say there's still time."

"This park has over forty square miles. Are you *sure* that's his car?"

"This time of night?" Angel asked. "How many vehicles would still be here this time of night surrounded by police cars that look *exactly* like his car."

"Well, if that is in fact his car, than we need to find his sister," Josh pointed out.

"Wouldn't the police have found her already?" Val asked.

"Not necessarily." Angel shook her head. "We know more about where to look than they do. As Val said, this park is forty square miles. She's a tiny eleven-year-old. We also know her name and roughly where she is. The police may be searching the park, but they have no idea where to go."

"This is true," Val said. "Let's go find her."

*   *   *

The park was stunning, and under other circumstances Jon would definitely enjoy the scenery and peace the park provided. However, he also knew by the terror emitting from Angel, as she went into further details of her dream on the way to the park, what dangers this park held. The nightmare that had occurred within its borders sent a chill up his spine. Demons were what killed Aden. He knew it was rough for her, but they had to know everything in order to know what they were walking into. It was times like these Jon wished he had the dream gift so his sister wouldn't have to go through the rough ones.

After a couple hours of searching, Angel stopped dead in her tracks. "There," she said, pointing to the bridge with a weeping willow right next to it, as the stream calmly flowed beside it.

Noting crushed grass, Jon turned and followed the tracks in the meadow toward the tree line. "Where do we go from here?" he asked Angel.

"This way," she said, following her dream. Feeling on edge as goosebumps coated her body, she knew they were in the right place. "Now would be a good time to have Jesse with us. I would like to know if they're still around."

"If they already did their job, I doubt they'll stick around," Val remarked. His spiritual sight kicking in, he suddenly stopped and looked up in a tree. "There's Lauren."

Looking up, Angel called out to her, "Lauren, my name is Angel. You can come down now. It's safe."

Lauren vigorously shook her head. "I don't want to until I see Aden. H-he said to wait for him."

"Honey, I need you to show me what direction he went in. We came to help. We need to find him too."

Pointing toward the east, Lauren said, "That way."

"Are you really going to make me climb up there?" Angel asked, with her hands on her hips.

"I don't know you."

"You don't, but we know Aden. We've been looking for you for about an hour."

"Prove it," Lauren challenged.

Remembering the dream, Angel said, "Aden brought you here to show you where he was going to ask Kara to marry him."

Knowing Aden wouldn't have told many about the upcoming engagement, Lauren slowly climbed down from the tree, dropping only a few feet from Angel. "What *were* those things? Where's Aden?"

"We're not sure," Angel said, kneeling in front of Lauren. Resting her other hand on Lauren's shoulder, Angel said, "I'm going to ask you to go with Val. He's going to take you to the police so you can get home to your parents. Will you do that?"

"Yes, ma'am."

"Good. When you get to the police, I want you to give them directions, so Val can bring them back here. I think I know where Aden is, but they'll need to come too."

"I-is Aden okay?" Lauren stammered, tears brimming her eyes as her bottom lip trembled.

"Honey, just go with Val. Okay?"

A tear escaped her eye and slowly crawled down her cheek. "Okay," she mumbled.

"You're okay." Angel wiped Lauren's tear away as Lauren sniffed and wiped her nose. "You're safe now, okay?" When

Lauren nodded, Angel finished with, "Go with Val. He'll keep you safe."

"Yes, ma'am," she said, and they left.

Once they were out of earshot, Jon asked, "Okay, where do we go from here?"

"Follow the trail," Josh pointed out. "They didn't hide it."

"You're a tracker?"

"Of course. You can't live on a ranch all your life and not be," Josh reminded him. "Come on."

Sandwiched between Josh and Jon, Angel nervously followed Josh, who was following the trail. "Seriously, even I can follow these," Jon said, looking down at the tracks. "Did they *want* us to…what if this is a trap?" he asked, a thought suddenly hitting him mid-sentence.

Angel and Josh stopped and looked at him, stunned. "Do ya reckon?" Josh asked.

"Don't know." Jon shrugged. "There's only one way to find out."

"Let's keep going, but stay on guard," Angel said, decisively.

After another several minutes, the scene they walked up to made Angel drop to her knees and threw up. Blood, body parts and matter, along with shredded clothing, covered the grass and splattered on nearby trees.

Glancing around the horrific scene, Jon gulped, "He's already gone."

*   *   *

Returning to the hotel after dealing with the police the next morning, Angel was beyond discouraged. Eating was the furthest thing from her mind as the guys somberly ate breakfast in the room.

"Please eat something," Jon begged for the umpteenth time.

Shaking her head, she dropped it into her hands while she sat cross-legged on the bed, with her elbows on her knees. "I...I can't."

"You need to keep up your strength."

"It was horrific! What Aden went through..." her voice faded. "Watching it. Seeing the scene afterward. I need to take a walk...by myself," she said and left the room.

Wanting to stay close to the hotel, she went down to the gym to walk on the treadmill. Thankfully the room was empty, so she prayed aloud. "Why did You do this?" Angel asked God.

"'Many are the plans in the mind of a man, but it is the purpose of the Lord that will stand.'" She heard Proverbs 19:21 in her mind.

Mulling the words over for a moment, she walked faster. "Look, while I understand that Your plans aren't the same as mine, I have to ask why he had to die? Why didn't You protect him? How am I supposed to trust this list if they're going to be taken out?" she asked the Lord aloud. "Never mind. I know. I know. We've had this conversation. You don't have to send the archangel again." She sighed. Stepping on either side of the treadmill, she looked up to God. "Why did he die? I'm sorry, but I *have* to know."

"*'Precious in the sight of the Lord is the death of His saints.'*"

"I know what Psalm 116:15 says," she said, rolling her eyes, "but that doesn't tell me why?"

John 14:1-3 slowly went through her mind, *"'Do not let your hearts be troubled. You believe in God; believe also in Me. My Father's house has many rooms; if that were not so, would I have told you that I am going there to prepare a place for you? And if I go and prepare a place for you, I will come back and take you to be with Me that you also may be where I am.'"* That verse was closely followed by John 10:28 and 29, *"'And I give eternal life to them, and they will never perish; and no one will snatch them out of My hand. My Father, Who has given them to Me, is greater than all; and no one is able to snatch them out of the Father's hand.'"*

"Look, I *get* that Aden is with You. What I don't understand is *why*. Why did he have to die? Why was he on the list if he was going to die? How is *this* in Your plan?"

Jeremiah 17:7 and 8 was whispered by the Spirit to her, *"'But blessed is the one who trusts in the Lord, whose confidence is in Him. They will be like a tree planted by the water that sends out its roots by the stream. It does not fear when heat comes; its leaves are always green. It has no worries in a year of drought and never fails to bear fruit.'"*

"This isn't making sense. Why can't You just flat out tell me? Why do I have to sort through verses and parables?"

"It is a lesson of trust," she heard the archangel behind her and jumped.

Turning off the treadmill, she snapped, "You need to quit doing that!"

"Doing what?"

"Popping up behind people. It makes one jumpy."

"Do not worry about being jumpy. Worry about trusting in the Lord. Why are you questioning Him?"

"Because we were given this list. I *assumed* those on the list were protected, you know, since they were *destined* to be A.N.G.E.L.s and all," a slight tone of sarcasm in her voice.

"Do you have free will?"

"Yes."

"Do others on the list have free will?"

"Yes."

"Demons unfortunately have free will too. It is just like when a loved one dies early. Free will takes them. It may not be in their fault, but the choice of another," the archangel explained, as they sat down on the side of the treadmill.

"But why? He was young. He was in the prime of his life. He was about to potentially be an A.N.G.E.L. or get married, whichever he chose."

"'*When you ask, you must believe and not doubt, because the one who doubts is like a wave of the sea, blown and tossed by the wind.*'"

"James 1:6." Angel nodded in understanding. "I *have* been doubting. Doubts cause problems. Doubts will pull me away."

"Correct."

"So what you're saying is that I may never know. That I just need to trust in the Lord."

"Correct."

"Fine," Angel said in a sigh.

"Trust Him," the archangel said, and then quoted Psalm 121:3. "'*He will not let your foot slip – He who watches over you will not slumber.*' He created this world with only His voice. He spoke this universe into existence. Do you not think you are important to Him? You are one of His A.N.G.E.L.s."

"Aden was supposed to be one of His A.N.G.E.L.s too."

"You are not immune to death as A.N.G.E.L.s. You *are not* immortal."

"Where were *you* during this?"

"Protecting the other team. I am only an angel. I am not God. I am not omniscient, omnipotent, or omnipresent. Only the Almighty One is."

"Then why did He not send someone else?"

"He did."

"I didn't see it in the dream," she accused.

"The angels were those streaks of light that slowed the demons from following them, giving Aden and Lauren the time they needed to enter the tree line. There were originally twelve demons, but only three slipped through. That gave Aden time to get Lauren to safety. Those angels gave Lauren the time to get up the tree. They gave themselves so Aden could get a head start, therefore protecting Lauren from being seen. The remaining demons chased after Aden. They did not find Lauren. Look, just because you do not see it or do not understand it, does not mean it did not happen. Angel, you are young, but you are not immortal. You need to face your immortality, along with the fact that you *are not* in control. Quit fighting Him. There *is* an army rising for the Lord. There *will* be casualties during this uprising. It is your job to get to those on the list, and get to them quickly. You need to find them and explain the offer to them. From there, it is their decision. Aden *may* have said no due to his girlfriend and pending engagement. Only God knows what his decision would have been, had he been given the opportunity. I am not saying that is the reason why he was taken either. He gave his life to save Lauren's life. He made a choice. He could have climbed that tree with her, but he chose to run to keep her safe. He is currently in Heaven with the Lord, reaping his rewards. John 15:13 says, *'Greater love has no one than this: to lay down one's life for one's friends.'* Aden answered the same call you have all answered, 'to follow Him, and if needed, lay down your life.' He did that. He laid his life down for Lauren. Now, you will not always get an explanation why you lose someone, such as with Amber or Aden. You will not always know why that person was taken or lost, but know this…you know the One who does. The Lord God protects you in many ways. However, He still gives you the gift of free will. As you know, that can be a curse or a blessing. He gave Aden the free will to choose to climb the tree with Lauren, or to run. He chose to run to keep the others from Lauren, and in essence, to save her life. Will you trust the Lord with your life without questioning Him every other second, or are you going to leave the team?"

"It's of that much importance?" she asked, stunned by the ultimatum.

"Yes. Trust Him with everything or not. He needs leaders who will trust Him."

After several moments, she decisively stated, "I will trust Him."

"You may never fully understand when things happen or why, but if you trust in Him, you need to understand and trust that He has a plan."

"I *do* understand that He has a plan. Jeremiah 29:11 tells me that. Why didn't he have a plan for Aden, though? You can't tell me that his plan and purpose was finished. His name was on the list."

Almost aloud, both heard the Lord's voice quote Isaiah 55:9 in their heads, "'*For My thoughts are not your thoughts, neither are your ways My ways, declares the LORD. For as the heavens are higher than the earth, so are My ways higher than your ways and My thoughts than your thoughts.*'"

"I will trust you," Angel said in a sigh as she stood. Then she more firmly stated, "I *will* trust you."

"Thank you," the archangel said, and then disappeared in a flash of light.

"Someday I *may* get used to this. Until then, I will have to trust You and Your plans."

*   *   *

"Hello?" Jesse said, answering his phone. The group was in the hotel room in Cork that afternoon getting ready to go meet Delaney at the pub for an early dinner. She was to bring Kai with her to meet them.

"Jesse, it's Jon. You need to know something. Angel should be the one to tell you, but she's spun out again."

"Seriously? How is she going to lead if she continues to do that?" Jesse snapped, irritated. "I thought she finally got herself grounded at the Haven before we left."

"She did, until we lost our London A.N.G.E.L.," Jon explained.

"What do you mean you *lost* him?"

"His name was Aden Knight," Jon started just as Angel walked into the room.

"Who is that?" she demanded.

"Jesse. Why?"

"Give me the phone," she said, putting her hand out. When she got on the phone, she said, "Let me talk to Rach."

Jesse handed the phone to Rachel, who looked at him confused. When she did, he just shrugged and mouthed, "*Angel.*"

"Great," Rachel whispered, rolling her eyes. Putting the phone to her ear, she said, "G'day, Ang. How ya going?"

"You needed to hear it from me," she said, glaring at Jon. "We lost our London A.N.G.E.L., Aden Knight."

"What do you mean you lost him?"

"He was attacked by the Unnaturals in a park yesterday, late afternoon."

"Unnaturals or demons?" Rachel asked.

"Same difference."

"No. An Unnatural is possessed. A demon is one of Cassius's crew."

"Seriously, does it really matter? He's gone!"

"Yes. If they're demons, then they're getting bold and don't care who sees them. It shows desperation. If it's an Unnatural, then they're operating under normal circumstances," Rachel explained. "Either way, out in the open is hardly normal. We need to know what we're dealing with here, though."

"They were demons. He gave himself to save his sister, who was with him. They were in a park at the time in broad daylight. They also said something about Calliope."

"You mean the muse Calliope?"

"You know who Calliope is?" Angel asked, stunned. With her background in archeology, she'd known who Calliope was as soon as she heard the name. Calliope was not a commonly referenced muse, so she didn't think many knew of her.

"She's supposed to be the muse of heroic poetry. We learned about her in school when we studied Greek mythology."

"Well, according to my nightmare, she's responsible for taking out Aden."

"Wow," Rachel said, taken aback. "They're *really* desperate if they did it in broad daylight as themselves. They could have been seen. Why didn't the archangel save him?"

"He said he was protecting you guys. That's the other reason I'm talking to you. You guys have something going on over there that you don't know about."

"Interesting."

"Whatever you're doing, hurry up and get out of there. If you haven't seen them yet, then they're there as Unnaturals. In the meantime, we're heading to St. Petersburg as soon as possible. We have two to get there, and we don't want to lose anyone else."

"I hear ya. We meet with a girl we've been talking to tonight. She's bringing another one."

"You have three there, right?"

"Yep."

"Then get them, and get out. They could be closing in on you and you don't even know it."

"We do now."

62

Chapter 3
The Purpose of the Lord Will Stand

"Thank you," Rachel said, and hung up the phone. Turning to the others, she explained, "Their A.N.G.E.L. in England was attacked and killed before they could get to him. Jesse, you have another name to add to the rock. Let's make sure not to have to add anymore."

"Did I hear you right? Did you say he was attacked by demons in broad daylight?" Jacob asked, not sure if he heard her correctly.

"Yes. That means they're desperate. Look, we have to convince Delaney that there's no more time. We need her, Kai, and Cori *tonight*. We can't afford to lose anymore. We're going to have to be as straight with them as we can without scaring them."

"But, we're only supposed to see Delaney and Kai tonight," Joe pointed out. "How are we supposed to convince all three tonight that they need to come with us?"

"We pray," Rachel said firmly, "and let God do the rest."

*　　*　　*

Walking into the pub that night, Rachel wouldn't admit it to anyone, but she was anxious. Looking at every person in the restaurant, she knew there were none from the other side there at the moment. She was grateful to have Jesse with them. Rachel knew Jesse would alert them if the other side was near, or closing in on them.

"Who's that girl with them?" Joe asked.

Almost star-struck by her, Jacob excitedly exclaimed, "That's Cori! She's prettier than the drawing!"

The girl with them had red, curly hair that dropped about four or five inches below her shoulders, along with sparkling blue eyes that seemed to have a faraway look to them.

"Is that a dog with her?" Joe asked, glancing under the table.

Excited God answered their prayers, Rachel squealed, "That's Cori! God did it! He pulled them all out of hiding! Come on! Let's go get our A.N.G.E.L.s!"

Delaney was on the end of the long table. She stood as the group neared them, and greeted them with a hug when they got near. "Guys, I'd like you to meet Cori Callahan and Kai Kearney. Cori, Kai, this is Rachel Sullivan, Jesse English, Joe Mason, and Jacob Armstrong."

"Such a pleasure to finally meet you both," Rachel said, shaking their hands. As the others sat down, they shook their hands as well. "We didn't expect to see Cori here too," Rachel said, pleasantly surprised.

"I felt led to come. When Delaney was talking to us about you, God told me to come," she explained with her thick Irish brogue.

"I'm glad He did. We've got a problem," Rachel said, just as Owen walked up to the table.

"While you're normally supposed to order at the bar, I can't help but come over to a table full of my favorite people. Cori, nice to see you! Feels like it's been forever, yeah?" Owen remarked.

"That sounds like Owen," Cori said quietly to Kai.

"It is," Kai responded.

"Wonderful! Lovely to see you too," Cori said with a smile.

"Is Charm with you?" Owen asked, referring to Cori's dog.

Instinctively, Cori reached down to scratch the black lab behind the ears at her name being mentioned. "Aye. Always."

"What can I get you fine folks this evening?" Owen asked, and then took everyone's order before disappearing into the kitchen.

Once he was gone, Delaney looked at Rachel, concerned, "You said we have a problem, yeah?"

"Yes. Our counterparts were in London trying to acquire another teammate, when he was attacked and killed...by the other side," Rachel explained in a low voice.

"What do you mean by 'the other side'?" Kai asked. "What *exactly* are we fighting here? Delaney tried to explain it to us, but I wasn't quite sure-like what I heard wasn't something out of a science fiction movie." Kai looked to be about six-foot, had shaggy brown hair that swooped to the side, at times covering his soft, brown eyes.

"No, I'm pretty sure ya heard her right," Joe said. "Unless you experience it for yourself, it's difficult to wrap your mind around it all."

"Where are you all from?" Cori asked. "I hear a variety of accents."

"Australia," Rachel said.

"Grew up in Mexico, but I'm an American, and now our home is Nevada in the United States," Jesse explained.

"I'm from Nevada in the U.S. too," Jacob said.

And, Joe finished with, "Texas."

"Variety. I love hearing the different accents," Cori said. "They're kind of like a mosaic of melodies woven together. Beautiful."

Jacob couldn't help himself. He liked Cori from the instant he saw her. The more she talked, the more he wanted to hear her voice. Usually girls bothered him, but the women of the A.N.G.E.L.s fascinated him more than anything. But this Cori was on a whole other level. "Don't think me rude, but were you born blind?" he asked.

"Yes. Charm is my second Seeing Eye dog. I've had her for about a year. She's my eyes. Before her was Clover. I make my own way around well enough with her, and have my friends to back me up."

"What about your families?" Jesse asked.

"My friends *are* my family. My dad was a drunk," Cori said, disgusted. "My mom puts up with him, but it ticked me off. When I turned eighteen, I couldn't handle it anymore and didn't have to, so I left."

"My family has its moments," Kai explained, "but haven't really had much contact since I left either."

"Seems we're all a bunch of misfits," Delany added, tongue-in-cheek.

"God doesn't call the qualified…He qualifies the called," Rachel countered. "There's no such thing as a misfit when it comes to the Lord."

"Good point. Now, you said we had a problem? That one of the London A.N.G.E.L.s was attacked and killed, yeah?" Kai asked, hoping to change the subject. "Does that mean we're all in danger-like?"

"Actually, yes," Rachel said bluntly. "We really need to get you guys out of here and to the Haven before something happens. I don't want to lose any more. We also have others we need to get as well."

Raising an eyebrow, Kai asked, "How will we be protected any better at the Haven?"

"God has placed angels of protection around the Haven. They're there twenty-four hours a day, seven days a week," she explained. "The archangel told us one time that each of the teams will have a safe haven of their own. One central location for each team."

"What happens if we don't go?" Cori asked.

"Honestly, you could have a target on you. I don't mean to scare you, but we weren't expecting what happened to Aden to happen to anyone on the list. And, there are still others we need to find as well."

"Here's your drinks, and your food will be here shortly," Owen said, dropping off their drinks. When he got to Rachel, he asked, "May I speak with you…privately?"

"I'm coming with her," Jesse asserted. "She doesn't go anywhere without me." He didn't trust Owen, and wasn't sure what he was up to.

"Fine. If we could step outside," he said, gesturing toward the front door.

Rachel groaned. More cold drizzle. She wasn't sure how they lived like this every day. A little rain here and there she could handle, but this continuous rain chilled her to the bone.

Once Jesse, Owen, and Rachel were outside, a van pulled up. Six men wearing ski masks jumped out, and jammed a needle in the necks of all three before dragging them into the van. They then peeled out of the parking lot at breakneck speed.

As Rachel went unconscious, she was grateful Jesse was with her. Slowly reaching her hand over, she grabbed Jesse's hand. He gave it a squeeze before he went unconscious as well.

*   *   *

After ten minutes, Jacob looked at his watch for the fifth time, and commented, "They're taking an awful long time to talk. Should one of us go see what's going on?"

Just then, another different waitress brought them their food.

Delaney furrowed her brow in concern. "Where's Owen?"

"We're not exactly sure," she said, setting the plates down at each place setting. "He said something about a break, but no one's seen him since," a girl whose nametag said 'Siobhan,' mentioned. "He's usually pretty good about that. Our manager put me on your table until he returns. So, don't worry-like. I'll take good care of you."

"Our problem is that he took those two with him," Kai gestured toward the two empty seats where food now sat.

"Which way did they go last?" Siobhan asked, slight alarm in her voice.

"Out the front."

"Wait here. I'll go see if they're still there," she said, and disappeared out the front of the pub.

When she returned, she went directly to the manager, who was suddenly at the table. "I understand our waiter is missing, along with two of your dinner mates."

"Yes, sir," Delaney explained. "He asked to talk to the girl, and one of the guys wouldn't let her leave without him. He's a pretty big guy too. Not that Owen's not in his own right, but this bloke was big!"

"I understand. We'll give them some more time to –"

"Sir, I don't think you understand," Joe jumped in, cutting him off. "Rachel and Jesse *would not* leave without telling us. They just don't do that. We're a team. There's something wrong."

"We'll keep an eye out. If it's too much longer, we'll notify the authorities. Chances are, they just took a ride somewhere."

"That's what we're afraid of," Jacob said under his breath, "and not of their own accord."

*   *   *

Rachel groaned as she began to regain consciousness. With a pulsating headache, she squinted to see what she could of the tiny room they were in. Noticing immediately that her hands and ankles were zip-tied to a chair, she groaned again. "What now?"

Looking over, she noticed Jesse was zip-tied to a chair as well, but Owen was nowhere to be seen.

"Jesse?" Rachel whispered. "Jesse, wake up."

He groaned, rolling his head toward her. "Where are we? What happened?"

"I don't know, but Owen's gone."

"Are you sure?" he asked. Glancing at the empty third chair, he asked, "Do you think they took him?"

"What do you reckon they want?"

"I don't know. They're not from the other side, though. Right now they're not near us," Jesse pointed out.

"I didn't have a chance to see the light or dark in the one's who took us before they gave us whatever that was, but I *do* know that whatever we've gotten into now is not good."

"Do you think the others are aware yet?"

"I hope so."

"Do you think they'll know how to find us?"

"That'll have to be a God thing, because none of us saw this coming."

"Agreed," Jesse said, a little more coherent as the minutes passed.

"Let's just pray they find us quickly."

"Rach, why do we seem to keep finding ourselves in these type of predicaments?"

"I know, right? Can't we just go on a mission and *not* have our lives threatened for once?"

"They'll find us," Jesse said, with renewed resolve as his mind cleared.

"No one knows where we are, though."

"God does," he said confidently. "And He's bigger than anything this world can throw at us. We'll get out of here."

"You think so?"

"I *know* so."

A burly man walked in, followed by two other men dragging Owen between them. "Sit," the burly man ordered as the two men let Owen go. When Owen sat down, the two who dragged him in zip-tied his wrists and ankles to the chair, and then left the room.

Rachel noticed the bruises on his face and knuckles, along with the blood from his mouth, and cringed. *What had they gotten themselves into?*

"He says you're a fighter as well," the burly man got into Rachel's face, resting his hands on hers, turning her attention back to him.

"Depends," she said, surprising herself at the calmness in her voice.

"On what?"

"On why I would need t' fight."

Nodding toward Jesse, he asked, "What if this lad's life depended on it?"

"Then the other one's not coming out of it alive," she said with a stern, authoritative tone in her voice. "I'm responsible for him, along with the others with us. I will fight to the death for each one of them."

"Ya may have to do just that, lass. Come on," he said, and cut the zip ties off her ankles. When he did, she kicked up. Everyone cringed as they heard his jaw crack. When she stood, she spun around and kicked his head. The man went back, bouncing his head off the wall and into the desk before he dropped to the ground, unconscious.

Reaching down, Rachel grabbed the knife that had dropped onto the ground, with her hands still attached to the chair. She then sliced the zip ties, freeing Jesse's hands before he used the knife to free his ankles, and then he released her wrists.

Just as Rachel let Owen out, he pulled a gun that was tucked into the back of his pants and ordered her to sit back down. "Uncle!" he yelled, aiming the gun at both Jesse and Rachel. When four other men ran into the room, he said, "She did that with her hands still bound. Still think I'm full of it?"

"Both of ya, have a seat," he ordered.

* * *

"I'm not worried anymore," Jacob confessed, "I'm downright scared. They've been gone a half-hour. I'm tired of everyone telling me to wait. *Something* happened."

"Give me a few," Delaney said, getting up from the table. Grabbing her phone from her pocket, she dialed it as she walked to a quieter part of the pub.

"Where's she going?" Joe asked.

"To call for back-up," Cori explained. "She's calling in the crew."

"What about the authorities?" Jacob asked.

"We're a bit more efficient," Kai assured him.

"Whatever you need, we can help," Joe offered. "Even though this is your territory, they are our teammates *and* leader."

"Which one?"

"Rachel's the leader. While she *is* the leader, we operate as a team. We each have different gifts, and bring different assets to the team."

"What do you mean by 'gifts'?" Cori asked.

"Well, Rachel can look at you and tell if you're one of the Lord's or not, or even if you're an A.N.G.E.L. or not."

"What does A.N.G.E.L. mean? I've heard you say that already. It's not a real angel. Is it?" Kai asked.

"A.N.G.E.L. stands for Available to Nurture God's Eternal Love. Anyone who is His can be an angel to another person," Joe explained. "You can be there for someone in need. You can bring them food. Even just witnessing to someone is being one of His angels. However, being an A.N.G.E.L. in the unit is a different kind of angel. We are given assignments by an archangel."

"Seriously? You've seen a *real* angel?" Cori asked, stunned.

"Seen the other side too," Jacob said under his breath, with a shudder. "They're scary. Count your blessings, Cori, that you'll never have to even picture one of them."

"Jacob!" Joe said, appalled at his comment.

"Oh, comments like that don't bother me. I'm pretty thick-skinned." Cori smiled. "Especially if he said it in a protective nature. I've come to terms with my blindness. I know God has heightened my other senses enough to compensate for my lack of sight. I have a vivid imagination. If you allow me, I can picture your faces by letting me touch them."

"Go ahead," Jacob offered.

As Cori ran her fingers over his face, his face flushed, and she giggled.

"What?" Jacob asked.

"I can feel that you're blushing. There's no reason to be embarrassed. You have a kind face…kind of round in shape. What color are your eyes?"

"Blue."

"And your hair?"

"Light brown."

Running her fingers down his neck, she went out to his shoulders. "You're not all that tall either, yeah?"

He cringed. "Not so much."

"But taller than my five foot four, yeah?"

"Yes," he said, heart skipping a beat in hope.

"You seem to have a kind heart and soul. Do all the A.N.G.E.L.s have this?"

"Yes," Jacob said, as she moved over to Joe.

"You're quite a bit taller, yeah?" Cori asked Joe.

"Only by about four inches," Joe said. "I'm about six foot. I have brown hair and dark brown eyes. Rachel has blonde hair, and brilliant blue eyes. And Jesse has blonde hair and green eyes."

Giggling again, Cori said, "I see."

"Why are you laughing now?" Joe asked, as she finished, running her fingers off his shoulders.

"Does she know?"

"Does who know what?"

"Does Rachel know ya like her?" Cori asked, with a knowing smile.

"How do *you* know?"

"I told you. I sense things. Just because I can't physically see, doesn't mean I can't see your feelings in your voice."

"I don't know if she does or not," Joe said, answering Cori's question, "but she and Jesse are a much better match."

"Always the big guys," Kai said, shaking his head.

"You're not all that small," Cori pointed out, nudging him.

"Not really muscular either," he countered.

"Okay," Delaney came back to the table, sitting down, "the group will meet in the student center in a half-hour."

"Jesse has the keys to our van," Joe pointed out.

Jacob added, "We're not normally apart."

"We need to call Angel and let her know what's going on. We should probably call the Haven as well, so they can be praying," Joe said, his southern accent getting thicker as he got more stressed.

"There's a phone booth over there if ya want some privacy," Delaney pointed to an old phone booth on the other side of the restaurant. "We'll wait here. I'll pay for dinner. By the way, we're joining your team as well, so we might as well start now. We talked about it earlier. This dinner was to give Cori and Kai a formal introduction to you."

"We trust her instincts. She's not the most trusting individual," Cori pointed out.

"Yes, now that we've met you, we are more than honored to be given the opportunity to be an A.N.G.E.L.," Kai added. "We know it's not the safest of positions, but we're supposed to be staying at what you called the Safe Haven. Pretty sure we're getting the better end of the deal."

"Thank you," Joe said, grateful. "We appreciate your help."

"They're part of our team as well, since we'll be joining you," Kai explained. "We'll be right here when you're done, and then we'll head over to the student center."

Jacob and Joe went into the booth and closed the door.

"Who first?" Joe asked, staring at his phone, feeling a pit in his stomach.

"Angel. Let's hope she's not in the air right now."

Dialing Angel's number, they were glad when she promptly answered, "This is Angel."

"Angel," Joe said, "This is Joe and Jacob. Not sure how to tell ya this."

Impatiently, Angel spouted, "Just go ahead and say it. We have a plane to catch."

"Not sure that you'll take this news well, but Rachel and Jesse were taken."

"Taken? What do you mean by taken? Taken where? By whom?"

"We don't know. We were waiting for dinner, and the waiter wanted to talk to Rachel. Jesse wouldn't let her go alone, so he followed them and, well, they're all three gone," Joe explained.

"When?"

"About forty-five minutes ago. Delaney, Kai, and Cori are helping with their contacts."

"Good. Was it the other side?"

"We don't know. The two who would know are the two who are missing," Jacob pointed out. "We're calling the Haven after we get off with you to let them know."

"The manager has also already contacted the authorities, but there's not much they can do without any information. No one saw anything," Joe said. "This will be up to God to give us help."

"Understood," Angel said. "Keep me posted...even if it's just through text."

"Yes, ma'am," Joe said, and hung up. "Well," he looked up at Jacob, "that went better than I thought."

"I don't think Daddy English is going to take it quite so well," Jacob pointed out.

"Who says she took it well? I think she's a bit distracted with losing Aden, and is trying to hold it together."

"I agree. Let's get it over with. We need to get back to the others."

Dialing the phone, Joe cringed when Mark answered, "Hello?"

"Mark, this is Joe and Jacob. We've got a problem."

*   *   *

"I don't *want* to sit," Rachel snapped, hand clasped around the knife she used to set Owen free. Glaring at all the men around her, Rachel's body felt on edge. Looking from man to man, her back was to the wall. "Why did you take us? What's going on?"

"We're going to give ya a little test, is all," the guy said innocently.

Three of the men jumped Jesse, and injected him with the sedative again before tying him to the chair. As Jesse went unconscious, Owen's uncle explained, "Time to test ya. We wanna see what you're made of, lass. *His* life depends on it," he said, nodding toward Jesse.

"No way!" Rachel glared. As fire flashed through her eyes, it turned them a steal blue. "I want answers!"

"*After* your test," he said sternly.

Two men, one on each side, jumped Rachel and dragged her out of the room, kicking and screaming. Finally, a third guy grabbed her legs to stop her from kicking the guys trying to carry her.

Throwing her into a cage, sending her to the other side, they locked it behind her. When she stood, she looked around, terrified. There were two levels to the room she was in, filled with people who were yelling and jeering. The cage she was in was round, with a single bright bulb in the center, lighting up only the cage. Having a difficult time seeing if the people were God's or not, Rachel prayed for intervention and strength. Just then, the cage door opened on the other side, and a large, bald man with a lot of tattoos and an angry face walked in. They slammed and locked the door behind him. He stood there with his arms crossed. No shirt, just jeans and boots. Rachel was sure he growled at her as she stared at him in wide-eyed terror.

*　*　*

"Guys, this is Joe Mason and Jacob Armstrong. They're friends of ours. Their friends were taken a couple hours ago from the pub. We need to find them *and* Owen. They were taken together," Delaney said to the group sitting at a table.

"Isn't Owen's uncle part of the underground?" one guy asked.

"I think so," a girl said. "He tried to recruit me once. I turned him down."

"What do we have to go on?" another guy asked.

"Just that they were taken from the pub. There are no cameras, and no one was outside at the time. There *are* tire tracks. Here's a photo of them," Delaney said, showing her phone to one of the girls.

"These look like standard van tire tracks, but let's head to the lab," the girl said, messaging the photo from Delaney's phone to her own before leaving with three others.

"Cori, Kai, and I will go to Cori's with these two to see what we can find," Delaney said, gesturing toward Joe and Jacob. "What if we meet back here in two hours?"

After Joe and Jacob described Rachel and Jesse to the group, they sent their pictures to those who needed them. The others already knew Owen. Afterward, they broke up into their perspective fields and started looking for them, agreeing to meet back in two hours.

Joe and Jacob knew it would be a long night, and that it would take a miracle to find Rachel and Jesse. They prayed for the Lord's will to guide and direct them to finding their teammates…mainly because they knew that's what it would take to find them.

C.J. Peterson

Chapter 4
Hide His Word in Your Heart

When they landed in St. Petersburg, Angel was already over being cold. It had been chilly in London, and wasn't any warmer in Russia. Being an American, living in Mexico most of her life, and then Nevada, she wanted the sunshine and warmth, but that would definitely be escaping her in the middle of September in St. Petersburg. With the average temperature between forty and sixty degrees Fahrenheit, she knew bundling would be a definite must until they got out of there…which she hoped was sooner rather than later.

Knowing they, as well as those on their lists, were being targeted, Angel was grateful when her Dad, Mark English, sent an older A.N.G.E.L. in Russia, Anastasia, to meet them at the airport. He called on her to lend them a hand in finding the two A.N.G.E.L.s in Russia before they lost another one to the other side. In the meantime, he sent Jerrod to Ireland to help Joe and Jacob find Jesse and Rachel.

"Welcome to Russia," Anastasia said with her thick Russian accent as she gave each of them a hug. "Mark said you need help to find A.N.G.E.L.s here in Russia?"

"There are two," Angel confirmed.

"What are the names?"

"That's the thing. We only have the last names and the city. No first names."

"Having said that," Josh added, "the Spirit usually seems to lead them to us."

"This is true. He is nice like that," Anastasia said with a smile. Her short, gray hair framed her etched face. The years had taken their toll on her, but she still seemed strong for seventy. "What are the names?" she asked again.

"Alexandrova and Kazakov," Angel said, glancing at the list.

"Oh!" Anastasia laughed as she clapped her hands in delight. "He is good!"

"Who?"

"The Lord, of course. Kazakov is my godson and grandnephew, Sasha, I bet. The second is a female by the ending of the name. Katia is the name that came to mind when you mentioned Alexandrova. I feel this is right. You are looking for my grandnephew and a young lady named Katia."

"How do you know?" Val asked, confused.

"Gifts of the Spirit," she simply said. Furrowing her brow, she asked, "You do not learn?"

"Is it like prophecy?"

"Like prophecy and discernment combined," Anastasia confirmed. "You will learn in time. Many gifts of the Spirit are used many different ways. To limit them, is to limit God. You would be foolish to limit God."

"Okay," Jon stepped into the conversation, "how do we find these two?"

"My godson is easy. He may know Katia. It works like that a lot."

"We need to find them quickly," Jon pushed. "We don't want to lose any more."

"Sasha is easy to find. Katia may not be so easy. May be elusive," Anastasia warned. "We will find Sasha after eating."

Resting his hand on his grumbling stomach, Jon agreed, "That'll work."

"Come. We get food."

"Yes," Angel said in relief. "Last time we ate was early this morning. I know it's only a three-hour flight, but we've been too stressed to really eat."

"Fill stomachs, then find them. This will be good."

"Let's hope so."

*   *   *

"So, you say he was attacked and killed before you could meet with him?" Anastasia asked, stunned, after Angel finished the story. "In broad daylight?"

"Yes," Angel confirmed. "The demons kept saying something about Calliope."

"Korax is the new second to Cassius," Anastasia, said, deep in thought. "I think maybe he pulled in this Calliope. Calliope

85

is a muse in Greek Mythology. May be another demon…maybe not. Only God knows."

"Whoever this Calliope is, they were cheering for her as they ripped him apart," Angel said with a shudder.

Resting her aged hand on Angel's, Anastasia said, "I am sorry you had to see this. His sister is okay, yes?"

"Physically, yes. She feels responsible for his death, though," Val explained. "She feels that if he didn't send her up the tree and run, he would still be alive."

"Maybe yes, maybe both would be dead," Anastasia pointed out.

"That's what we told her," Val agreed.

"You have kind heart," Anastasia observed. "How do you fight as A.N.G.E.L. with your heart?"

"It's not easy," Val admitted.

"And you. You are different," she said to Josh. "What is your gift?"

"Language," he responded.

"Do you speak Russian?" Anastasia asked, noticing that he seemed to be listening to a conversation near them.

Turning back toward her, he said, "I speak any language known to man. I've been tested more times than I'd like."

"Your accent? You are English or Australian? Not American?"

"No. I'm not an American. I'm Australian."

"With the U.S. team?" she asked, confused.

"They're no longer limited to one country," Angel explained. "That's why we're here."

"You are not here to start Russian team?"

"No. Our teammates are from all over the world. When the scrolls were opened, they were broken into four sections of the world."

"I see. Things are changing."

"Very much so."

"How is the other team doing?"

"They haven't lost anyone, but they have their own trouble. Two have been taken. Dad's sending them help," Angel explained.

"Oh dear! By the other side?" Anastasia asked.

"We're not sure *who* took them. That's up to Jerrod, Joe, and Jacob to figure out. We've already lost one. We don't want to lose any more. We have our assignments. We need to stay focused."

A young man who stood about six foot two, with short, spikey black hair said something in Russian to Anastasia as he walked up to the table. His dark brown eyes cautiously scanned the crew. Giving Anastasia a hug, he asked her a question.

"He said, '*Well, if it isn't my favorite godmother.*' And then he asked who we are," Josh translated for the others.

"You know Russian?" the young man asked, surprised. "With your accent, I would not think this."

"Sasha, this is Josh Sullivan. He knows many languages. He is with Jon and Angel English, brother and sister, along with their teammate, Val Thibodaux. They are A.N.G.E.L.s. A.N.G.E.L.s, this is my grandnephew and godson, Sasha Kazakov. I do believe you were looking for him. God led him here."

"Interesting," Sasha said, shaking each of their hands. "How do you know me? Why were you looking for me?"

"I told you. They are A.N.G.E.L.s," Anastasia explained. "You need to go with them."

Sasha shook his head. "Oh, I do not think so."

"You are being called, young one," Anastasia pointed out. "Are you going to tell Almighty One no?"

"Not going to agree to anything until I know what is going on."

"Then sit. We talk." Anastasia gestured toward the empty seat.

* * *

"Father," Rachel said, looking toward Heaven, "Please help me. I need Your strength, not mine. I need to save Jesse's life. We were brought here for a devious purpose. We have another mission we need t' fulfill for You. I know this can't be it."

"'*Fear not, for I am with you; be not dismayed, for I am Your God. I will strengthen you, yes, I will help you, I will uphold you with My righteous hand,*'" she heard Isaiah 41:10 in her mind.

"Thank you, Father," she said, and looked toward her opponent, who stood there, bulky arms still crossed. Kneeling down, she tied her boot, and then slid the knife out of her hiking boot. "Okay. Here we go," she said, concealing the knife in her hand. She would rather not use the knife, but if she had to, she would. By the size of him, she would need every advantage she could find.

Standing, she studied him. "You're a big one, aren't ya? Why do they have such a big guy against a sheila like myself?" Louder, as she looked around, and shouted, "Are ya afraid of tiny little ol' me? You have to send your biggest guy against a little girl?" Shaking her head, she crossed her arms and said to the guy in her normal voice, "I feel bad for you."

"Why is that?" he growled.

"Because when I beat you, you'll be teased unmercifully."

"Ya think?"

"I *know*. You know why?"

"Why is that, lass?"

"Because I'm not fighting with *my* strength. I fight with the strength of the Lord Almighty!" she said, and ran at him. When she was almost to him, she jumped and kicked him in the stomach, sending him back five feet. He stumbled, but didn't fall. Running behind him, she jumped on his back and got him in a sleeper hold.

"What are ya trying to do, lass?" he demanded, slamming her against the fence over and over again, swatting at her as if she were just an annoying mosquito.

"*'The Lord is my light and my salvation,'*" she said, quoting Psalm 27:1. She grunted when he slammed her against the pole of the fencing. "*'Whom shall I fear? The Lord is my strength.'*" She groaned when he slammed her again. Tightening her grip, she went on, "*'Strength of my life; of whom shall I be afraid?'*"

"You *should* be afraid of me!" He shouted.

Sliding the knife down her hand, she placed the blade on his throat, and he froze. "Ya got one choice, mate. You can give up, or you'll never see the light of day again," Rachel said, giving him an ultimatum.

"You think so, lass?" the guy said, and then flipped her over his head. She hit the ground, hard, leaving a nick on his neck.

"This is gonna be tougher than I thought," she said aloud to herself, rolling over just in time to miss getting stomped by him. If she could tire him out, she may have a chance. Also in her favor was that his blows were predictable due to his size.

Scrambling off the ground, she kept the knife secured in her hand as she dodged his throws left and right. She went to sweep his legs, but when she kicked him, his legs didn't move. Right leg throbbing, she hopped, looking at him wide-eyed as he turned back to her.

"Oh God, I need Your strength for this," she whispered, trembling in fear.

Before she could move, the man's fist landed on the side of her head. Flying through the air, she slammed into the fence of the cage. Bouncing off, she landed with a thud. The world spun around her. Shaking her head, she did her best to focus on the giant in front of her. Even though there looked to be three of him, she decided that if she went after the one in the middle, she may have a chance of actually hitting him.

"Had enough?" he snarled, as blood from the nick trickled down his neck.

"Not by a long shot!" she said, standing up. Swaying side to side, she felt blood run down her cheek as the area he'd hit pulsated in pain. Meanwhile, the back of her head throbbed where she hit the ground, messing with her vision. Squinting to see better, she tightened her hand around the knife handle. "Why do you find it such fun to pummel little girls? I would think your mum would have raised ya better."

"You do *not* have the right to bring my mum into this!" he growled.

Crouching down, she prayed for clarity as to what to do next. Psalm 18:32 and 33 came to mind. Saying the verse aloud, she gathered strength with each word, "'*It is God that girdeth me with strength, and maketh my way perfect. He maketh my feet like hinds' feet, and setteth me upon my high places.*'"

"What are you saying, lass? Are ya delirious?"

"'*The Lord will give strength unto His people; the Lord will bless His people with peace,*'" she went on to quote Psalm 29:11.

Shaking his head, he crossed his arms. "You're mumbling nonsense, and I haven't even started. Enough of this!" he snapped, and slammed his fist into her mid-section.

Feeling a couple of ribs crack under his fist, she let out a howl as she flew backward, slamming into the cage again before dropping to the ground, taking her breath away. Groaning, she slowly pushed herself up to her hands and knees, holding her ribs. The jeering of the crowd echoed in her mind. Between the pounding, the pain, and the shouts and cheers, her mind was on overload. Taking a moment, she collected herself before looking back at him with a look of determination.

"You're a stubborn one, aren't ya?" he said, visibly impressed. "Why don't ya just stay down?"

"'*My flesh and my heart may fail, but God is the strength of my heart and my portion forever*,'" Rachel said, quoting Psalm 73:26, as she staggered to her feet once again.

"Ya got a death wish, lass? Stay down!"

When he went to swing again, she ducked and ran behind him. Before he could turn around, she climbed on his back, pushing her feet against his lower back to straighten her legs so he couldn't reach her. She didn't put her arm around his neck this time. She didn't want to give him a way to flip her again. Leaving one hand on his shoulder, she used the other hand to press the knife into his neck at the carotid artery. "Move an inch, and I jam the knife in. You will be dead within a minute," she hissed.

Reaching back over and over again, flailing his arms, he realized he couldn't reach her. Feeling the knife go deeper, cutting into his neck, he knew she meant business. "I'm done," he said, raising his hands as the blood drizzled down his neck in a faster stream. "You win."

Objections were heard throughout the arena while she climbed off his back.

Shaking her hand, the guy admirably said, "You're a tough lass."

"Honestly, without my knife, I'm sure you would have won," Rachel replied, relieved to be done, as she gingerly held her ribs. Sliding the knife into her pocket for safekeeping, she looked around and yelled, "Now, where's Jesse? I fought! We are to be set free!"

Suddenly, doors to the arena burst open and gunfire showered the area. The guy she'd fought jumped on her, covering her with his body, as the ear-piercing screams and shouts vied with the deafening gunfire for which was louder.

After what seemed like minutes, but in reality was only a few tense moments, silence and smoke filled the air. "Rachel?" a voice yelled. Shoving the now-dead guy off her, she cautiously looked around. "Rachel?" she heard again.

"Jerrod!"

"I'm here!"

"Get Jesse! He's in the office!"

"The boys are getting him," Jerrod said, coming to the cage. He shot the lock on the cage. Then he jerked the door open. Keeping an eye for any movement, he helped her up. "We need to get out of here...fast!"

Stumbling to her feet, she staggered from the cage. "No need t' ask me twice." They met Joe, Jacob, and Jesse, and were out the door to the waiting van in seconds. As soon as they were in, Delaney floored the van out of the parking lot.

"You okay?" Jesse asked, grabbing Rachel in a hug. "I was so worried about you."

"Owwww!" She flinched in pain, so he let her go.

"What happened?"

"Broken ribs. I won thanks to the knife I keep in my hiking boot," she explained, still shaking. She wasn't sure who was shaking more – her or Jesse. "Just as he gave up, gunfire splattered the area."

"It wasn't just us. We had some help. Their friends are in the van behind us," Jerrod explained, feeling her ribs to see which ones were broken. "Feels like three of them." Absentmindedly, as he continued to check her over, he explained, "I jumped on a plane as soon as Joe and Jacob called, and got in early this morning."

"How long have we been gone?" Rachel asked, stunned, as Jerrod looked at the blood in her hair to find the source.

"Two days," Jacob said from the front seat. "You guys scared us to death."

"Good news is, we got three new team members," Joe explained from the second seat. "Bad news is, we have to go the round-a-bout way to get home. Your luggage is there," he said, nodding toward the bags in the back of the van. "We have to go to Dublin to catch a ferry to Liverpool. Then from Liverpool, we're catching a train to St. Pancras in London.

From there, we taxi to Heathrow. From Heathrow, it's a measly sixteen hours until we land in the good ol' US of A in Reno." Joe smirked. "It's the safer way to get you two outta Ireland. It also keeps us off radar until we check in at Heathrow."

"Chances are, they'll expect us to catch a plane outta Cork or Dublin," Cori added. "This may seem a pain way to do it, but it's the way that will give you time to recover, as well as get us outta Ireland undetected."

"You'll not hear any argument from me," Rachel agreed. "You all did a great job in finding us and forming a plan to get us out of here. I don't want to know what will come of this situation. I'm pretty sure we angered the wrong people."

"You did," Delaney confirmed over her shoulder as she drove.

"They're not good people to get mixed up with…even worse to tick off," Kai pointed out, while Jerrod checked Rachel's head for more damage.

"Ouch!" Rachel cringed and jumped when Jerrod touched the cut on her cheek with gauze doused in providone iodine. "Easy on, mate!"

"Have to clean it. Sorry."

"You're not sorry."

"No, I'm not," he said, as he finished cleaning her wounds. "However, we need to get you cleaned up. We don't want people to give us odd looks while we're traveling. You'll also need your Lovenox shots to stop your blood from clotting until we land in Reno. We have a plane change in the U.S., so I'll give you another shot then. With your injuries, you know that's a concern."

"Definitely," Rachel agreed. "Might as well start now," she said, lifting her shirt, exposing her abdomen. Pinching her skin, she took a deep breath before he stuck it in and emptied the syringe. "Ouch," she groaned. "That feels like a bee sting."

"I know. Sorry, but not really. It's for your health. Here's a clean shirt." He tossed it to her before he made his way to the front of the van while she changed.

Once he was in the front, Jesse turned to Rachel. Putting his hands gently on her shoulders, he spoke quietly. "Look, I know you can handle yourself. I'm grateful you were willing to fight for me to the death. However, please don't ever do that again."

"I will do what I have to for my Lord and my team," Rachel snapped.

Seeing the fire flash through her eyes, he sat back on his feet. Looking deep into her eyes, hoping she would understand, he pleaded, "If anything happened to you, I don't know what I would do."

"You would probably lead this team."

"Not without you," he said, resting his hand on the side of her face.

Stunned, she placed her hand over his and took a deep breath. Still shaken by the events of the last few days, she shook her head. Looking down for a moment, she collected her thoughts. She had to stay in control. Looking back up at him, she explained, "Thank you, but the entire team does not rely on one person, except the Lord."

Sighing, he shook his head. "Please understand? I don't think you know what you mean to me."

"I do. And, I'm sure you know what you mean to me. I have to keep a level head, though."

"Why won't you let yourself feel what we both know we're feeling? In doing what we do, we need to take it when we get it. Life is short. It's even shorter for an A.N.G.E.L. – you know this."

"I get that. Trust me, I do! I also know we're only starting this journey. I know we have a long trek ahead of us."

"Starting with you getting healed before we take off again."

"That's not going to be easy."

"I know you can handle it. You're a tough little cookie," Jesse said, and gave her a gentle hug. It would be hard for him, but he would do his best to pull back in regards to his feelings for Rachel until she was ready. Deciding he would do his best to wait, he knew he would have to make a move soon. Her answer would be the deciding factor on if there were to be a future for them or not. Until then, he would hold out hope.

"We have a long trip over the next few days, folks," Jerrod pointed out. "We'll need to get the rest where we can. Rach, you're going to need to clean yourself up before we get to the ferry. We can't take you on it looking like that."

"Not that you don't always look good, darlin'," Joe added, "But, blood and torn shirts are not really in style."

"Enough said," Rachel said, picking up the shirt. "Everyone face forward. We have to get out of this country. Sooner rather than later, eh?"

Chapter 5
All Things Work Together for Good

"Being an A.N.G.E.L. is a choice. It is a choice to let God not only rule in your heart and life forever, but to have control too. You are strong, young one," Anastasia said, resting her hand on Sasha's shoulder. "You have taken care of me for years. Now you need to choose a path for yourself."

"I do not know if I can do it. I promised Mother to take care of you."

"Take courage. Joshua 1:9 tells you, '*Be strong and of good courage; do not be afraid, do not be dismayed, for the Lord your God is with you wherever you go.*' He will give you the strength you need. You only need to hide His words in your heart. He will be with you. You need to do this."

"I have a choice, yes?"

"You always have a choice," Angel stepped into the conversation. "God gave us all the free will to choose. He hopes you will choose the path He has for you, but if you don't, there will be another to step up and take your place. Having said that, *you* are the best person for the job."

"How do you know this?" Sasha asked.

"We have a portion of the list," Angel explained.

Anastasia's face went pale. "You have the box with you?"

"We know where it is," Angel confirmed.

"You have seen it open?" she asked, stunned. "Not many have seen this."

"Yes. We were there when the Colonel opened it." When Angel mentioned the Colonel, Jon cringed.

"What is it?" Anastasia asked, noticing Jon's face.

"He was like a second father to me," Jon explained. "When he passed, it was not only a loss to the A.N.G.E.L.s, but a deep wound to me."

"I am sorry to you for this loss. When the Colonel went, it was a hard loss to all the A.N.G.E.L.s, but deeper for you, yes?"

"Yes. Thank you, but that's not our concern at the moment," Jon said, refocusing the group. "Our concern –"

"Our concern is getting to those on the list before the other side does," Angel cut Jon off. "We already lost one in England. We don't want to lose any more."

"I understand, but this is not an easy thing you ask of me," Sasha pointed out, his Russian accent thick as he spoke English.

"I'm not asking you anything we have not done ourselves. And, technically *I'm* not asking – God is," Angel pointed out.

"This is true," Sasha said, sitting back in his seat, mulling things over in his mind. "When do you need my answer?"

"We still have to find Katia. Once we get an answer from her, we'll go. But, I feel you need to be warned. The other side has already killed the A.N.G.E.L. from England. The other side got to him before we did."

"They *killed* him?" Sasha asked, making sure he heard her correctly.

"Yes. Now, just because you choose to be an A.N.G.E.L. doesn't mean you're protected. You will be one of God's warriors as an A.N.G.E.L., but you're still mortal. Granted, we have a little supernatural help, but we *are* still mortal."

"I understand."

"Do you have any idea where we can find Katia?" Angel asked.

"Katia who?"

"Katia Alexandrova."

"St. Petersburg is big place. How do you expect to find this girl?"

Angel shrugged. "Not sure. God tends to lead us where we need to go."

"Well, then I hope He shows you the way to her," he said, and got up and left.

"Well, then," Josh huffed. "Do we take that as a maybe?"

"I think I will," Angel said, watching him walk out of the restaurant and down the street. "This has all been up to God so far, so I'm going to leave it in His hands."

"This is good, I think," Anastasia agreed. "He has a stubborn streak. He will come around. Have patience. God will work on his heart. In the meantime, you find Katia."

"Sounds like a plan. After all, '*all things work together for good to those who love Him, who have been called according to His purpose,*'" Angel said.

"Romans 8:28. Yes, this is true," Anastasia agreed. "God is good."

"All the time," Jon finished. "And all the time."

"God is good," Val completed.

*   *   *

"Liliya?" Katia called out as she walked into their shabby apartment. Sparsely decorated, the pair had been orphans since Katia was eight and Liliya was two. Finally being emancipated at eighteen, Katia had taken her sister with her when she left the orphanage. That was four years ago.

"Liliya!" Katia called out more loudly, as she continued to search the apartment. Working at a local shop during the day, and as security at night, Katia was able to let Liliya go to school. Unfortunately, Liliya had to function as if Katia wasn't around, due to the hectic schedule.

"Seriously, little one! Where are you?" Katia demanded. Finally finding the note on the counter, she scanned it to find that Liliya had gone out with her good friends, Tatiana, Grisha, Dmitry, and Stepan. "Well, at least *one* of us is having fun," Katia sighed. Looking toward the heavens, Katia said aloud, "Pastor says You are there, and will never leave us. He says You see everything that goes on with us, and are right beside us. While I believe in You and in Jesus, sometimes I feel lost and alone," she admitted, and then looked down, upset. After a moment, she looked toward the heavens and said, "If You are really there, why won't You cut me a break? Just once?"

Hearing a knock on the door, she answered it to find Liliya's friends all looking stressed and terrified. "Is she here?" Tatiana asked, panicked. Everyone spoke Russian. "Is Liliya here?"

"What do you mean?" Katia asked. She held the note up. "Liliya said she was with you. Is she not?"

"We were at the club when she went to the bathroom, and then disappeared," Stepan explained. "She was gone for too long when we sent Tatiana after her."

"She was not in there. No one was in there," Tatiana added.

"When was this?" Katia searched their faces for answers.

"About an hour ago," Grisha said. "We searched, hoping to find her before we came to you for help."

"Did you ask the manager?" Katia asked.

"Manager, waiters, bartenders…everyone we could find," Dmitry said. "No one saw her after she left the table. There were so many people. We could not find her anywhere."

"Let's go," Katia said, grabbing her keys before they all ran out of the building together.

* * *

Katia called off work that night in order to search for Liliya, but to no avail. She even called off the next morning to continue the search with Liliya's friends. Katia didn't feel she would be able to get any rest until Liliya was found. Liliya was her only family, and the only one who Katia truly loved besides the Lord. Without Liliya, Katia would be alone in the world…and that was something Katia did not want to face.

"Please, if you see her, tell her to come home?" Katia asked the clerk at the store Liliya went to when she was home alone.

"I will. I am sorry. Have you told the authorities?"

"I am going there next."

"I hope you find her. This is not a good area for a young girl to be alone, especially at night."

"I know. That is what is worrying me," she said and left.

Stopping to make a report, she felt it was almost useless, as the officer didn't think anything could be done, but took the report anyway. As far as he was concerned, Liliya was a runaway. Brokenhearted, Katia walked out of the station.

"I heard you tell them she was at the club last night," a voice behind her said, and she spun toward the college-aged man who followed her out of the station.

"Yes. Do you know something?" she asked, as they spoke in Russian.

Looking both ways to make sure he wasn't heard, he said, "You didn't hear it from me."

"Of course not. Now talk!"

"I know there is a group who frequents the clubs."

"What *kind* of group?" Katia asked, crossing her arms, getting impatient.

"One that likes young, pretty girls. They use them to sell."

"Like slaves?" Katia shook her head, confused. "Are you talking slaves?"

"A *kind* of slave," the guy hinted.

Katia narrowed her eyes. "Meaning?"

"Meaning the kind that sells girls for profit."

With a look of angry realization on her face, she asked, "Are you telling me what I *think* you're telling me?"

"That your sister may be caught up in a sex trafficking operation? Yes."

Narrowing her eyes, she demanded, "Where do I find these people? Give me a name!"

"I-I can't."

Grabbing him by the collar, she walked him backward until he slammed into the brick wall of the building. Growling, she ordered, "Give-me-a-name!"

"S-Sergei Petrenko. Do not tell him I told you."

"If I find out you lied to me, I don't care that I do not know your name. I will figure it out, and I *will* find you!"

"I believe it!" he said, putting his hands up in surrender.

"So, going to ask you one more time. Is Sergei Petrenko the one I need to be looking for?"

"Y-yes," he stammered. "He is at the top. You have to work your way up there."

"Where do I start?"

"I heard Stepan Rusnak is where you start. He is one of those in the schools."

"Stepan Rusnak?" she asked, taking a step back. "Are you *sure* that is who I should be looking for?" she asked, confused. "That is one of her friends. He was with her last night."

"Yes. He leads them to a club where they get kidnapped. How long has she known him?"

"Only about…about a couple of months."

"He changes schools a lot. He and a couple of others are like scouts. They find candidates, and get to know them. They get close to them and get them to trust them. Once they have trust, their job is to get them to where they will be taken. Before the authorities catch on and get too close, they change schools."

"How? How do they get them to trust them?" she questioned.

"Once they befriend them, they start taking them to the clubs. After a few times, once the girl is comfortable in a particular club, they are kidnapped from the bathroom. Once they are kidnapped from the bathroom, they are taken to a house. I am not sure where the house is located. From the house, I have no idea *where* they go."

"Then *who* do I talk to in order to find out?"

"I would start with Stepan."

"I mean it. I *will* find you if you are lying."

Hands in the air again, he said, "I know. I know. I'm not. You seem like a nice girl…well, you did before you slammed me into the wall. You are looking for your sister. I hope you find her. I lost mine. That is how I found out as much as I know. Unfortunately, I have never found *my* sister. I hope you find yours."

Taking another step back in shock, she asked, stunned, "You *never* found her?"

"No."

"What is her name?"

"Elena Yukova."

"Your name?"

"I do not want to tell you," he whined.

"I'll find out anyway. Make my life a bit easier," she said, crossing her arms, finally letting him go.

"Erik," he admitted, as he stuffed his hands in his pockets, looking down.

"I will do my best to find Elena as well, Erik. Here," she wrote her number down on a piece of paper from her wallet and handed it to him. "This is my number. You call it and leave a message that it is your number, and when I find her I will let you know."

Furrowing his brow, he said, "She has been missing for two years. She was fifteen when she was taken. How will *you* find her when no one else has been able to?"

"When I get to Liliya, we will find Elena as well. They are both seventeen. I will not stop until I find both of them."

"You mean, you will really help me?" he asked, with hope in his eyes for the first time since she saw him.

"I will get you an answer of some kind. It will be my mission to find both of our sisters."

"Thank you! God bless you!" he said, and quickly hugged her before taking a step back.

"I will start with Stepan. I feel he needs a 'come to Jesus' moment, and I intend to give it to him."

*   *   *

As they finished ordering their dinner at the restaurant that evening, and the waiter left to turn their order in to the kitchen, Val turned to the others, "So, how are we supposed to find Katia?"

"God has a unique way of bringing the people we're looking for to us," Josh pointed out before taking a sip of his soda.

"I am sorry," their waiter, Stepan, said, speaking English as he returned to the table, "we are out of Kotlety. Is there another choice you would like?" he asked, handing Jon the menu.

"Hmmm. What about the Golubsty?"

"Yes. We have this. Same sides?"

"Yes, please."

"Thank you," Stepan said, and disappeared back into the kitchen.

"Okay, I know Kotlety is like a meatball, but what is Golubsty?" Val asked.

"That's meat-stuffed cabbage leaves," Jon explained. "Their food is good, but not what I'm used to. I have a feeling we're going to experience a lot of new food, so I'm going to make the best of it."

"And pray it doesn't mess with your stomach," Val said, popping a fish oil capsule.

"What's that for?" Jon furrowed his brow.

"It's to help with, um, irritable bowel. It's really messed up with all this new food. I'll get used to it, though… hopefully."

"What would you do if it did get to me?" Jon asked, curiosity getting the better of him.

"Well, if your stomach gives you issues, I have ginger for nausea, red raspberry for diarrhea, and hops for upset stomach."

"Not sure how you fit everything in your suitcase," Josh said, shaking his head with a chuckle. "You seem to have a complete herbal medicine cabinet in there."

Nodding, Val's attention was suddenly drawn to the hostess stand, when a young lady with a loud voice came in.

Furrowing his brow, he tapped Josh, and gestured toward the hostess.

"Gde Stepan?" the girl demanded.

"YA ne znayu, Katia," she stammered.

"Well, *that's* interesting," Josh remarked.

"What?" Angel asked.

"That girl just demanded to know where Stepan was…and her name is Katia," Josh explained.

"*Really*?" Angel said, turning to Katia. "Looks like God's looking out for us after all."

Reaching over the stand and grabbing her by the collar, Katia pulled the hostess toward her and demanded, "Gde on, Alina?"

As the group looked at Josh, he translated after each sentence, "She wants to know where he is again…and the hostess's name is Alina."

"Na kukhne," Alina relented.

"She just told her that he's in the kitchen. Be prepared for some yelling. She's not happy," Josh remarked. "She said something not very nice under her breath as she let her go."

"Well, Katia is *very* pretty," Val remarked, intrigued, as he watched the angry Katia storm by.

"Obviously *something* has her riled up," Angel said, studying her.

Just then, they heard Katia yelling in the kitchen at Stepan. Everyone in the group looked at Josh wide-eyed, as he translated, "Apparently she's looking for a girl named Liliya, and thinks Stepan did something to her."

"That would explain her anger," Val said, looking toward the door.

Suddenly, Stepan was thrown through the double doors, landing on the floor, as Katia flung the kitchen doors open. Poised between the open doors with her hands in balled fists at her sides, Katia shouted in Russian with fire in her eyes.

"She said, *you will tell me what you have done*," Josh said, watching the pair, wide-eyed.

Stepan stammered in his response. When the group looked at Josh, he quickly translated, "He asked, *What are you talking about? Do you know where she is?*"

Picking him up off the ground by his ear, Katia pulled Stepan behind her out the door. The group got up and followed them out the door to see Katia slam him against the wall, shouting less than an inch from his face at him in Russian.

"Whoa!" Josh looked at them, stunned. "She, uh, said that Stepan *sold* Liliya. She says that Stepan gave her to them, and demanded to know where she is again."

"He *what*?" Angel asked, floored. "Did you say what I *think* you said?"

"Yes. Now, shush!" Josh hushed her. "I can't hear."

As the conversation went on, Josh translated. "He said, *Sold her? You've lost your mind! She was my friend!*"

Katia growled as she got in Stepan's face. The group looked from the pair, to Josh, for him to translate. "She said, *She is my sister, and you sold her as a sex slave! Give me a name so I can track them down and get her back!* Oh boy!" Josh added on the end of the translation. "This isn't good. Liliya's been sold! We have to help her!"

Just as they were about to go over to Stepan and Katia, the police could be heard barreling down the street, so Katia let him go and took off. Before she left, she let him know that she would find him again, and that he'd better be ready with information.

"That's not good," Josh said, as the group returned to the table. "What can we do to help her?"

Sitting down at the table, Angel said, "We have to do what we can. Without her sister found, there is no way she'll join us. We'll have to help find her sister."

"We'll have to find Katia again first," Val pointed out. "She's quick!"

"We don't know where she *is*," Josh said, "but we know where she'll *be*."

"What do you mean?" Angel asked.

"We know she'll be looking for Stepan," Josh pointed out. "If we stay near him, *she'll* find *us*."

"Ooo! Good point!" Val agreed.

"Then that's our plan of action," Angel decided.

"Many apologies," Stepan said, coming to their table. "Dominika will be taking over this table. I must speak with someone. Dominika speaks English as well."

"No problem." Angel smiled. "Are you okay?"

Taking a deep breath, he slowly let it out before he admitted, "It was scary. Not sure why she did that. I will be okay. I must speak with authorities, so Dominika will take over. Many apologies again."

"Your English is very good. Would you mind helping us a bit while we're here?" Josh asked.

"We'll pay you," Angel added, hoping the incentive would entice him. "We're not here for very long, and could use as much help as we can."

"I will," he said, grabbing a napkin. He scribbled his name and number down on it before he gave it to Angel. "You call me, and I will meet you. Again, many apologies," he said, and disappeared back into the kitchen.

"Good thinking," Val remarked. "I feel so sick talking to him though. What if he really did what she accused him of doing?"

"Then we know she'll find him again," Angel said with a shrug. "It'll be in our best interest to be near him when she does."

"Will she be able to trust us after that?" Val asked. "We'll be hanging out with her sister's kidnapper."

"We'll just have to have our translator explain why we're with her," Angel said, resting her hand on Josh's arm. "Right, hon?"

Josh leaned back and crossed his arms, letting Angel's hand slip off.

"What's wrong?" Angel asked, almost hurt.

"There's a lot going on," Josh said, deep in thought. "Not a good time to start anything."

"What do you mean?"

"We'll talk about it later," Josh said, and got up to go to the bathroom.

He splashed water on his face, and then looked in the mirror. *How could she even think of any type of romantic notion at a time like this?* Angel seemed to target him as soon as she saw him, and let everyone know it. He never made it a secret, though, that he wasn't interested in anyone right now.

Josh imagined what *he* would do if it were Leah or Rachel who were taken. That thought alone was deeply upsetting, but for such a grotesque reason just added insult to injury. At that moment, he made a personal vow to the Lord to help Katia find Liliya…whatever it took.

*   *   *

After returning to the table, Josh ate most of his meal in silence. Deep in his own thoughts, he let the conversation swirl around him without adding his comments. His thoughts were with Katia and her sister.

"We need to find Stepan," Josh finally said after Dominika took away their empty plates, and left the check.

"We will…tomorrow," Angel said decisively. "If we call too soon, he'll think something's up."

"I didn't say to call him. I said to *find* him. He's our only lead. You can bet for certain that he's not far from Katia's eye either. Where he is, she'll be close behind."

"Why are you so fixated on finding Stepan?" Angel asked. "We have his number. We'll just call him tomorrow. What's the big deal?"

"What if we lose him before then?" Josh argued. "He said he had to go talk to someone. Who's to say it's not the bloke who took Liliya?"

"He said he was going to the authorities," Angel said, not bothered by the situation. "We'll just catch up with him tomorrow."

"You don't understand the urgent urgency here."

"All right. What *is* the urgent urgency? Stepan's our lead. We wait and talk to him tomorrow."

"No!" Josh snapped.

Never seeing Josh snap before, the table was stunned silent.

Turning to Jon, Josh asked, "What if it were Angel who was taken? Would *you* wait until the next morning to call a lead?"

"No," Jon said, understanding Josh's perspective.

"I would be willing to bet that Katia hasn't slept since she found out her sister went missing. And to find out it was a friend who got her kidnapped?" Josh shook his head. Pounding his fist on the table to make sure his point was heard, he sternly said, "We *have* to find Stepan…*now!*"

"I agree," Val said. "If it were one of our team members, we wouldn't hesitate to find them *tonight*."

"Me too," Jon agreed. "If it were Angel or Rachel, we wouldn't be sitting here arguing about it. We'd be out that door."

Feeling a twinge of jealousy at the attention Josh was paying toward Katia and her sister, Angel struggled inside. "Look, it's not like the other side is after her," she said, as she stirred her soda with a straw. "It's dangerous to go out in a strange country at night. This can wait until the morning."

"How can you be so callous?" Josh shook his head. "Some days I don't even know who you are."

"Fine," she said, dropping the straw and crossing her arms. "We'll go. Tell us, oh wise one, how *exactly* are we going to find him now? It's been at least a half hour since he left."

"Some days you can be a brat!" Jon snapped. "What if it were Jesse or I taken? I realize we're big guys, so you generally don't have to worry, but where is your empathy and compassion for another? There are days I seriously question the choice to make you leader. I thought you'd worked this out already. Why does it have to be such a struggle to get you to lead? Why should doing the right thing even remotely be in question here?"

"It's not!" Angel shot back. "I can't *afford* to have compassion and empathy in my position. I have to consider the safety of all of my team. I have to look at the risk versus safety factors."

"We're *all* God's children," Val argued. "He put us here for a reason. You don't think it was a coincidence that we *happened* to have Stepan as our waiter tonight, do you?"

"No. But, you guys are proposing that we look for someone who is connected to sex trafficking in a foreign country…at night," Angel explained her side.

"I realize that, but in this case time is of the essence," Josh disagreed. "There are people's lives on the line here. This is not an instance where caution should be used. Now, do we need to watch what we do out there? Oh yeah! But finding this girl is super important. Not just for what it does for Katia, but for what it will do for Liliya as well."

"What if she still chooses not to come, and one of you is injured during the process?" Angel challenged.

"I'm not doing it just because I want her on the team. I'm doing it because it's the right thing to do. It's the same reason we helped Ashley when it came to Allie and Callie," Josh said.

"And that got her killed," Angel pointed out.

"No, the other side took her out. The alternative was that those little girls, who were taken, would have been left in the hands of the other side, and only God knows what they would have done to them. Look, I know it's a risk, but I'm willing to take that risk in order to help Katia and Liliya," Josh said, putting his foot down. "This is not up for discussion as far as I'm concerned. *I'm* helping!"

"Me too. I'll take the risk," Val agreed.

"I'll take that risk too. Their lives are just as important as mine," Jon added.

"Fine." Angel put her hands up in surrender. "I know when I'm beat." Standing, she added, "Let's go find him."

After paying the bill, the group went outside. "Where do we start?" Val asked.

Seeing Dominika standing against the corner of the restaurant toward the back, smoking, Josh told the others, "Stay here." He then headed toward Dominika. "Hi," Josh said in Russian as he approached her. "Nice night tonight."

"I thought you only spoke English?" Dominika replied, surprised.

"I speak many languages." He shrugged. Leaning against the wall next to her with his hands in his pockets, he turned the conversation back to English for the benefit of the others, and asked, "Remember that guy who waited on our table?"

"Stepan. Yes. What about him?"

"Well, he gave us his number to call to show us around the area," he said, showing her the napkin with the number on it. "Do you happen to know where he went? We wanted to get in touch with him tonight to show us around to some of the clubs. He said something about going to the authorities, though, which is probably why he's not answering."

"He probably did go to the authorities. That girl was crazy tonight! Knowing him, and how stressed he looked, he will probably go out afterward. He goes to this club a lot," she said, taking the napkin. After writing the name of the club down, she handed it back. "He goes there just about every night after work."

"Thank you. And, thank you for taking care of us tonight."

"No problem. Come back again soon?" she asked, hopeful.

"Maybe," he said, flashing a smile. "The food was really good. In the meantime, have a good night." Walking back over to the group, he held up the napkin, "He's probably here," he said, handing it to Angel, who snatched it from his hand with an angry look on her face. "That's where we start."

Chapter 6
The Thief Comes Only to Steal
and Kill and Destroy

After stopping by the hotel to change into something a little more suitable for a club setting, the group called a taxi to take them to the club. "This is…nice," Angel said, hesitantly, as her eyes adjusted to the lack of light in the club.

The loud music was almost deafening, the flashing lights blinding, and the smoke suffocating as they made their way through the crowd. The guys surrounded Angel to protect her, as people continuously bumped into them. Those dancing didn't seem to pay attention to anyone else there. They just bounced around, dancing, without a care in the world. Angel now understood how easy it would be for someone to go missing. It was almost too perfect a setting for a kidnapping.

"Does anyone see him?" she yelled over the noise.

"No," Josh said, looking in every direction.

"What about Katia?"

"Not…wait!" Jon said, catching a glimpse of her. "She's over there." He pointed to a table in the corner.

Slowly making their way across the club, they walked up to Katia's table. "Hi," Josh started. "I know you don't know us, but we know you need help finding your sister, and we're here to help."

"What do you mean? Who are you?" she asked in English, stunned.

Angel shoved past Jon and Josh, and explained, "We're A.N.G.E.L.s – which stands for Available to Nurture God's Eternal Love. We are sent on missions for God, which is Who led us here."

"Have you misplaced your brain?" Katia asked.

"Um, I *think* you meant to say, have you lost your mind," Val offered, stifling the laugh that wanted to escape.

"The jury's still out on that one," Angel chuckled. "Look, we know Liliya's disappearance has to do with Stepan and this club," she said, producing the napkin showing his number and the name of the club.

"Real smooth, Angel," Josh said under his breath.

"Why do you care?" Katia questioned.

"Because we want to help," Angel said, simply.

"I do not know you. I do not want your help. I will take care of my own affairs and my sister, just as I have all my life. Please leave."

"We're still going to help," Josh explained. "We're going to try to get close to Stepan to do it. If you see us near him, that's what we're doing."

"I do not care. I do not know you." She stood. "Please leave."

"Wait!" Angel put her hand on Katia's arm, but Katia pulled away.

"Touch me again, and I *will* break you in half!" she threatened, taking a step back, looking for an exit.

"We need to find Stepan first. Is he here?" Jon asked.

"That way," Katia said, pointing over their shoulder.

When they looked toward where she pointed, they didn't see him. When they turned back, she was gone.

"Great. She's a runner." Val sighed, shaking his head. "This is going to be more difficult than we originally thought."

Angel shrugged. "Well, at least she now knows who we are, and what we're doing with Stepan."

"I don't think that was a good way to tell her. Could ya have presented it in a much less insane manner?" Josh rolled his eyes as he crossed his arms. "Not everyone is okay with the whole spiritual side of Christianity, and you just *blurted* it out, expecting her to be perfectly fine with it."

"I told her the truth," Angel said in her defense.

"You know what? I'm tired of this. I'm going to find Stepan. Jon, she's all yours," Josh said, wondering out to the dance floor to take a look around the club.

"What's *his* problem?" Angel asked, watching him leave.

"You," Jon shot.

"What do you mean?"

"You're not the most tactful when handling others. Maybe Val should be the next one to talk to her. I don't think she likes you."

"I don't know why not. I was honest with her."

"She thinks you're certifiably insane."

"I can't help that."

"Yes, you can," Jon said, putting his hands on Angel's shoulders so she would look at him. "It's all in how you say it. In order to be a good leader, you *need* to learn how others perceive you, not how you *want* them to perceive you. You need to learn how to talk to people so they know you care."

"I can't afford to do that. I don't have time for that."

"You can, and you'd better!" Jon snapped. "The enemy has come to steal, kill, and destroy. If you don't use the basic human instincts of empathy and compassion, then you might as well be working for the other side."

Crossing her arms, she glared at Jon. "That's the meanest thing you've ever said to me!"

"Stop this! You're acting like a two-year-old, while a young girl's life is on the line! How would you feel if this were Rachel, Allie, or Callie? You would do *anything* you could to find them, right?"

"Of course!"

"Then why won't you help Katia?"

"Because she doesn't *want* our help!"

"That doesn't mean we stop helping her. That just means we have to do it a different way."

"You're losing it!"

"Probably," Jon chuckled, "but it won't be the first time."

"Are you using your brain, or –"

Narrowing his eyes, he growled, "Don't you *dare* finish that!"

Taking a step back, Angel knew she'd crossed a line. She'd never seen him that angry before. "I-I'm sorry."

"You *should* be!" Jon crossed his arms, angry. "I use my brain when it comes to people. I've *never* gone after a girl just to take advantage of her, and you know it! I look at the heart."

"Okay. Okay." Angel put her hands up in surrender. "I'm done arguing. Where do we start?"

"Finally!" Jon threw his hands in the air. "About time you came around. As far as I'm concerned, we do what Josh said. We look for Stepan. When we find him, Katia won't be far behind. He's also our only lead to finding Liliya."

"All right, then," Angel relented. "Let's go."

*   *   *

Searching the club for hours, the group finally sat down at a table around one o'clock in the morning, exhausted. "*Please* tell me this wasn't a search in futility," Angel groaned, dropping her head on her crossed arms.

"Do I know you from somewhere?" Stepan asked in Russian, walking up to the table. "I know I have. I would remember those eyes anywhere," he said, resting his elbow on the table and his chin on his hand, as Angel looked up at him. He'd obviously had a few too many.

"Do you speak English?" she asked.

Josh glared at him as he narrowed his eyes, knowing full well what he'd said.

"Oh, yes, baby," he said in English, looking longingly at Angel. "I said I would know those beautiful eyes anywhere. You are gorgeous. I have not seen you here before. Where do I know you from?"

Seeing how drunk Stepan was, Josh stood, bracing his hands on the table. "I think you may need to sleep that off, mate," he said, watching every move Stepan made in case he suddenly got aggressive.

Angel put her hand on Josh's arm. "No, no. He's got a point. I would remember him anywhere too. You were our waiter tonight, yes?"

"At the restaurant! *That's* where I know you," he said with a smile. "Of course."

"Angel," Jon said, uneasy. "What are you doing?"

"I'm fine. After all, what can a waiter do to me with you guys around? He's a cute one at that." She giggled. "Aren't you?"

"Yes, as are you," Stepan said with a dreamy smile.

"You're playing with fire," Val warned. With a sick feeling in his stomach, he said, "You *know* what you're doing is wrong."

"Relax, Val," Angel said, "I also know Who is on our side."

"God is not a toy," Jon argued.

"I know, but he looks innocent enough. Aren't ya?" She asked, leaning closer to Stepan.

Stepan smirked. "Yeah. Yeah, sure."

"See? He's perfectly harmless. Aren't you?" she asked, batting her eyes at him.

"Ohhh, you are trouble," Stepan said, starry-eyed.

"God's not going to let me get hurt, guys. Relax."

"God's not a wish box *or* your personal bodyguard," Josh said, angry. "He is the Lord God Almighty! You work for Him. He *doesn't* work for you!"

"Relax. We have nothing to worry about. Do we, Stepan? You're an innocent young man. Right?"

"Do you have to work hard to be like that, or is it a gift?" Josh said, disgusted. "He's way too young for you. I'm done. You're on your own. I'm going back to the hotel. She's all yours, mates," he said, and left to catch a cab back to the hotel.

"Well, *that* was fun. What do we do for fun now that he is gone?" Stepan asked. "There is more dancing. Want to?" He offered his hand to Angel.

"Don't," Jon warned.

Taking his hand, Angel went out to the dance floor with him.

"This is a bad idea," Val said, shaking his head. "She's going to get us in big trouble."

"Problem is, she's going to have to answer to God for this. Personally, I wouldn't want to be in her shoes if this goes south," Jon pointed out.

"Me neither," Val said in a sigh. "Me neither.

*　　*　　*

Walking into their room at the hotel, Josh was still upset at Angel. Sitting on the bed, he sighed, dropping his head into his hands. "Lord, help me. I don't know what to do here. She's purposely throwing herself in trouble one minute, arguing with us about doing the right thing the next." Looking to Heaven, he said, "She's being reckless. What do I do?"

"'*Commit to the Lord whatever you do, and He will establish your plans,*'" Josh heard Proverbs 16:3 go through his mind.

"But, what if those plans go against Your ultimate plan?"

"The Lord has others keeping an eye on you at all times," Josh heard the archangel, as he suddenly appeared beside him.

"I understand that," he said, not even fazed by the archangel's appearance next to him. "However, she's arguing with us one minute, and then throwing herself in danger the next. I don't know what to do with her anymore. I expect her to do the right thing, but she never does it without a strong discussion. How is she supposed to be a leader when she's behaving this way? How are we supposed to be a team, when we're always fighting with her?"

"She is growing into her position. She is the youngest. She is used to her brothers cleaning up her mess. You, Jon, and Val have now filled that position in her eyes."

"Exactly. What happens next time when we're not there?" Josh asked. "She puts herself in bad positions. And when she's not, she's arguing with us on doing the right thing."

"She will have to answer for her actions."

"I'm afraid she's going to lead us into a trap if she's not careful. I guarantee Rachel would *never* do this to her team!"

"Maybe not, but they are two different women. The Lord made them different on purpose. They both have their own path," the archangel pointed out.

"Why does Rachel seem more up to the challenge than Angel?"

"Because she is."

"Then why is Angel in a leadership position?"

"It is her path."

"Is it also *our* path to die because of *her* choices?" Josh challenged. Then, realizing whom he was talking to, he said, "Look, mate, I'm sorry. I just don't know what to do right now. While I trust the Lord, *and* you, I don't know so much about trusting Angel anymore. I thought she had these problems worked out at the Haven."

"She still has her struggles. She was doing better until she lost Aden Knight in England. She is scared, and is doing her best not to lose anyone else."

"In doing so, she's shutting us all out. She's alienating herself from the rest of the team. To her, this isn't a team. It's a dictatorship. She only listens when we fight her."

"Then, you need to sit her down and explain this to her. She needs to find her heart again."

"Tell me something I don't know," Josh said in a sigh.

"She needs *you* to show it to her. Jon is too sensitive to her feelings in order to be tough with her. Val is too sensitive to understand how to talk to her when it is something so vitally important. He is not confident enough in himself yet. You? Well, you already have her heart."

"What if I don't want it?"

"That is your choice. However, right now, that is the only way you are going to reach her."

"I don't *want* to do that. It's not my position."

"You may have to step up and temporarily take the leadership position if she is unable to complete the work," the archangel said.

"I would rather take over, than have to have that conversation with her," Josh said, crossing his arms as he stood. "I don't know how to go about it."

"You have two sisters. You are the one best suited to speak with her regarding this matter. If you choose not to speak with her through her heart in love, then choose to speak with her through her heart as a sister."

"I don't know that I could ever consider loving her in the mental state she's in now." Josh shook his head. "I look at the heart…and hers isn't very pretty right now."

"I understand your point of view, *and* your position. All I ask is that my team work together to get the job done. And, in this case, this is a 'no man left behind' situation," the archangel pointed out, using one of their sayings.

"I understand. I'm just not sure how to do it. I can speak any language known to man…except 'woman,' obviously."

Chuckling, the archangel said, "In time, you will learn."

"Not soon enough, mate."

"I like you," the archangel said, resting his hands on Josh's shoulder. "You will do well in His service. Thank you for saying yes when the call was put out to you."

"Ha! Like I had a choice!"

"You *always* have a choice," the archangel pointed out. "God has given each of you free will."

"No way, mate." Josh shook his head. "When the Lord calls, *I'm* not gonna be the one to tell Him no. That may be the biggest mistake I'll ever make. He is the Lord God. He spoke this world into existence. He can speak me out of existence just as quickly, but that's not Who He is. It's Who He is, is why I serve Him without question. I trust Him with everything."

"Then, trust Him during this time. How easy is it for Him to keep you all safe through this situation?" the archangel asked.

Sitting back on the bed, dropping his head into his hands, Josh knew the archangel was right. "I trust *Him*," he admitted, looking back up at the archangel, "it's *her* I don't trust."

"Then trust the One who put her in her position. The devil has come to steal, kill, and destroy. He is trying to tear this team apart. Do not give him a way in. Do not let him use the cracks this team has to destroy you. You are all a part of not only this unit, but also something that is even bigger than yourselves. You are part of the Kingdom of the Lord."

"I know. That's why I'm still here. Is it still okay to question her if I feel she's making the wrong choice?"

"That is your duty. Once you are comfortable in her decisions, then you can back off. For now, though, let God work on her heart. If the time comes, you may be called upon to take over for a bit. Until then, however, you will have to learn to trust *both* of them."

"I've had this conversation before at the Haven."

"I realize this may be a test for you, and her, but trust Him. He knows what He is doing."

"Well, He hasn't let me down yet."

"And, He never will."

"All right, mate," Josh relented, "I'll talk to her."

"God *is* still looking out for you."

"And, in the meantime, we'll keep doing our job."

"That is all that is asked of you."

*　　*　　*

That night, when Katia walked into her apartment, her heart broke at the silence. Knowing she was of no use as tired as she was, she fell onto her bed, asleep in seconds. Calling off work again would not be an option if she wanted to keep her jobs. Fearing there was way too much on her mind to let it slow down, her body proved her wrong, and she immediately went into REM sleep as soon as her head hit the pillow.

*　　*　　*

"You will fetch a good price, kitten," the guy with Liliya sneered in Russian, as he tucked a portion of her blonde hair behind her ear. Then he gently rubbed her cheek with his finger.

Turning her face away from him, she felt like she would throw up. Chained to a ring on the wall, she sat on a bare, horribly stained mattress on the floor, looking disheveled at best. Being kept in a dirty basement with several other girls, she knew she would do her best to fight his ill intentions. "Don't touch me!" she shouted at him. "I am *not* your kitten."

"You may be as yet."

"Never!"

When he went to touch her face again, she bit him. When she did, he pulled back and punched her jaw. "Teach you to never do that again. You must respect me!"

Spitting blood from her mouth, she glared at him.

"Fiery little thing, aren't you! Yes, you will fetch a good price, I think."

"Just try it!" Liliya challenged.

"You will submit, in time."

"In your dreams!"

"Liliya!" The girl next to her looked at her, stunned. Speaking in English, she told Liliya, "He will hurt you worse than he already has."

Knowing from experience that the man didn't speak English, Liliya responded to the girl in English as well, so he would not understand their conversation. "I will not submit to him. He can die for all I care!"

"What are you saying?" the man demanded in Russian.

"Wouldn't *you* like to know," Liliya shot back in Russian.

"He will continue to beat you, and keep you here like he did me," the girl said to Liliya in English.

"I would rather die than submit to this…this *boy*!"

Grabbing her chin, the man jerked her head toward him so she would look at him. "*What-are-you-saying*?" he demanded in Russian.

"If you leave her bruised and beaten, she will not fetch a good price, Sergei," the girl cautioned the man in Russian.

"Do you want me all to *yourself*, Elena?" Sergei let Liliya go, and sat down next to Elena on her mattress. She did her best to move away from him, but he grabbed her arm, yanking her next to him. Breathing on her neck, he quietly said to her, "*You* want to be my little kitten?" He ran his fingers down her light brown hair before rubbing his hand on her arm. He then added, "That can be arranged."

"Not now." Elena tried to sound like she was interested, yet strong enough to brush him off. "I need to look after Liliya, since you bloodied her."

Shoving her away from him, he snapped, "Fine. You do that. You also teach her manners and respect." Before leaving the basement, he added, "If you don't, *you* will be the one to pay for it!"

Once the door slammed behind him, Elena scooted next to Liliya to look at her face in the dim light. "You okay?"

"Not really. How long have you been here?"

"Two years, I think. You tend to lose track down here. I see the sun rise and set through those windows many times. It is best not to dream of escape. If you do, and he finds you again?" She shook her head. "It will not end well."

Bottom lip trembling, Liliya admitted, "I want to go home."

"Home," Elena sighed. "I have not seen my family in a long time. I almost forget what home looks like. I feel this is my life now."

"Has he –?"

"What?"

"Has he touched you?"

"Sometimes you do what you have to do so you can live another day – never say never, my friend."

"I do not want to," Liliya said, tears rolling down her cheeks. "I want to go back to my sister."

"I know you do. I was the same way. If you want to stay here, then keep doing what you are doing, and he cannot sell you."

"*Sell* me?" Liliya squeaked out, her big blue eyes wide in horror. "What *is* this place?"

"I know you just woke a little bit ago, but are you really going to tell me you do not know what you are doing here? You *really* have no idea what these other girls are doing here?"

Shaking her head, Liliya's thoughts spun, as she glanced at the other seven girls in the dingy basement with them. "I do not want to do this!"

"You speak English. Sergei knows this. This will fetch a higher price for you," Elena said, ignoring the young girl's concerns, as she wiped away the blood from Liliya's mouth. Seeing a bruise forming on her cheek, Elena pointed out, "With this? You will be here for at least a few more days. He will not fetch a high enough price if you are damaged. This has to go away first."

"But, if I keep being damaged, he cannot sell me?" Liliya asked, forming a plan in her mind.

"Not to another, but he will probably take you for himself. These other girls have only been here for a few days. Some will be leaving tomorrow, some the next day. Others will come in their place. I see this time and time again. Each time, I still remain here to do Sergei's bidding."

Looking at the young women, Liliya's heart sank. *Could she stall long enough for Katia to find her? She knew Katia was looking for her, and it would only be a matter of time. Should she bide her time, or plan an escape?* "Where are we?" Liliya finally asked.

"Do not know. We are not allowed out."

"How are you still here?"

"I perform well for him," Elena admitted, red-faced. Looking at her, with desperation in her voice, she begged, "Please do not think bad of me! I do it to stay alive."

"I understand. I will *not* be staying, though. I *will* find a way out."

"Please? If you do find a way out, please do not tell my family what has become of me? I would rather they think I am dead, than know what is truly happening to me. It would bring dishonor to the family."

"It is as you said. You are doing it to stay alive. You do not do it out of love or joy. You do not go out and get others, bringing them into here. You do not want to be here any more than they do," Liliya said, nodding toward the other girls.

"How…?" Elena looked around and listened for a moment to make sure no one was listening, before she asked, "How are you planning to get out of here?"

"Do not know yet," Liliya said, looking around. "Give me time."

"That may be something you do not have," Elena warned, and moved back to her mattress, which was on the floor next to Liliya's. Chained to the wall at the head of her mattress, with a longer chain than the others, she sighed, and pointed out, "You may only be here a few days. This is the way it has been for me for years. I do not remember what the sun feels like," she said, looking longingly at the sun slowly rising in the distance. "Will be day soon. Things will happen tonight. Some girls will leave. You want to get away? You watch them. There is a pattern in the day. Problem? You are chained. The only way out is the key. It dangles from Sergei's neck on a necklace. I see it often."

"Why do you not get it while he sleeps?"

"I am still in chains upstairs. I have much a shorter chain up there. There is no escape, or I would have figured it out by now."

"If there is, I will find it," Liliya said with determination. "I *will not* stay."

"I pray you are right. This is a dark place."

*   *   *

Sitting up in her bed, sweating, Katia's heart was racing. Looking out the window, she saw the sun rising. *Could the dream have been real? Could she really have seen where her sister was being held? If it was, how was she going to find this house? There were a million of them in St. Petersburg.* Aloud, she made a vow, "I will find you, sestra. Trust me. I *will* find you."

Chapter 7
Guard your Hearts and Minds

That morning, the sun streamed into the bedroom of the team in St. Petersburg. When it hit Angel, she groaned, feeling the four measly hours of sleep she got, longing for more. "Is it morning already?" she asked, looking around. While Jon and Val were still asleep, Josh was awake in a chair at the table, reading his Bible. "You're awake." She smiled. "You were asleep when we came in last night. You looked like an angel while you slept. It was very sweet."

"It wasn't real sleep. You lot are louder than an elephant in a china shop," he said, not taking his eyes off the passage he was reading.

"Think that's a *bull* in a china shop," she corrected. When he didn't smile, she asked, "Are you okay?"

"No. Not really. Liliya's still out there, lost, and you throwing yourself at that waiter last night didn't help anything."

"I was trying to get close to him!" she defended herself.

"Did it work? Are you close to him?" he asked, shifting only his eyes in her direction, not moving a muscle otherwise.

"What do you mean by that?" She sat up, narrowing her eyes at him. "I was doing my job. What's the difference between what I did last night, and what you did with *Dominika*?" she asked, disdain evident in her words.

"All I did was get information. I *never* hit on her. That's *not* my job."

"You used your looks to get information and you know it!" Angel challenged.

"What are you going on about? All I did was tell her we may be back. It was good food," he said innocently.

"You are *so* full of it!"

Turing toward her, he sat forward, and reminded her in a stern tone, "*I'm* not the leader. *You* are. My job is to get information. At no point did I throw myself at her. *You* on the other hand are to be held to a higher standard, as you *are* the leader. You threw yourself at that bloke. I saw it. I went back to the club to apologize to you. When I walked in, I saw you rubbing on him while dancing with him." He shook his head. "I left, sickened by the scene. As an A.N.G.E.L., at *no point* do I feel the Lord would *ever* want you to throw yourself at a bloke to get information. That's *not* His way."

"Oh really? And, how do *you* know what His way is?"

"This," he said, sitting up as he waved his Bible. "You should read it sometime," he said, setting it back down on the table, open to the passage he was reading.

Clicking her tongue in objection, she snapped, "Judgmental much?" Getting off the bed, she stormed into the bathroom, slamming the door behind her. As soon as she did, both Val and Jon jumped up, immediately on alert.

"*What* was *that*?" Val asked, his heart in his throat as he grabbed his chest.

"*That* was our fearless leader, acting like a two-year-old *again*," Josh said, and sat back in his seat to continue reading Proverbs 31.

"She's ticked! What did you say to her?" Jon asked, wiping his eyes from sleeping. "I can feel the tension, and it's suffocating."

"I only pointed out that she threw herself at Stepan last night to get information. She then decided that I did the same thing with Dominika, so it was okay."

"You may have used your charm, but you never threw yourself at her," Val pointed out. "There's a massive difference between what you did and what she did."

"That's what *I* said. I also let her know that I went back to the club to apologize…that is, before I saw her rubbing all over Stepan." Closing his Bible, he set it on the table. "And she has the nerve to say that I did the same thing? No way. There are some days where I find that woman impossible!"

"That was not even close to what you did," Jon agreed.

"Are you three finished?" Angel said, coming out of the bathroom.

"Depends," Josh said, leaning back in his chair, interlocking his hands behind his head. "Are *you* ready to listen? Are you ready to admit what you did?"

"I did the *exact same thing you did*!"

"No. He didn't," Val said, shaking his head. "You went beyond asking questions. You crossed a line."

Angel crossed her arms in a huff. "Why are you guys ganging up on me?"

"You've been fighting us left and right since we got here. In England, you were a different person. Since we left London, you've been back to your old self," Josh pointed out. "And, that's *not* a good thing, for the record. Angel, you're gonna rip this team apart if you keep fighting us. We can't keep cleaning up your messes."

"I have no idea what you're talking about."

"How could you not?" Val asked, stunned. "It doesn't take Jon's gift to feel the tension."

"You keep fighting us between doing the right thing and you being callous," Jon pointed out. "Come on, Angel. You're not a little girl anymore. You are responsible for this team."

"And I personally don't want to end up dead, just because you're having a temper tantrum," Josh added.

"This is ridiculous!" Angel threw her hands, exasperated.

"Oh really?" Josh challenged. "Then why did the archangel and I have a conversation about your behavior last night?"

Pale, Angel asked, "What? Are you serious?"

"Yes. He said for me to talk to you about it. That's why I went back to the club last night. You were otherwise occupied, or I would have told you when I apologized."

"And now?"

"Now, I'm not going to. You crossed a line. Did you do it to make me jealous? 'Cause just so ya know, I'm not interested," Josh said bluntly. "I look at a woman's heart, and yours, right now, isn't all that pretty…despite the packaging."

She dropped on the bed, floored. "I-I don't know what to say."

"How about 'I'll consider your feelings, what's right, and what God would want us to do from now on'? That would make me happy," Jon offered.

"Me too," Josh agreed.

"And me. If things don't change, I'm going to Rachel's unit. I wanted to give you a chance," Val explained. "I was hoping your old ways had changed."

Suddenly a streak of light shot into the room, and the group heard, "So was I."

Seeing the archangel, Angel hung her head in her hand. "Are you serious? Why are *you* back again?"

"Because you are tearing your team apart," the archangel explained. "Would you like Josh or Jon take over for a bit while you work out your struggles?"

"We can both take it, and just put our heads together, showing how well we work together as a team," Josh offered.

"I think that is a wonderful idea," the archangel agreed. "You all need to work together as a team. Angel, while you *are* the leader, you *are not* the only person on this team."

"Yeah, this isn't the Angel English show," Jon jumped in. "We're not just accessories."

"We're also *not* your bodyguards," Josh added.

"We need to operate as a team, or we're not only going to lose Sasha, but we're going to lose Katia as well, or worse yet, completely lose Liliya's trail, and she is never heard from again," Val pointed out.

"They all have a point," the archangel jumped back in. "You have lost your way again, Angel."

Angel stood, determined. "I'll prove to you guys that I am a good leader!"

"Not at this time," the archangel overruled her. "Due to your actions last night, you are being replaced by Jon and Josh. They are choosing to work together. If you disagree, Josh has the final say."

"Yes, sir," Jon and Josh said in unison.

"Make me proud," the archangel said, and then disappeared in a streak of light.

As soon as he disappeared, Angel grabbed clothing from her suitcase, and ran into the bathroom in tears.

"Not quite how I wanted this to go down," Josh said. "I still have a heart. She needs to learn some hard lessons, though."

"Pretty sure she just did," Val pointed out. Then, with a sigh, he added, "Well, *this* is an interesting way to start a day. I haven't even had a cup of coffee yet."

"Not a way she wanted to start either," Jon added.

The bathroom door flew open. Standing there, shaking, Angel announced, "I'm going out."

"Where are you going?" Josh asked.

"Somewhere where I don't need my bodyguards," she said, and threw her dirty clothes on top of her suitcase. Grabbing her purse and coat, she stormed out of the hotel room, leaving the trio with their head's spinning.

"Ummm, *what* just happened?" Val asked after a moment.

"Not sure. Reckon we should follow?" Josh asked Jon.

"Na. She may just need some time," Jon said, getting off the bed for a shower.

"Let's hope," Josh said, picking up his Bible to continue reading.

*   *   *

"Unbelievable!" Angel sighed, wrapping her coat around her as she left the hotel. Walking quickly as she slipped her gloves on, she hoped that between walking fast and tucking her coat around her, the cold wouldn't cut through. Autumn in Russia was more than she'd bargained for. She couldn't wait to get back to the warm weather.

"That's it!" Angel said, when an idea hit her. "I'll prove to them that I not only belong on this team, but that I *am* leader quality! *I* will find Liliya and get her back...by myself!"

Running back to the hotel, she stopped at the desk and asked to use the phone. Once Stepan answered, Angel said, "Stepan? This is Angel from the club last night."

"Oh! Wonderful to hear from you!" he said in his best English.

"Um, are you busy?"

"I am at lunch right now. I have school until four. And then I go to work until eleven."

"Oh," Angel said, disappointed.

"Do you have something in mind?" he asked, intrigued.

"Well, the boys are being party poopers, and I want to go out and play."

"Really? A real party lady, yes?"

"Yes."

"I think I can get out of here. Want to meet me at the club? It opens in an hour."

"Perfect!" she said. "That'll give me some time to get a shower."

"Yes. I will see you at the club in an hour," he said and hung up.

Ideas swirling, she ran to a gym near the hotel to grab a shower, and then to the store to buy a dress. She could have gone upstairs, but she didn't want to tip off the guys as to what she was planning. She hoped to get close enough to Stepan, that he would give her some information about Liliya. This was the break she needed to get the boys to know just how good she really was. Josh would be impressed, and she could salvage whatever relationship they had left.

Catching a taxi, she went to the club.

*   *   *

When she arrived to the club, several people were already there. It didn't take long for her to find Stepan sitting at a table, with two sodas and a plate of fries. Snacking on the fries, a smile crossed his face when he caught sight of Angel.

Standing when she walked up to the table, he gave her a welcome hug. "Nice to see you today."

"Thank you," she said, sitting across from him as he retook his seat. "Um, is this for me?" she asked, picking up the soda in front of her.

"Of course. I take care of my ladies," he said with a sly smile.

Over the next few hours, Angel shared different stories from her life. Only ones she felt comfortable in sharing. Ones that seemed vague, yet allowed her to seem invaluable.

"So, let me see if I understand," Stepan said after several more hours, "you speak English *and* Spanish?"

"Yes."

"You have a college degree?"

"Yes."

"A good family?"

"Yes."

"Then, *why* are you here?"

"My brother, his friends, and I are here on vacation. We took a break from the heat, and the U.S., to experience a new culture."

"I'm sure I can arrange that," Stepan said.

By now the club was filling up.

"If you'll excuse me, I need to use the restroom," Angel said, standing. "The multiple sodas are taking their toll on me."

"Would you like something else? I could order while you are gone?"

"Actually, whatever you think," she said with a smile. Not understanding why they were watching him in connection to a missing girl, Angel felt extremely comfortable with him.

As she walked into the bathroom, one of the stall doors opened behind her. She went to the mirror to check out her hair. "Not bad," she said, impressed.

Suddenly, a hand covered her mouth, while another arm wrapped around her, pinning her arms to her body. Another guy came out of the same stall holding a syringe, and jammed it into her neck.

At first the room blurred, and then spun, until she felt her eyes roll into the back of her head. Her body went limp as the world around her went dark.

* * *

Leaning on the railing of the ferry, Rachel inhaled the salty air, while the cold wind brushed her face. The seas were slightly stormy as they crossed from Dublin to Liverpool, and the sun was nowhere in sight. Rachel knew she could relax, as they were out of Ireland, but she still felt on edge.

"Hey, Rach," Jerrod said, walking over. Leaning on the railing beside her, he said, "I know we should be off-duty and you should be in recovery mode, but I can't help feeling that we've missed something, or that something big is coming."

"I know what you mean. We got Delaney, Cori, and Kai, but I wonder if that's the last we heard of our friend Owen?"

"We made some really bad enemies coming in after you two, but I wouldn't change anything we did."

"Me neither. Having said that, why do I have a sick feeling in my stomach?"

"I'm the same way. I wish I knew," Jerrod said, looking out at the water, feeling the coolness of the wind on his face.

"Angel said one of ours was taken out in London."

"I know. She called us, and talked to Mark. She was a mess."

"We're heading back into London. What if Calliope and her fellow compatriots are still there, and are waiting on us?" Rachel asked.

"I guess we'll just have to trust in God, that He's got us covered. He's not let us down so far."

"But, He let Angel down."

"You think so?"

"Wouldn't you feel like that if you were her?"

"I would," Jerrod agreed. "However, I also know God doesn't do surprises. He knows what's going to happen, and has made arrangements to care for us per His will."

"Why didn't he care for Aden? What do you reckon Angel is feeling right now? She just got herself turned around."

"So, you're saying that sick feeling in your stomach is –"

"Maybe that something has happened to Angel," Rachel finished.

*   *   *

"So, how long do we let her sulk?" Jon asked. "We've given her all day."

"Okay, mate, where do we start?" Josh asked. "She's been out for several hours. She's your sister. Where would she go?"

"Maybe the club?" Jon offered.

"Sounds good," Val said, and the guys got ready to leave.

As they walked out of the hotel, Val felt something to the right of him. Turning in that direction, he caught sight of Katia. "It's Katia," he said, pointing her out to the others.

When she saw them, she ran, and the boys gave chase. Running through the streets, Jon wasn't sure if they would be able to find their way back to the hotel, but he didn't care. Katia had obviously been watching them. He intended to find out why.

Seeing her duck into a warehouse, the three ran in after her. As they walked through the paper warehouse, Val, Jon, and Josh took a moment to get their bearings. The smell of cardboard, mixing with the chemicals from the factory, was almost overpowering. The overhead lights never moved from their position above them. However, the shadows of the racks seemed to move, sending a shiver down Jon's spine as they made their way through the building. Jon wasn't sure exactly what they were getting into when it came to Katia.

Keeping a lookout in every direction, they searched the vast warehouse for the young woman who had ducked in only moments before. The few times they'd seen Katia around town, she looked to be about five-eight, with medium brown hair that hung just below her shoulders. She had a thin build from working two jobs, while trying to care for her younger sister.

To Jon, the eyes were windows to the soul. Katia's dark brown eyes showed the hard life she lived in her short twenty-two years. He admired her beauty and spunkiness, but her running was starting to get to him. After losing Aden several days ago, Jon wanted to get Katia and Sasha, and get out of Russia before anything else happened. Knowing the other side was hunting them, and that they seemed to have a bit of an edge over the A.N.G.E.L.s lately, unnerved him. With Calliope and her minions after them, he wanted to get back to the Haven. He wished this trip was as easy as it was when they recruited the last two members of the team, but this was simply not the case.

"She's in here," Val said, as he, Jon, and Josh scoured the warehouse. Val's heart raced, while the trio searched the dimly lit shelving units, stacked ten to twenty feet high throughout the warehouse. His spiritual sight told him she was in the shelving units, but where, he wasn't sure.

"Can you see her?" Josh asked Val.

"She's in the shelf–" Val's words halted as an arm reached around. Katia rested her arm on Val's shoulder, pulling him toward her. Afraid to speak, he gulped, feeling the cold steel blade to his neck she held in her right hand. They didn't have to look any farther for Katia…she'd found them.

Katia growled something in Russian.

"W-what did she say?" Val asked, his voice shaky.

"She wants to know what we want," Josh translated, hands in the air. "Katia, we know you speak English. In fairness, how about we all speak it? If not, you need to know I can speak Russian too."

"I am aware," she said in English, studying the three men. "Why are you following me?"

"*You* were watching *us*," Jon pointed out.

"I saw your friend earlier. I assume you followed her too?" Katia asked.

"C-can we just lower the knife?" Val asked, his hands still in the air.

Pulling him closer to her, she said down near his ear, "Not. Yet. You need to answer questions. This," she said, tightening the knife, "will get me answers."

"We'll answer whatever you want. Please just take the knife off our friend's neck?" Jon asked, hands still in the air.

"Not yet," she said firmly.

"No worries," Josh said, doing his best to ease the tension. "So, um, did you say you saw Angel?"

Nodding, Katia confirmed, "She was with Stepan. Please know, Stepan, he –"

Josh nodded. "We know."

Narrowing her eyes, she asked, "You know where Liliya is?"

"No, but we're hoping to help you find her."

"Why? Why do you care?"

"Because if it were *my* sister, I would want as much help as I could get."

"Question," Jon asked. "If you were watching Angel, why were you at the hotel?"

"Because she is not at the club any more," Katia said. "I think maybe she comes back to the hotel."

"She's not at the club anymore?" Jon asked, hoping he didn't hear her correctly.

"No."

"How long has she been gone?"

"An hour. Maybe two."

Wide-eyed, Josh asked, "Do you…do you know where she went?"

Confused, Katia asked, "You do not know?"

Jon dropped to a crouched position, feeling sick to his stomach as he held his head. "She's missing," he groaned. "Please don't say it's what I'm thinking." Looking toward Heaven, Jon said, "Please, Lord, don't say she got taken too."

Katia lowered the knife as she climbed off the shelf. Sliding the knife back into the sheath on her hip, she said, "We are in same ship, then?"

"Same boat," Val corrected. "And, yes."

"Your sestra is missing, thanks to Stepan, and so is mine."

"Yes," Jon said, feeling like he would throw up right then.

Kneeling in front of Jon, Katia put her hand on his arm. When he looked up, she simply said, "I understand."

"I know you do."

"What if we join teams?"

"That's join forces," Val pointed out. "And, please don't take offense that I'm correcting you. I find your misspeaking of our sayings cute. Unfortunately, this situation is not cute." Crouching next to Katia, he added, "We need to find both of them…and fast."

"Then, we start with Stepan," Katia said firmly. "It all begins with Stepan."

Chapter 8
Trust in the Lord

Going back to the hotel, the four sat in the room, and ate a dinner of sandwiches and chips, each one deep in their own thoughts. Jon and Val were stretched out on the beds with their legs in front of them in a seated position, while Josh and Katia were at the table.

"When's the last time you had decent sleep?" Josh asked Katia.

She shook her head as she took another bite. "Do not know."

"When's the last time you had something decent to eat?" Val asked, noticing how hungrily she ate her sandwich.

"Do not remember."

As the phone to the room rang, Jon looked at Josh. "You're the one who speaks Russian," Jon pointed out.

"Too true," Josh said, getting up to answer the phone. With the conversation in Russian, Josh started with, "Hello?"

"You speak Russian. Is this Josh? The A.N.G.E.L.?" a young man asked.

"Who is this?"

"This is Sasha Kazakov. My godmother is Anastasia –"

"Oh yes," Josh cut him off. "How can I help you?"

"I have a feeling it is *I* who can help *you*," he pointed out.

"What are ya going on about?" Josh asked in English.

"Pardon?" Sasha asked, not sure he understood the phrase.

"What are you talking about?" Josh corrected himself, as the conversation switched to English.

Sasha explained, "I need to meet with you. Is okay if I come to the room?"

"Where are you?"

"Downstairs."

"Oh! Come on up, mate!" Josh said, excited. "We're in room 325."

"I will be there in a moment."

"Great!" Josh said, and hung up.

"What's going on?" Jon asked, sitting up.

"Sasha's on his way up," he said, sitting back down at his seat to continue eating.

"For those of us who *don't* speak Russian, what's going on?" Val asked. "We only got half the conversation."

"Who is this Sasha?" Katia asked.

"We're trying to recruit Sasha to be an A.N.G.E.L. as well," Josh explained.

"That girl Angel was being honest?" Katia asked, stunned.

"More than ya know," Josh said. "Anyway, he's downstairs and wanted to know if he could come up."

"Did he say *why*?" Jon asked.

"Nope." Josh shrugged. "Guess we'll find out soon enough."

Katia raised an eyebrow. "Do you get people who do this often?"

Josh nodded. "More or less."

Hearing a knock on the door, Val answered. "Hey, Sasha," he said, opening the door for him to walk in. "Come on in!"

Closing the door behind him, Sasha came in and sat on the same bed Jon was on, so Jon scooted over to give Sasha room. Noticing Katia, Sasha asked, "Who are you?"

"Katia. You?" she asked, snacking on her chips.

"Katia Alexandrova?" Sasha asked, stunned.

"Yes. How do you know?" Katia asked, as she glared at him, not putting her sandwich down.

"My godmother said she was the other one. How did you find her?" he asked the others.

"God led her to us," Josh explained. "It's a long story."

"How did you know my name?" Katia pressed.

Changing to Russian, Sasha explained, "My godmother worked with a group called A.N.G.E.L.s all of her life. They go around the world helping others in the name of the Lord."

"It is real?" she asked, wide-eyed.

"Oh yes! Have you ever had something happen that just cannot be explained?"

"Maybe," she said, uneasy.

"I have, too. Just listen," he said. Turning to the others, the conversation continued in English. "I am here because I have heavy thoughts that show me things."

"Like premonitions?" Jon asked.

"Yes!" Sasha said, relieved they knew what he was talking about. "I get those. I have been praying about being an A.N.G.E.L., and today God gave me a…what was the word?"

"Premonition," Jon said again.

"Yes, that is it. God gave me premonition about Angel and two other girls."

"Were they in a house? In the dark? Sort of underground?" Katia asked. "Like a…what is the word?"

"Like a basement or dungeon?" Josh offered.

"Yes. How do you know, Katia?" Sasha asked.

"I had the…" she looked at Jon for the word.

"Premonition," Jon said again. "How about visions? Would that be easier?"

"Yes. Much," Katia said with a grateful smile. "Mine was a dream."

"Nice!" Val said, excited. "We have two with premonitions!"

"Have two what?" Katia asked.

"Two A.N.G.E.L.s," Sasha said.

"Meaning?"

"Meaning two on the team with visions," Val explained.

"Who said I am on a team?" Katia asked.

"No one," Val said. "Look, we can argue semantics for days. What we *need* to do is focus on finding Angel and Liliya."

"This is true," Katia conceded.

"So, do you have an idea where this house is?" Jon asked.

"I have something that may find us a…what do you call it? Oh! A lead," Sasha explained.

"Where?" Katia asked.

"Moskow Victory Park. You know this?" Sasha asked.

"Over that way." Katia pointed in the direction of the park. "Only a few roads over."

"How do you know this lead is in the park?" Val asked.

"There is a park that has a monument to soldiers from World War Two. This is particular monument is only found in this park in St. Petersburg. There is a meeting tonight. That is the lead," Sasha said. "There will be two men and one woman."

"I know that monument!" Katia said, excited. "It has trees around it that we can hide in and not be seen."

"When?" Josh asked.

"We need to leave quickly," Sasha said, with a sense of urgency. "It will be anytime."

"Then let's go," Josh said, grabbing his coat and gloves.

Just as they left the room, Katia ran back in and grabbed the other half of her sandwich before running back out after them, locking the door behind her.

* * *

As the ferry docked, Rachel and the others exited the ferry and took a couple of cabs to a local hotel in Liverpool. Their train was to pull out the next morning at eight.

"Oh, to be on a nice bed again," Rachel said, gently lying down on one of the queen-sized beds in the girl's room.

"Mind if I share with you?" Delaney asked Rachel. "Nothing personal, Cori, but I don't think it'll be very comfortable sharing a bed with me, you, *and* puppy," she said ruffling his head as he wagged his tail.

"It's a good thing we're close. You know the rules about petting Charm," Cori reminded her.

"Not in public," Delaney confirmed.

"Right. Now, as far as sharing a bed with Rachel, I'm not offended, luv," Cori waved her off. "You know we're pretty hard to offend. Up, Charm," she said, tapping the bed as she sat down on it. The black Labrador happily jumped up and lay down behind her on the bed. As Cori lay her head down on Charm's mid-section, she asked, "So, what are we doing for dinner?"

Rachel groaned in pain. "Not sure. Don't care to eat right now, though. Too much pain."

"Want me to get Jerrod?" Delaney asked.

Rachel nodded. "Please."

As Delaney left to the boy's room next door, Cori felt her way over to Rachel's bed and sat down beside her. Rubbing Rachel's arm, Cori said, "I can feel how much pain you're in. I'm sorry you got mixed up with Owen. He's normally a good person. Seems he's gotten worse over the last several months."

"Don't know. Don't care. Just know it hurts," Rachel said, wiping the few tears that escaped.

Delaney came back into the room, closely followed by all the guys. "They were still settling," she commented, going over to the side of the bed where Cori was sitting, so Jerrod could get to Rachel more easily.

"Talk to me, Rach," Jerrod said, brushing her hair out of the way.

"My ribs hurt so bad. I feel like I'm going to throw up," she moaned, holding her ribs.

"Can you all go back over to the guy's room?" Jerrod asked. "I need to check something out."

As they all left for the boy's room, which had two queens and a twin bed, Rachel quietly mentioned to Jerrod, "If it's internal bleeding, I'll have to go to the hospital here. That'll not only put us on the radar, but also keep us here longer."

"I know," Jerrod said, watching the others leave. As soon as the door closed behind them, Jerrod had Rachel roll over onto her back and lift her shirt so he could see the area where the broken ribs were. "Jesse is beside himself," he mentioned, as he examined her.

"What do you mean?" she asked, and then jumped and groaned when Jerrod touched her ribs.

"He feels absolutely sick that you're hurt, and that he couldn't do anything to help you."

"He…ow!" she yelped and jumped again. "That hurts!"

"Okay, I don't see anything out of the ordinary, nor do I feel it. You may just be finally feeling it since the adrenaline has gone down. I have some pain medicine in the room. In the meantime, sit up for a minute." Once she was sitting, he wrapped her mid-section with an ace bandage to brace the ribs, putting a little pressure on them. "Wrapping the ribs is controversial, but it's always worked better for me in the past with the guys I worked on."

"Thanks," she said, as he gingerly lowered her back down to the bed.

"As you also know, you're going to have to lie on the side where the ribs are broken so no bleeding will go into the lungs.

You're also going to have to occasionally take a deep breath to reduce your chances of getting pneumonia."

"Got it. Thanks," she mumbled.

"I'll go get you your pain medicine. It'll knock you out. I would *really* like you to eat first, if you could."

Looking at him, another couple tears crawled down her cheeks.

"Okay, but tomorrow you *will* eat," he said sternly. "I'll be right back," he said, leaving the door ajar behind him while he ran next door.

"Ohhh, why?" Rachel whispered. A few more tears escaped her eyes as she looked toward Heaven. "Lord, this hurts so bad. When I'm hurting as badly as this, I'm not on alert as I should be."

"Then, you need to rely on your team," Jesse said, walking into the room with a pill bottle and a bottle of water in his hands, closing the door behind him. "Sorry to step on your prayer, but I thought you may want this sooner rather than later. Jerrod sent me."

"He said you were struggling," Rachel said, adjusting to a more comfortable position.

"We're going to be ordering in, and staying in the other room for a while. Delaney said she'll do her best not to bump you in her sleep." Sitting on the side of the bed, he got the pain pill from the bottle. "Look, I'm sorry you felt the need to put yourself through this in order to protect me."

"I would have done it for anyone," Rachel said. Putting the pill in her mouth, she let Jesse help her drink water, and then a little more to wash the pill down.

"I know you would have," he said, gently setting her back down. "But, you shouldn't have to."

"You are not immune to having things happen, ya know?"

"I know. I am, however, stronger than the average guy," Jesse pointed out. "And, being a guy, it's normally in my nature to protect the ones I care about," he said, rubbing his finger on her cheek. "I know things can't go anywhere right now, but I want you to know that I am always here for you."

"I know. I'm sorry I can't do anything at the moment."

Chuckling, Jesse tucked a portion of her blonde hair behind her ear, "You amuse me even when you're in tremendous pain."

"I need," she put her hand on his arm, and jumped in pain, "I need ya to be on alert. I'm not focused. And with this medicine, I'll be even less so. This is a team, and I need my team to help with the load until we can get back to the Haven."

"No need to ask. Of course we'll be right here, looking after our fearless leader," he said with a wink. "Now, you need to not worry your pretty little head about a thing, except getting some sleep. Trust us. Trust in the Lord to keep us all safe."

"I don't know if I can sleep right now."

"Want me to stay with you for a bit?" Jesse offered. "You know, until you're sound asleep."

Looking at him for a few moments, Rachel finally relented.

Sliding onto the other side of the bed, Jesse put his arm under her neck, and she slowly rolled toward him on her broken ribs, allowing him to wrap his arm around her. Stroking her hair, he prayed for her as she went into a deep, painless sleep.

Chapter 9
Lean Not on Your Own Understanding

Groaning, Angel struggled to clear her vision. Shaking her head, she moaned as she put her head back, hitting…*concrete*? Snapping to full awareness, she was immediately on edge. Pulling her arms, she realized she was chained to a wall.

Hearing a phrase she didn't understand, Angel cocked her head to the side, and asked, "What? Was that English?"

"Many apologies," the young girl said. "You are American?"

"Yes. What's going on?"

"I said to be quiet. And to not let him know you are awake."

"Who? Why? What's going on?"

"Shhh! You need to lower your voice. I will talk if you will be quiet."

"Yes, ma'am," Angel said, with the feeling of fear slowly suffocating her.

"Good. Now, my name is Elena. You?"

"A-Angel," she stammered. "Where am I?"

"I am Liliya," another girl said, who was on the other side of Elena. Both girls were chained to the wall, and they each sat on a filthy twin mattress, the same as Angel.

"Liliya? As in Liliya Alexandrova?" Angel asked.

"Yes," Liliya said, confused. "I do not know you."

"I know your sister," Angel explained.

"My sestra? You know Sarai?" Liliya asked.

"Her name is Katia," Angel said firmly.

"You *do* know her!" Liliya grinned. "How do you know her?"

"We were working with her to find you."

"Well, you did. How do we get out now that you have found me?"

"You take me with you, yes?" Elena asked, hopeful.

"Of course, along with anyone else still here," Angel agreed.

"Wonderful news!" Elena said, excited.

"First, we need to figure out where *here* is," Angel said, looking around.

"I am here for a long time, and still I do not know," Elena explained.

"How long have you been here?" Angel asked.

"About two years," Elena said in a sigh. "I have a feeling I will be here until the end of my life."

Angel's jaw dropped. "*Two years*?"

"Others have come and gone, but not me. Sergei likes me too much."

"Meaning?"

"He takes me when he wants me."

"Oh my! Elena, I am *so* sorry," Angel said, tearing up as her heart broke for Elena.

"I am here not so long," Liliya explained.

"Has he…has he done anything to you?" Angel asked, not sure if she wanted to know the answer.

"Just this," Liliya said, and turned her head toward Angel so she could see all of her face.

"Oh!" Angel looked at her, wide-eyed, at seeing the large bruise on her left cheek.

"He is not a nice man," Elena started. "He does not know English, so that is how Liliya and I talk around him."

"Well, I don't know Russian, so this could be interesting," Angel said in a huff.

"He will be here soon. When he does, you pretend to be asleep still. He will leave you alone. He does not want to damage you. Not fetch a good price for you."

"But, if he does, you may get a couple extra days," Liliya added.

"How long does he normally keep girls here?" Angel asked.

"Three to four days," Elena explained. "He puts the girls on the computer, and highest bidder gets the girl. I see this when he takes me to his room."

"Seriously?"

"Yes. Need to take a good photo, though. No bruising. Not fetch good money if you are damaged."

"I see," Angel said, forming a thought in her mind. "I need to think and pray."

"You do. Get help."

"I will. Shhhh," Angel said, and closed her eyes as she put her head against the wall.

Praying in her head, Angel said, "*Lord, I need serious help here.*"

She heard the Lord's response in the form of Galatians 5:1 in her head. "*'Stand fast therefore in the liberty wherewith Christ hath made us free, and be not entangled again with the yoke of bondage.'*"

"*I do stand firm in what Christ has done for me,*" she continued to pray in her head, "*I wouldn't be here if I didn't. Unfortunately, I have also screwed up beyond recognition. I have taken things into my own hands without going to You first. That is my fault. I am not the savior of these girls. You are. I am not the one who will rescue them. You will. Help us, Father!"*

"'Count it all joy, my brothers, when you meet trials of various kinds, for you know that the testing of your faith produces steadfastness. And let steadfastness have its full effect, that you may be perfect and complete, lacking in nothing.'"

"I am aware of what James 1:2-4 says. I am having a hard time rejoicing in this trial, though. What these girls go through is horrific. To be a slave to someone else's whims is no life at all. Each time they're touched, it slowly kills their soul. The idea of escape has even eluded Elena. She has been held here for two years, chained to a wall, having her virtue taken whenever this Sergei wants her. Then there's Liliya. All she wanted was to relax and enjoy being a teen. Next thing she knew, she was thrown into this pit. The only way she is able to still be here is to be bruised? What is this? How is this a trial we are to rejoice in?"

"'Now the God of peace, that brought again from the dead our Lord Jesus, that great shepherd of the sheep, through the blood of the everlasting covenant, make you perfect in every good work to do His will, working in you that which is well pleasing in His sight, through Jesus Christ; to whom be glory for ever and ever.'"

"The words of Hebrews 13:20-21 will bring me peace in this," she prayed, *"Thank you, Father, for those words. I will trust in You to get us out of here…mainly because You are the only One who can. To God be the glory forever and ever. Amen."*

Hearing someone on the stairs, Angel opened her eyes to see a man, about six-foot-two, burly, with black hair, steel blue eyes, and a scar on the left side of his face. Shuddering, she took a deep breath. Knowing what she had to do to buy some time, she was determined to do what she had to do in order to get them out of there.

As her head cleared, and he entered the room, she heard the Spirit whisper to her Proverbs 3:5 and 6, *" 'Trust in the Lord with all thine heart; and lean not unto thine own understanding. In all thy ways acknowledge Him, and He shall direct thy paths.' "*

"It's okay, Father," Angel whispered a prayer to God, "I know I screwed up. I can fix this. Please give me the courage to do what I need to do."

As he neared, Angel glared at him. With a sneer, she said, "Well, if it isn't Sergei."

"Angel!" Elena gasped. "Stop!"

"What did she say?" Sergei demanded in Russian from Elena.

"Sh-she just said, 'If it isn't Sergei'," Elena explained in Russian.

Turning toward Angel, he glared at her. Grabbing her face, he jerked it toward him. "Translate!" he growled at Elena in Russian. "You will tell her that she needs to submit to *my* authority!"

"O-okay," Elena agreed. In English to Angel, Elena said, "He said you will submit to his authority."

"I submit to *no one* except the Lord!" Angel shouted, and then spat on him.

"You have one more chance," Elena translated as Sergei shouted in Russian. "Please Angel, do what he say," she added.

"Never!" Angel shouted.

Grabbing Angel by her chin, Sergei pulled her closer to him, spitting as he growled in Russian.

Elena translated, "You *will* submit. If you do not, you will *never* see the light of day."

"I will. God is not finished with me yet. You wait and see!"

As soon as Elena translated, Sergei shook Angel. Elena looked at him wide-eyed as he shouted Russian. When he snapped at her, Elena explained, "He said you are godforsaken. He said you will *never* get out of this alive. God will not get you out of this. You are now Sergei's, not God's."

When she finished, Sergei pulled Angel to him so she was less than two inches from his face. Cocking his head to the side, he studied her for her reaction. When she stared at him defiantly, he slammed her against the wall.

Groaning in pain, she felt a trickle of blood go down the back of her head. Angel shook her head, seeing stars. Pulling her back to him, he demanded, and Elena translated, "You will listen to me and do as you are told."

"Never!" Angel shouted.

Seeing him reach back, she braced for impact while the other two cringed. Swinging toward her, he pounded his fist into the side of her face, slamming her head into the wall once again.

As the black cloud drew her into unconsciousness, she heard Proverbs 16:18 in her head, *"'Pride goes before destruction, a haughty spirit before a fall.'"*

*   *   *

As the guys and Katia entered the park, Jon asked, "Where are we going?"

"Over there. In a few minutes, two men and a woman will appear," Sasha explained, pointing to a tall monument, that had a statue of Russian soldiers with their flag, perched on top of a tall stone pedestal. There were trees behind it that would provide good coverage for them. "One man will give other man an envelope. That is end of the vision."

They took positions behind trees. Val and Katia were in one section behind a tree, while Sasha and Jon were on the other side of the monument across from them, and Josh was somewhere in the middle. They were well positioned to see the monument from three different angles, with one Russian speaker with each group. The monument was off to the side, so it would be a convenient place to have a covert meeting, and not be seen.

If it wasn't for the vision Sasha had, it would be a serene scene. The leaves from the trees all over the park coated the ground. As the breeze carried them, they would pile around the various monuments. When the wind occasionally gusted, it would kick the leaves up like a wave, but for the most part, it gently pushed them around, creating a gorgeous sea of red, yellow, and orange.

As they were tucked in their spot, Val asked Katia, "Who do you think we're waiting for?"

She shrugged. "Do not know."

"Any ideas?"

"Hoping Sasha has them. He is the only lead to Angel and Liliya right now."

"This is true. God will provide the one we're looking for to help."

Taking her eyes off the monument for a moment, she cocked her head to the side, studying Val. "You seem wise," she observed. "Quiet ones usually are."

"A wise person learns from others, a discerning person knows who to listen to," Val pointed out.

"You are both," Katia said confidently, as she turned back to the monument. "I stick to you."

Chuckling, Val said, "That's stick *with* you."

"Whatever." Katia shrugged. "I know who I stay beside."

"I don't mind."

As the silence hung heavily over the park, a weird feeling fell over Sasha. The hair on the back of his neck suddenly stood on end. "Jon?" he asked, looking at every shadow he could see to figure out where the feeling was coming from.

"What's up?" Jon asked, not taking his eyes off the monument.

"Jon," Sasha tugged on Jon's arm, as the feeling got worse by the second.

"What?" Jon asked. When he turned to Sasha, he saw the color drained from Sasha's face. "What's wrong?"

"Suddenly a bad feeling."

"What does it feel like?"

"Everything in my body is on edge, tingling. Hair on my neck is standing," Sasha said, rubbing the back of his neck.

Jon turned back to the monument to see a man walk out of the shadows, and he instantly knew Sasha had another gift. Sasha could sense those on the other side. "You have Jesse's gift," Jon whispered, more to himself. When Sasha gave him a questioning look, he explained, "You can sense the other side." Wishing with every bone in his body that they had some means of communication, he cringed at what he knew was standing before them. The man who walked out was an Unnatural.

*   *   *

Waking in the morning, Rachel was surprised to see that Jesse was still holding her. "Jesse?" she whispered.

Jesse smiled as he opened his eyes to see her still in his arms. "Hey, Rach."

"Why are you still in here?" she asked.

"Because you were sleeping so well, we didn't have the heart to wake the two of you," Cori said from the other bed, where she, Charm, and Delaney had slept.

"Are they awake?" Delaney asked.

"Yeah. Want to help me take Charm outside to go to the bathroom?" Cori asked her.

Getting out of the bed, shuffling to the bathroom in the room, Delaney mumbled, "Let me go first."

After she closed the door, Rachel mentioned, "Still in a lot of pain. Jesse, can you go get Jerrod? I also need to talk to the group as a whole."

"Let me get Charm out before you meet with everyone," Cori asked. "We won't be long. I promise."

"No worries," Rachel agreed. "I still need to talk to Jerrod first. And," she put her hand on Jesse's arm to stop him from getting off the bed, "And, you come back with him. I need to meet with you both before we meet with the others."

"Okay," he agreed, and left the room.

"Have an interesting dream?" Cori observed.

"Not quite. More like instructions I know they won't like. Something's happened, and we need to bail as quick as possible."

"How do you know? You've been unconscious since we've been here."

"God," Rachel said, struggling to get into a better position.

"Better make it quick-like. We have an eight o'clock train to catch, yeah?" Cori pointed out. "And, it's," she hit the button on her watch that told her the time, "six-thirty."

"I know."

"All right, let's take puppy out," Delaney said, coming out of the bathroom. She looked at Rachel concerned, "What happened?"

"Why do you ask?" Rachel asked.

"I have the gift of discernment, remember? I also gauge feelings extremely well."

Rachel nodded in understanding. "Like Jon," she said aloud to herself.

"So?" Delaney pressed, putting her jacket on as Cori got hers as well.

"You'll find out. I need to talk to Jerrod and Jesse first."

Wide-eyed, Delaney said, "This sounds big."

"Get Charm taken care of and hurry back," Rachel said, and the three of them left her alone.

A moment later, Jesse and Jerrod came into the room. "What's up, Rach?" Jerrod asked.

"Extreme pain," she groaned.

"I was worried about that."

"That's not all. We have to split up. Remember that feeling we both had on the ferry?"

"Yeah. You figured out what it was?"

"Yes. The team in Russia needs help. They've run into Unnaturals."

"How do you know?" Jesse asked.

"God told me."

"Okay then," Jesse said, taking a deep breath. "What do we do? You're not in shape enough to help anyone."

"No. I'm not," she agreed. "And, I need Jerrod with me. Jesse, you need to take over the team. I need you to be strong. They need your gift. I feel Angel's in serious trouble too. You guys need to get ahold of them. You'll have to change your tickets to a plane to St. Petersburg. Cori and Kai are coming with Jerrod and I, so they can set up at the Haven. You may also need Delaney and her language gift in the field."

"Are you sure?" Jesse asked.

"Yes. I'm one hundred percent sure."

"Okay," Jesse relented.

"We need to meet and tell the others before we catch the train," Rachel explained. "Hopefully we can change your tickets before we get on the train, so you are set once the train gets to London. In the meantime, I need to get to better health at the Haven."

Jerrod nodded. "Agreed."

"They may need you to come back out," she told Jerrod. "They may need your tactical military skills."

"If they do, Jesse will let me know." He looked at Jesse, who nodded.

"Then it's settled. As soon as Delaney and Cori come back in, we'll fill the others in," Rachel said decisively. "I have faith in you all. You guys are a strong team. Don't let the problems of the other team wear off on you all. I want my team back the way it was. We'll have to adjust to new people as it is. I don't want to have to settle petty issues as well. Jesse, you'll be working with Jon and Josh."

"What about Angel?" Jesse asked.

"That's the problem. She's in trouble. Can you work with Jon without problems?"

"Yes. We may be brothers, but we work together pretty well. We each have our own strengths."

"And Josh has his," Rachel said. "It'll be all of your jobs to find those out, to work to your strengths in order to get this fixed. We'll get Cori and Kai to shift some of the tickets to get you all to St. Petersburg as soon as possible."

Chapter 10
Be Strong and Courageous

Jon thought about texting, but he knew that would light up everyone's phones. "Help, Father?" Jon said, looking to Heaven for help.

"What *is* that?" Sasha asked, shuddering, feeling as if bugs were crawling and scratching him all over his body.

"*That* is an Unnatural. They are possessed by demons."

"*What?*" Sasha looked at him, stunned. "Oh!" he said, rubbing his arms as the feelings intensified. "It getting worse."

"There's more of them," Jon said, confidently.

Just then, a beautiful woman wearing a white fur coat walked onto the scene. Her long brown wavy hair hung to about her mid-back. Her eyes were an odd shade of yellow on her flawless, milky white skin. "Wild," Jon whispered, surprised.

"What?" Sasha whispered back.

"Do you see her eyes?"

"Forget her eyes! Look at *her*!"

"She's stunning, yes. The other side preys on the weaknesses of others. Beauty is only on the outside with this one, though. That I guarantee," he said, studying her.

Just then, Stepan came into view.

"Stepan," Katia said, and went to jump, but Val grabbed her arm. "What? We can take out the other two."

Val shook his head. "No, we can't."

"Why not?"

"Because I have the gift of Spiritual sight, and that is *not* a man *or* a woman."

"What do you mean?"

"They are Unnaturals. There are demons in those two. Stepan has no idea what he's talking to."

Looking back at the trio next near the monument, they saw Stepan talking to the pair in Russian. Katia translated for Val, and Sasha translated for Jon. Josh just hung out where he was, keeping an eye on everything he could, straining to listen to the conversation from his position.

The man of the duo stood to about six-foot-four. He had blonde hair, and the same yellow eyes the woman had. Both had pleasing physiques. While they spoke in Russian, Josh heard it all in English.

"Sergei contacted us and told us of your success," the woman remarked, pleased. "You have done well."

"I am only doing my job," Stepan said, blushing. "Thank you for the opportunity. Speaking of which?"

"Oh yes. Your money," the man sneered, pulling a thick envelope out of his pocket. "Before we do. Do you happen to know who was here in Russia with Angel?"

"There were three men."

"There is also another young lady, yes?" the woman asked knowingly.

"Yes, but Sergei already has her sister," Stepan pointed out. "She can be used to get to Katia if need be."

"Really?" The woman smiled. "You have been invaluable."

"Thank you. Now?" He gestured toward the envelope.

"Not so fast," the man said, putting his hand on Stepan's shoulder.

Trying to back away, Stepan was surprised when the man's hand clenched tighter, and he was unable to move. Looking at the pair wide-eyed, Stepan asked, "What is going on?"

"While you have been most helpful, you now know what we look like," the man explained. "We cannot have that," he said, and the man's eyes suddenly shifted to black, and a bat-like creature took his place. Its scales, which coated its skin and wings, were reddish-black. On the end of its hands were long, sharp talons. And its yellow eyes did not miss much, as they bore a hole in Stepan's soul. While its wings fanned out behind it, it slashed right through Stepan's abdomen, sending his intestines to the ground.

Looking at them, stunned, Stepan dropped to his knees. The creature laughed before he slashed Stepan's throat to finish him off. In that instant, Stepan fell back onto the hard concrete. Stepan's life ebbed away, as his blood began to coat the brightly colored leaves near the monument.

After Stepan took his last breath, the woman and the creature turned to leave. Between steps, the creature turned back into the man. Calliope playfully kicked a couple piles of leaves with a joyful giggle as they left, arm-in-arm.

When they were sure they were alone, Katia turned to Val, pale. "*What* was *that*?" she asked, sick to her stomach.

"*That* is an Unnatural. The woman should have changed too," Val said, confused. As the others made their way over to them, it hit Val, "I know who that was."

Seeing him go pale, Josh asked, "Who is it?"

"An Unnatural," Jon explained. "Sasha has Jesse's gift. He felt them coming."

"While that's cool," Val started, "you need to know that the woman was Calliope. And since he's more red than the other demons we've seen, I'm pretty sure the other one was Korax." Seeing the shocked faces, Val finished with, "And, the worst part? If Katia's translation is correct, Korax and Calliope have direct access to Angel and Liliya."

*   *   *

"This train ride feels like it's taking forever," Jacob complained, feeling the thumping pace from the train vibrate through his body.

"It's only three and a half hours," Cori said, sitting beside him.

"I'm glad our flight to St. Petersburg is only three hours. Three hours seems a lot shorter on a plane than on a train."

"At least it's not the sixteen or so hours *we* have," Cori pointed out, with Charm on the floor at their feet.

"Sorry you guys can't come with us. I was just getting used to having you guys around."

"We'll see you at the Haven when you come back. That'll give us time to set up."

"This is true. It's going to be weird being in the field without Rachel," Jacob said.

"She's strong," Cori pointed out, "but she has three broken ribs. She's not going to be much use to you. And if she's right, you'll already have your hands full."

"True."

"I've never heard of real life angels or demons. I thought that was just in the Bible."

"Where there's light, there's dark," Jacob pointed out. "We saw some in Australia."

"Going around the world must be exciting," Cori said, admirably. "This is my first trip out of Ireland."

"What you're doing is just as important."

"What do you mean? You're in the field fighting this stuff, yeah? That sounds more exciting to me."

"What *you* do, though, is just as important," Jacob said. "You're watching our backs with your computer know-how. And, thanks to Jerrod's connections, you have a bit more access than most."

"We would have it anyway," Cori said with a smile.

"How?"

"Well, let's just say we have our ways, and leave it at that. The less you know, the better. Trust me. It's plausible deniability for you. It's also for your own protection."

Jacob chuckled. "Probably."

"Well, I hear you have some unique gifts of your own," Cori pointed out.

"Not as unique as some of the others."

"What you do with regular everyday stuff is wild! Your hunting skills, I've heard, are amazing as well."

He shrugged, blushing. "There's nothing amazing about me."

"That's not what I heard when I asked around."

"Really? Why did you ask around about me?"

"Well, I, uh, wanted to know who we were working with," she said nonchalantly.

Jacob nodded in understanding. "Gotcha."

"Also," she added, resting her hand on his, "I like to know about those who pique my interest."

"Oh!" He looked at her, wide-eyed, as his heart skipped a beat. With a smile, he blushed. "Thanks."

Across the aisle, Delaney and Joe sat together, talking. "So, do you travel often?" Joe asked her.

"Not really. Been in Ireland all my life. You?"

"Just since running into the A.N.G.E.L.s." He smiled, showing his dimples. "I've experienced all sorts of new things around them."

"Ohhh, you are *so* trouble." Delaney chuckled, shaking her head. "Cute *and* adventurous."

"You don't seem too bad yourself."

"Thank you. I *am* a little nervous about all of this."

"Why? It's just a short hop to Russia."

"It's more what's waiting for us *in* Russia. If Rachel's right, we're walking into a firestorm, yeah?"

"This is true, but we have something bigger than what's waiting for us in Russia, darlin'," Joe pointed out.

"What's that?"

"We have God, and all of His army. Satan may think he's better than God, but he's far from it. While this is his playground, God's stronger than anything Satan may have in his arsenal."

"Glad you have the confidence."

"I do. I've seen what God can do. Once *you* do, you'll feel more confident about being an A.N.G.E.L. too. You have to be strong and courageous in where you stand with your faith. Doubt and fear are the enemies of faith and trust. When your faith and trust in the Lord are replaced with doubt and fear that the Lord won't take care of you, then the other side has won. Trust Him. He's got us."

"I hope your right. I have a feeling we're headed into a mess."

*   *   *

Slowly opening her eyes, Angel groaned in pain. Once her new world came into focus, she groaned again at seeing she was still in her concrete cell. Glancing toward where the girls were before, she was relieved to see that Liliya and Elena were still there. "Where are the other girls?" she asked, noticing the others who had been in there were now gone.

"Sergei. He tell them they suffer same fate as you if they do not behave," Elena explained.

"They listened," Liliya added. "He sell them yesterday."

Stunned, Angel asked, "How long have I been out?"

"You were out for a day and a half," Elena explained.

Angel sighed. "Great."

"You see okay?" Liliya asked. "You hit your head pretty hard."

"Yeah," Angel said, slowly sitting up. "Wow. I'm hungry…and dizzy. And, my head is pounding."

Elena nodded toward the bowl of oatmeal next to Angel's bed. "You need to eat."

Picking it up, Angel took a spoonful of the oatmeal, and then watched it plop back into the bowl. "How long has it been sitting here?"

"Sorry to say, a couple of hours," Elena said. "No more until tonight."

Dejected, Angel sighed again. "Great."

"Your friends and my sestra will find us, no?" Liliya asked.

"Oh, of course. It's just going to be a matter of when. God knows where we are. He's given me the confidence of knowing He won't leave us alone."

"Will we make it out alive?" Elena asked.

"I don't know. I'm just glad I know that when I die, I'll be with Him."

"How do you know?" Elena asked.

Jaw dropped, it never occurred to Angel that Elena and Liliya may not be Christians. "I-I'm sorry. Are you not a Christian?"

"What is a Christian?" Elena asked.

"A Christian is a follower of Jesus Christ, Son of the living God."

"Who is this Jesus Christ? You say Son of the living God, but why have we not heard of Him?" Elena asked.

"You've *never* heard of Jesus?"

"My sestra talks about Him," Liliya said. "I do not want to go to church, though. People are…how do you say it?" Snapping her fingers to come up with the word, she said, "They do not do what they say. They think they are better than me."

"They're not. I promise you. I'm sorry they act that way," Angel said, heartbroken.

"Will this Jesus get us out of here?" Elena asked.

"Yes, He will," Angel said confidently.

"Is He with your friends right now?" Liliya asked.

"What? No. Yes. Well, sort of. Oh, boy." Angel dropped her head in her hand. "Okay. Let me start from the beginning." As Angel talked, Liliya and Elena listened to every word. "Long ago, God created the world in seven days, according to the scriptures in Genesis. He spoke the world into existence. On the sixth day, He created man, and called him Adam. Adam named all of the animals in the Garden of Eden, since God gave him dominion over the animals and the plants. The only rule God gave Adam was that he couldn't eat from the Tree of Knowledge of Good and Evil."

"That is all?" Elena asked.

"Yep. After a while, God noticed that Adam was lonely, so He put Adam to sleep, and used Adam's rib to create a woman, Eve. Adam, of course, was thrilled. He showed Eve all around the garden, and told her about the one rule. Well, even longer ago than the garden, there was an angel named Lucifer. Lucifer was an angel pretty high up. After a while, Lucifer thought he was better than God, and managed to convince multiple other angels he was too. Well, when God found out, he kicked Lucifer out of Heaven. We know him today as Satan. God also kicked out the angels who followed him, known today as demons."

"There are no demon or angels today, right?" Liliya asked.

"Oh no," Angel shook her head. "They're here. They could even be right here in St. Petersburg. See, Satan knows that when Christ comes back, and God re-establishes His Kingdom as stated in Revelation, he's going to be thrown into a bottomless pit. And he wants to take as many with him as he can."

"I see," Liliya said, mulling over the new information.

Seeing the wheels turning in their minds, Angel went on with the story, "Anyway, back to the Garden. You see, Satan saw his way in to mess with God's new creation, the human race. He approached Eve in the form of a snake, and tempted her. He twisted the one rule she knew. He told her that God didn't want her to be like Him, that's why He didn't want her to eat the fruit from the tree. Eventually, she gave in and ate it. Then she gave it to Adam, and he ate it too. Once the Lord God found out, he punished man, woman, *and* the snake. Snakes are forever to live on the ground, under the foot of man. Man would forever be forced to forage for themselves from the land and water. They had to work for their food. And, women would forever experience severe pain during childbirth. And, if all that wasn't bad enough, they were kicked out of the Garden, which is even now being guarded by angels with fiery swords. The biggest punishment, and most severe, was that the direct communication would be shut off between God and man. The only way to ask for pardon for sin, at the time, was to sacrifice a perfect animal by shedding its blood on an altar."

"Wow. Did not know this." Elena shook her head. "Is this all true?"

"Oh, there's much more. I'm just giving you the short version, for sake of time," Angel explained.

"I see. How do I learn more?"

"It's in the Bible. *When* you get out of here, you can read it for yourself."

"Okay, but where is Jesus?" Liliya pressed. "How will this story help us find Him?"

"Patience," Angel said with a smile. Despite where they were, she enjoyed telling others about Jesus. "You see, over many years, God's people went through a lot. So much so that God got together with Jesus and the Spirit, and they came up with a plan to help man. Jesus agreed to come to Earth in the form of a man, and to sacrifice Himself to put the bridge of communication back in place between God and man. Jesus's sacrifice would also create a way for man to spend eternity with God and Jesus in Heaven."

"Wait. You said a sacrifice was killing an animal on an altar," Liliya said, furrowing her brow. "You said man needed to shed the blood of an animal."

"I did."

"So, if Jesus was to be sacrifice, then…" Liliya's voice trailed off as it dawned on her what had happened.

"Yes. Jesus came to Earth in the form of man. He was born to the Virgin Mary. He grew up, knowing what man faced on a day-to-day basis, so man would know Jesus understood them.

He, however, was perfect. He was without sin. He was even tempted by Satan himself, and won."

"So, what happened to Jesus? You speak in the past tense," Elena observed.

"Glad you're paying close attention." Angel's eyes twinkled. "You see, during Jesus's ministry, He clashed with the teachings of the Sadducees and Pharisees. They were the religious leaders of the day. They wanted the power and prestige, but Jesus was doing many miracles in God's name. He was giving the Lord the credit. Well, after a while, the religious leaders got together to figure out a way to kill Jesus and take Him out of the equation. They were losing people daily to Jesus, and they wanted their power back."

Elena nodded. "I can see that."

"Well, during Jesus's time, He kept a close inner circle of men around Him. They are known as apostles. The religious leaders got ahold of one of them, named Judas."

"Oh! That means traitor," Liliya said, excited she finally recognized something from the story.

"Yes. Judas betrayed Jesus to the religious leaders, who falsely accused Jesus for various things. They had been trying to get Him for a while, and finally succeeded. In order to do this, they needed Judas. Key to this is that Judas betrayed Jesus for thirty pieces of silver, and with a kiss."

Elena wrinkled her nose, disgusted. "Not nice."

"I agree," Angel said. "Now, the night Jesus was betrayed and arrested, He had a dinner beforehand. He had His small band of men there, and served bread and wine. This is where the communion that we observe in remembrance today, came from. During this meal, Jesus informed the men that one among them would betray Him. Judas, at that point, had already made the deal with the religious leaders, so as soon as Jesus said it, Judas knew He was talking about him."

Liliya shook her head. "Bet he felt like punched."

"Do you mean like *he got* punched?" Angel asked, making sure she was following her.

"Yes. That is it."

"Yes. He was so upset that he left the dinner. Also, during the dinner, Jesus told Peter that he would deny Jesus three times before the rooster crowed the next morning. Peter felt horrible! How could Jesus think this of him?"

"I would feel horrible too," Elena pointed out.

"Me too," Angel agreed. "Well, after the dinner, Jesus wanted to go to the Garden of Gethsemane to pray. He asked the others to watch out for Him, to make sure it was safe. Jesus went to pray to the Father, which is what we call God today. Jesus told Him that He was willing to go through with the sacrifice, but if there was any other way, He was willing to listen. Jesus was praying so hard to the Father, that He was even sweating actual blood."

"Wow," Elena said, shaking her head.

"Oh, that's wow, but what's also wow, is that Jesus took a moment for a break, and went to the men who were supposed to be watching out, and found them asleep."

"Yikes!" Liliya looked at her, wide-eyed. "Even with Judas and those bad men coming? Very bad!"

"Definitely! Well, of course Jesus wasn't happy. After a reprimand, Jesus went back to praying. It was then that the religious leaders and Judas came to the Garden. As they approached, Jesus went back to his friends. When He got there, Judas met Him with a kiss. That was the signal to the leaders which man was Jesus. Once he kissed Jesus on the cheek, the religious leaders arrested Jesus. This is where it gets really bad."

"Worse than being betrayed by His own friend?" Liliya asked, horrified.

"Yes."

"How is this possible?" Elena asked.

"Just listen," Angel encouraged. "You see, after they arrested Jesus, Peter went to the courtyard near where they took Jesus to see if he could get some information on what was going on. While he was there, three different people accused him of being one of the men who was always with Jesus. He denied it all three times. Shortly after the third time, the rooster crowed, and Jesus was taken through the courtyard to face even worse torture. When He did, Jesus looked directly at Peter."

"What did Peter do?" Liliya asked. "I would be sick!"

"I'm sure he was. He ran away for the moment. In the meantime, the soldiers beat Jesus with this horrible thing called a cat o' nine tails. It's a whip with multiple tails on it. They beat Jesus with this, ripping the flesh from His bones and muscles."

"Oh!" Liliya said as she and Elena looked at her in shock.

"Afterward, they placed a purple cloak on Jesus's back. Purple back then meant royalty. They also shoved a crown of wooden twigs with thorns three inches long onto Jesus's head. You see, between the crown and cloak, they were in essence mocking Him being King of the Jews."

Nodding, Liliya solemnly said, "I see."

"Well, after the blood dried, they ripped the cloak off Jesus's back, therefore reopening the wounds on His back. They then ripped the cloak into shreds and cast lots to see who would get the different shreds as a souvenir."

"That's horrible!" Elena said, horrified.

"Yes. Well, *then* His trial came about."

"*After* all that?" Elena's jaw dropped.

"Yes. However, Pilate, who was basically like a governor at the time, didn't want to convict Jesus, because he didn't think Jesus had done anything wrong…which He hadn't. Anyway, Pilate decided to give the people the option of who to crucify."

"Crucify?" Elena looked at her wide-eyed. "Meaning like the Crusades?"

"Yes."

"After everything they did to this Jesus, they were going to crucify Him too?" Liliya asked, stunned.

"Yes."

"I see," Liliya said, taking a deep breath. "Okay."

"So," Angel went on with the story, "Pilate took the worst of the worst from that day and age – a murderer named Barabbas. He gave the people the option of releasing one of them. Unfortunately, they chose Barabbas. Pilate couldn't believe it! He went over to the washbowl, and informed the crowd that he was washing his hands when it came to being responsible for the death of Jesus."

"Wow," Elena said, shocked. "They let a bad man go, but killed a good man?"

"Yes," Angel confirmed. Going on with the story, she explained, "The next thing that happened was the crucifixion. In those days they made people carry their crosses through the streets, all the way to where they would be nailed to the cross, and hung there until they died." Hearing gasps, Angel went on, "Jesus was already wounded beyond belief. So when it came to carrying His cross, as He walked through the streets being spat on and shouted at, He finally collapsed. They made a man from the crowd carry it the rest of the way. Once they finally reached Golgotha, where He and at least two others were to be crucified, they nailed Jesus to the cross by His hands and feet with three-inch spikes. They also left the crown of thorns on His head, and placed a plaque on the top of the cross, which said 'King of the Jews' on it. Once everything was in place, they put the cross upright, putting all His weight on his hands and feet, ripping into the skin that was already damaged by the spikes."

Liliya looked away for a moment, and took a deep, cleansing breath at the picture she had in her mind.

Elena's jaw dropped. "Oh my!"

"There's more," Angel said. "As He hung there, the skies got dark. One of the guys on one side mocked Jesus, demanding to know why, if He were truly the Son of God, He didn't come off the cross and save them all. Meanwhile, the other one snapped at the man, and asked, '*Don't you fear God, since we are under the same sentence? We are punished justly, for we are getting what our deeds deserve. But this man,*' meaning Jesus, '*has done nothing wrong.*' He then asked Jesus to remember him when Jesus went into His Kingdom that day. Jesus told that man, '*Truly I tell you, today you will be with Me in paradise.*' Jesus made sure to take care of that man, even as He was hanging there dying. Also, Jesus looked to John, and asked John to care for Jesus's mother, Mary. Again, making sure to care for others while He was dying. Even going through torture, His mind and heart was on others."

"Amazing," Elena said, shaking her head.

"During this time, from noon to three, darkness came over the land. It was as His blood was being shed that the sins of the entire world were put on Jesus. There was so much sin, that God actually turned His back on Jesus. When He did, Jesus called out, asking God why He had forsaken Him. Once that happened, they gave Him vinegar on a sponge to quench his thirst. Once Jesus took a sip, He let out one last cry, and died."

Elena shook her head. "That is heartbreaking."

"Wait a minute!" Liliya looked at Angel in fear, when a dreadful thought hit her. "If He is dead, how will Jesus help us?"

Elena looked from Liliya to Angel, surprised she hadn't thought of it herself.

"I'll get there. Give me a minute. You see, once Jesus died, the veil between where the priests used to commune with God in the Temple, and where the normal people would go, was torn in two, reestablishing our direct line of communication with God through Jesus's sacrifice. Now, you're right, Jesus *did* die. He died, but three days later He resurrected from the dead, bringing with Him the keys of Heaven. He showed Himself to His apostles, even taking Peter aside, forgiving him three times – in essence, negating Peter's denial of Jesus. Jesus was also seen by over five hundred other witnesses."

"When was this?" Elena asked.

"Almost two thousand years ago."

"And, now? Where is this Jesus now?" Elena pressed.

"I'm getting there," Angel said, trying to get through the rest of the story before Sergei decided to come down. "You see, just before He went back to Heaven to be with the Father, Jesus wanted to make sure we were taken care of as well, so He left the Holy Spirit here to guide us. Jesus then went to Heaven on a cloud. Those of us who are His children are still awaiting His return. All of this is in the Bible."

"If Jesus is in Heaven, how will He help us?" Liliya asked.

"He *is* in Heaven, interceding for each of us. Meanwhile, the Spirit, along with His angels, are fighting every day we are here, for as long as we are on this planet. *That* is how He will help us."

"How do we become one of His children?" Elena asked.

"All you have to do is confess your sins to Jesus in prayer, and ask Him to be your Savior. He has already taken the penalty for your sin, which is eternal death in the depths of Hell, on Himself at the cross. You see, because of that original sin, each of us is born with the penalty of that sin. It's inherited. Once we reach the age of accountability, which is different for each of us, we are then responsible to make the choice to accept Jesus's gift of paying the penalty. If we don't before we die, we are then doomed to eternal life in the Lake of Fire in the pits of Hell."

"That place is real?" Elena asked, wide-eyed. "And, I thought life here on Earth has been hell."

"Nowhere near what it's like in real Hell. And, yes, just like there is a real Heaven, there is a real Hell. Just like there are real angels, there are real demons. There are real spiritual battles going on all around us every day. Whether you see them or not, or whether you believe it or not, they *are* going on."

"And, we stop it by asking this Jesus to forgive us of our sins?" Elena asked.

"You'll never stop the battles, but you *will* be able to go to Heaven when you die. You will also be a child of God, so the angels will fight as many battles for, and with you, as they can. You have a job to do as well, though. It'll be your job to keep the relationship with Christ. Your job is also to tell others about Him."

"And, if we don't ask this prayer, when we die, we go to hell with Satan?" Liliya asked.

"Yes."

"We just have to pray?" Elena asked again.

"Yes."

"I want to do this."

"Me too!" Liliya said, making sure they heard her.

Angel led the two of them in prayer. As each girl prayed, they felt a massive burden lift off. Knowing that no matter what happened to them on Earth, that they would be in Paradise with Jesus when they died, gave them a hope that neither had felt for a long time.

Chapter 11
The Lord will be with You Wherever You Go

Somberly sitting in the room, the group was once again deep in their own thoughts and prayers. Praying for guidance, they hoped for some clue as to which way to go next.

"How do we find them?" Katia finally asked. "Sitting here not doing anything is no help!"

Pacing, Sasha stopped and looked at her. "I know Liliya is your sister. Angel is now all our sister. We need to find these girls."

"There is another girl," Katia said, and they all stared at her. "The man who gave me Stepan's name, his sestra was taken too. That is how I find Stepan. Her name is Elena."

"So that's *three* women we need to find?" Jon asked, and she nodded.

"If we stop them, we save more than three," Josh pointed out. "We save many other's daughters. Each one of those girls is someone's daughter."

Val shook his head, beside himself. "I don't understand how someone could do this to another human, let alone an innocent girl."

"There are a lot of things I have seen in doing this over the years, and I still can't figure out, for the life of me, why or *how* someone could do it to another human being," Jon said. "You can't let it get to you, though. Once you disassociate yourself from your heart, you take the human factor out of your choices and decisions. Once that happens, humanity is doomed. People don't place enough stock in how much their heart plays in their decision-making. People need to follow their heart, but they sometimes forget to take their brain with them."

"Here! Here!" Josh agreed. "It would solve a lot of problems if people were alert, and used their brains, hearts, *and* instincts."

"I also do my best to follow what God tells me to do," Val added.

"What if you lose your way?" Katia asked.

"You can't lose what is always at your side," Val said, holding up his Bible. "When you see the world through the heart of Jesus, that allows you to see the world differently. If you don't have it handy, memorize some key verses like we do in the games."

"Games?" Sasha asked.

"You'll know soon enough," Jon said with a smirk. Remembering Jacob's trouble with the challenger/aggressor game, he chuckled to himself.

"With all the bad, how do you see good? It is a dark world, no?" Katia asked.

"You take the blinders of what the world wants to offer you, and put on what Jesus wants to offer you, and then you have a lot fewer questions," Jon explained. "He has an amazing plan for you. You only need to say yes and follow it. In Jeremiah 29:11, it says, '*For I know the plans I have for you,*" *declares the Lord, "plans to prosper you, and not to harm you. To give you a hope and a future.*' He's always looking out for His children, we only need to listen."

"Yes. This is true," Sasha said, realizing the answer to a question he had been agonizing over since first meeting the A.N.G.E.L.s that day at lunch. "You are right. And, now I know. Yes, I will join you. I will say yes to God's call. My godmother said God has taken care of her long before me, and He will do it long after me. I will stay with you."

"Great!" Jon grinned. Then reality dawned on him once again. "Now we just need to find our sisters, so we can move onto the next assignment."

"Problem is, Stepan was our only lead," Jon pointed out, as he laid back on the bed, resting his hands behind his head, while watching the fan on the ceiling slowly spin. "And, now Stepan is gone."

"This is true," Josh said, sitting back in his chair with his arms crossed. Stroking his chin in thought, he added, "Of course, there's always the lead of Calliope and Korax."

"How did you know that man was not human?" Katia asked Val.

"I have the gift of Spiritual sight," Val explained. "It's the same way I knew you were on that shelving unit in the warehouse. When I looked at Korax and Calliope, I saw a shadow figure within them. What I can't figure out, though, is why Calliope didn't change when Korax did?"

"She is a muse!" Sasha said as it hit him. "Now I know why I know that name. Calliope is a myth from ancient time!"

"Sooo, maybe *not* a myth?" Josh posed.

"Okay, that brings us to the next question of how do we locate a myth and a demon?" Jon asked. Chuckling, shaking his head, he added, "Only *we* would run into a problem like this. And the kicker? They probably know *exactly* where Angel is." Pulling his legs up as he sat up on the bed, he dropped his head on them, and finished with, "And, if they get to her first, she's done for."

"We need backup," Josh said, picking up his cell phone. Dialing Mark, he was relieved when Mark answered on the second ring. "Oh! Praise God!" Josh said, relieved.

"We already know," Mark answered.

"*How* do you know? *What* do you know?" Josh asked. When he did, the others looked at him in shock, so he put the phone on speaker so the others could hear. Surrounding he and Katia around the table, the group joined the conversation.

"We know Angel's in trouble, and it has to do with the other side," Mark said.

"She's in deeper trouble than she's ever been in before, Dad," Jon explained. "She's been kidnapped and plopped in the middle of a sex slave ring."

"*What*?" Mark asked, stunned.

"That's not the worst of it."

"How could it get worse than *that*? How did this happen?"

"Just wait," Jon said, in the middle of the worst conversation he has had with his father to date. "Last night, our only lead was killed in the middle of a park, by Calliope and Korax."

"Please, for the love of God, tell me this is some kind of war game you are playing, and this is the scenario," Mark said, his voice shaking.

"I wish it were. We're in deep over here, Dad."

Taking a deep breath to stay in control, Mark went out onto the deck to get away from Casey and the girls. He didn't want Casey to overhear the conversation until he could sit her down to explain. Closing the sliding door behind him, he demanded, "How in the *world* did *that* happen? Tell me *everything*! And, I *mean everything*!"

"Dad, this started because of her behavior and choices," Jon said, trying to calm his dad down enough to get the help they needed from him. "She threw herself at our only lead. When she was cornered on it by us *and* the archangel, she did a slingshot in the other direction."

"What is a slingshot?" Katia asked.

"It means she went completely the opposite direction to the one she should have gone," Val explained.

"Who is that? Who all is there?" Mark asked, as he paced the deck.

"We've added Sasha Kazakov for sure," Josh explained. "He's the godson of Anastasia. Katia Alexandrova is still thinking things over. However, it's Katia's sister, Liliya, who was originally taken by the sex trafficking operation. That's how we ran into our lead, Stepan. Angel took it upon herself to try to find Liliya by herself. We're thinking she did it to prove herself. However, they took her too."

"Then," Jon jumped back into the conversation, "last night, Sasha came to us and told us of a meeting in the park. We went down there, and that's where we saw the human form of Korax and Calliope. Korax turned into his true form and slashed Stepan to death."

"Right in the middle of the park?" Mark asked, appalled.

"It was late at night," Jon explained, "but yes."

"Wow. This group is either brazen or desperate."

"Or both," Jon finished. "Look, Dad, we took a lot of them out at Black Rock, and they're looking for revenge. They've thrown the general operational guidelines they used to follow out the window. They've killed one A.N.G.E.L. in broad daylight in London, and now they know where Angel and Liliya are. They are more than likely going to beat us to rescuing them. We need serious help or we're going to lose them both…forever."

Running his hands through his hair in nervousness, Mark stopped pacing, and looked out at the vast high desert landscape behind the house, deep in thought. After a few tense moments, Mark sighed, and then said, "We knew it was bad, but we didn't know it was *this* bad."

"It is," Jon confirmed.

"Well, at this point, Rachel is severely injured. She has at least three broken ribs that we know of. Her, Jerrod, and two of the new ones from Ireland, Cori and Kai, are already on their way back here. Jesse, Joe, Jacob, and Delaney, the other new one from Ireland, are on their way to you guys. They have to wait until later this morning because there's only one flight from Heathrow to St. Petersburg, and it takes off at nine-twenty each morning. They missed it yesterday. They'll land around two-thirty today. Anastasia will meet them at the airport, and bring them to the hotel. Make *sure* you're there."

"We will."

"In the meantime, Derek and I will take the next flight out. Once Jerrod gets back, which should be in a couple of hours, I'm going to have him turn around and come back out to Russia. This is an all-hands-on-deck situation."

"Have an idea," Josh jumped in.

"What's that?"

"What if I call my dad and have him come up too?"

"He's a good asset as well," Mark said. "If he's willing, that would be great! See if Danny and Charlie will come too? I know Ethan's already out doing something for Danny."

"If it were Rachel, I promise you they'd be here. I'm pretty sure it'll be the same in regards to Angel," Josh said confidently.

"Give him a call and send me a text. Derek and I are scrambling as soon as I get off here."

"Thank you, Dad," Jon said, relieved for the help.

"Josh, call your dad. We'll be there as soon as possible. Jon, I'll text you the information once the tickets are purchased. We'll have Anastasia pick us up from the airport as well. Once people get there, I want them to get to the hotel room. Reserve two more rooms. We're going to need at least three total with everyone coming in. Stay in your room until we get there, *except* for sleeping and getting the rooms. I don't want anyone running around out there, or we could lose more."

"Sounds good."

"Love you guys. In the meantime, be careful and…watch your backs."

"Yes, sir," Josh said, and they hung up. "Well, that was both encouraging and discouraging. If he's calling out the troops, than we're in bigger trouble then we thought."

"Call your dad," Jon said, as he started pacing.

"In the meantime, we all need to be in prayer," Val added. "Mark said it was an all-hands-on-deck situation. We need to get as much help as possible."

"G'day," Josh said on his phone. "Willow, is Pop around?...Thank you," he said, and waited. To the others, he explained, "My sister-in-law is going to get him."

"G'day, Josh! Great t' hear from you," Nico answered the phone, as Josh put it on speaker for the others to hear.

"Wish it were under good circumstances," Josh said.

"Right-o. What happened?"

"We're in trouble. Mark and Derek are on their way here, and I was hoping you would be able to come help too. If you can find them, Mark asked if Danny and Charlie could come as well?"

"Is Rachel okay?"

"She's injured, and is on her way back to the Haven. Problem is Angel's missing. She's been taken."

"What happened?"

"She was taken by a sex trafficking ring."

"Wait! *What*? How did *that* happen?"

"It's a long story. That's not the worst of it, Dad. Remember Korax?"

"Isn't that Cassius's new second in command?"

"Yes. Korax has recruited a new one to help. Her name is Calliope."

"Isn't that a muse in Greek mythology?"

"We thought so too. Unfortunately, she isn't. She's something entirely different. Just what? We're not sure. The other side killed the London A.N.G.E.L. before we could get to him. And last night, Korax and Calliope killed the only lead we had to Angel. Dad, they also know where Angel is."

"Bloody hell!"

"Dad!" Josh snapped.

"Sorry. Haven't heard anything this bad in a while. Yeah. Let me chat with your Mum, and I'll find Danny and Charlie. Where are you?"

Josh hung up after giving Nico the information about where they were. "Now, it looks like we wait for reinforcements."

"In the meantime, we look for Sergei," Katia simply said.

While everyone looked at her stunned and confused, Josh asked, "Sergei? Who is Sergei?"

"Sergei Petrenko," Katia said, trying to figure out why they didn't know who she was talking about. "The man who has Liliya."

"Wait. What?" Josh asked, shaking his head, confused. "You never told us about Sergei."

"Yes, I did," Katia said, adamantly. "Why do you not know this? I told you already."

"No. You didn't," Val said. "We would have remembered *that* one. We thought Stepan was our only lead."

"Didn't Dad say Delaney was coming?" Jon asked. When the others nodded, he explained, "Delaney is one of the computer people. She's supposed to be support at the Haven. When she gets here, I'll bet she can find this Sergei. We only have to wait until they land at two-thirty."

"In meantime, we look too," Katia said, almost desperate. "We can't wait. If Korax and Calliope want to take Liliya and Angel, we need to find Sergei first."

"Okay, where do we start?" Jon asked.

"I-I do not know," Katia admitted. "I hoped you knew. We *have* to do something!"

"We *are* doing something. We wait. Help is coming," Josh reminded her. "Rachel's team'll be here in eight hours. Mark and Derek'll be here early tomorrow. My dad'll be bringing Danny and Charlie with him, and they'll be here tomorrow. And Jerrod should be here tomorrow or the next day as well. They're coming. We just have to wait before we make things worse."

"Dad actually reminded me to wait," Jon said, looking at his phone. "Just got a text with his flight information. He said to wait at the hotel until everyone gets here so we can come up with a plan."

"Liliya could be shipped off before then!" Katia objected.

"We could die if we don't," Josh countered. "We're not dealing with normal people here. We're dealing with what you saw last night. You *really* wanna face that without back-up?"

"I fear for her," Katia said, hoping the others would understand.

"I understand that," Jon said, kneeling in front of her. Taking her hands, he said, "Angel is one of the Lord's. She's also an A.N.G.E.L., and she's strong. The Lord will be with her wherever she goes. Is Liliya a Christian?"

"No. She did not want to go to church. I go when I did not work," Katia explained. "I fear for her."

"The choice is ultimately hers," Jon explained. "In this world, we don't have control over much. We need to learn to work with what we *can* control. In this case, we can't control Korax or Calliope's actions. We need Delaney to help us find Sergei. And, we were ordered *not* to go after *anyone* until the others get here. My dad and Derek are former special operations Air Force guys. Jerrod is former Navy Corpsman, who also worked with the special ops guys. Josh's dad is former FBI. Danny and Charlie have been A.N.G.E.L.s for years. Danny's former military, and Charlie's an Aboriginal. They all have a lot of assets, training, wisdom, and experience they've gathered over the years. If those guys can't help us find three girls, or in this case, an entire ring of people, then no one can. That's *not even* taking into consideration who *else* we have on our side."

"Who?"

"God, and all of His Army…including the archangel."

"Is that archangel a real angel?" Katia asked, confused.

"Yes," Jon said, as a sudden streak of light filled the room.

When the light dissipated, the archangel stood in the middle of the room. "You are all in trouble," he announced.

"Tell me something we *don't* know," Josh said, as Katia and Sasha stood in shock at seeing the archangel.

"You see him?" Katia asked Josh.

Snickering, Josh answered, "Yes."

Katia walked up to the archangel and pushed on his shoulder. When he moved, Katia took a step back in shock.

Chuckling, the archangel said, "Yes. I am real."

Shaking his hand, stunned, she said, "I am Katia."

"And I am Sasha," Sasha said, awestruck as he shook the hand of the archangel.

"I know. And, I am an archangel of the Lord God," the archangel explained. "I am glad you have chosen to answer the call. I understand you are still in doubt?" he asked Katia.

"I have my sestra," Katia explained, upset. "I want to see how this goes before I commit. Also, afraid of care for her if I am not home."

"She can stay at the Haven with my family." Jon shrugged. "That's an easy one. We'll get her to the U.S. where she can start school. Her world will be wide-open from there."

Katia looked at him, unsure. Turning back to the archangel, she said, "Much respect, but scared for sestra."

"I am aware," the archangel confirmed. "I am also aware of who else is here. I know what happened last night too."

"Great. No disrespect, but now that we're all on the same page, what are we going to do about it?" Val asked.

"Mark, Derek, Nico, Danny, Charlie, and the others are coming," the archangel pointed out. "One of my angels is getting Danny and Charlie for Nico. They will be heading out soon."

"When you say *others*, do you mean some of your fellow angels?" Jon asked. "We're in serious trouble. We've already lost one. If we lose Angel and Liliya, this isn't going to be pretty."

"I understand."

"I don't think you do," Katia said, anxiety and stress written all over her. "Liliya is all I have!"

"Patience, young one," the archangel said, resting his hand on her shoulder.

When he did, a feeling of calm washed over Katia. Looking up at the archangel, Katia asked, "Will she be okay?"

"She is not alone," the archangel explained. "She is also now one of the Lord's children. Angel led her and Elena in a prayer to Jesus."

"I understand. If she dies, she will go to Heaven," Katia said, still upset. Looking back up at the archangel, she admitted, "But, I need her here."

"Katia, calm down," Val said, going over to her, putting his hands on her arms. As she looked at him, he explained, "You said that you would stick with me, right?"

"Yes."

"Well, I'm sticking with the Lord, and following His lead in this…no matter what the outcome is."

"This is *my* sestra!"

"I understand. And, Angel's *my* sestra," Jon said, coming behind her, resting his arm across her shoulder. "And, no matter *what* the outcome is, I'm still following the Lord as well. I'm scared to death for Angel, but I also know the Lord is capable of far more than you ever thought possible. Having said that," he looked toward the archangel, as he added, "if something *does* happen to Angel, I will *still* follow the Lord. I will still be an A.N.G.E.L. no matter the outcome. I answered the call to the Lord, not to Angel. Angel and Jesse being A.N.G.E.L.s as well is just a benefit. My mom and dad will gladly take Liliya in if she makes it through this. If Angel doesn't, my family will mourn, but we will also have the assurance of knowing we will see her again. And, now," he turned back to Katia, "thanks to the archangel, you have this assurance in regards to Liliya as well."

Josh stood and rested his hand on her head, while Sasha walked over and put his hand on her lower back.

Once everyone was in place, Jon started, "Father, I bring before You Katia, Angel, and Liliya, along with all our other A.N.G.E.L.s who are travelling here. You know the situation. You know our hearts. I ask You to place Your mighty hands on each one of us, giving us the strength and endurance to finish this. I ask You to place Your hands of protection around each of us, bringing us all through this."

"Father, I bring before you Katia," Val jumped in. "She is still young in the faith. I ask You to wrap her in a blanket of comfort and peace. Allow her to have the confidence that nothing going on in this world is a surprise to you."

"Heavenly Father," Sasha continued, "please send angels to help us. We need help. You are the ultimate power. Everything starts and ends with You. You are the Alpha and Omega, Beginning and End. You please take this situation, and work it out per Your will. Thank you."

"Dear Lord," Josh prayed, "You *are* the Lord God Almighty. You own the cattle on a thousand hills. *Nothing* goes on in this world that You don't know about, and have not already taken into consideration. We love, honor, and respect You, and Your sovereignty. We know if we don't come through this, that we have the blessing of knowing we'll be with You in a split second. We just ask that whatever happens to Angel, Liliya, and Elena, happens per Your will, and quickly. If they are to come to You, please do not let them suffer. We ask all of this in the name of Jesus. Amen," he finished, and everyone looked up.

Hanging her head, Katia only nodded in response as her heart broke. Tears slowly ran down her cheeks at the thought of what might be happening to her sister.

As the others drifted away from Katia, the archangel lifted her chin so she looked at him. While he wiped away her tears, he said, "Do not give up hope, young one. It is not finished yet. Choices made may well alter what I know. Free will, will determine the outcome. But know this, young one, you are *not* alone. In this family, you will *never* be alone."

"You call me young one. Why?"

"Because you are still young in the Lord. However, the Lord has big plans for you if you choose to follow His call. That is something only you can do. You have to make the choice. Make it for you, not for Liliya. She has a different path."

"I am scared," she admitted.

"I am aware. I will also be watching over all of you as much as possible."

"What will happen to Liliya?" Katia asked.

"That is known only to God."

"Can He give me hint?"

Chuckling, the archangel shook his head. "I am sorry. That is not something I can answer for you. You know, though, that Mark is on the way with Derek, as is Nico with Danny and Charlie."

"We know," Josh confirmed.

"They will help you. Listen to them. They are wise and have much experience in this type of situation. And know that the Lord is always with you as well."

"Thank you," Katia said, grateful.

To the others, he added, "Glory to the Lord forever and ever."

"Amen," they responded.

With that, he disappeared in a streak of light, leaving everyone standing there, still unsure what to do.

"So, angels and demons are real?" Sasha asked, breaking the silence after another minute.

"Yes. The other side is what you felt when Korax and Calliope walked into the park," Jon explained. "Korax is *definitely* a demon. We're not exactly sure *what* Calliope is."

"Trouble," Josh said.

"Understatement," Val added.

*   *   *

"Angel, will Jesus help us out of this?" Liliya asked.

"I don't know." Angel shook her head. "I *do* know He's here, and won't ever leave us…no matter what happens."

"Angel? Are you awake?" Elena asked, waking up herself at hearing voices.

"Yes."

"You had us worried," she explained. "You did not wake up for dinner."

"Not sure if I would qualify *this* as dinner," Angel said, wrinkling her nose. Picking up the bowl, she slowly ate the mush they attempted to call oatmeal.

"Is food, no?" Liliya pointed out.

"Yes. That it is," Angel agreed. "Even though I would still be hesitant to call it that."

"Why would Jesus not help us out of here like you said?" Liliya asked.

"Jesus will help us by standing with us. He'll never leave us. Even when the world comes against us, He'll walk through it all with us, even if it's all the way up to Heaven."

"So, He will not help us out of here?" Liliya asked, confused.

"God gave us, as His children, a gift of free will. That darn free will." Angel sighed, shaking her head. "Free will gets us in trouble sometimes, and gives us blessings other times."

"We make our own choices, like to accept Jesus," Elena said in understanding.

"Exactly. We make choices every day. God knows what choice we will make, but still gives us the choice."

"How will we know what is the right choice?" Liliya asked.

"Well, God gave us His Word, the Bible. People, at the core, were the same a long time ago as they are today. Cultures may be different, but people, deep down, are still the same. We like to take control of situations. None of us has ultimate control, though. We each make choices that may affect another. The best way to make a wise choice is to read the Word of God. When you do so, it gives you wisdom and direction. The other way involves the Holy Spirit I told you about yesterday."

"The One Jesus left?" Elena asked.

"Yes. He will help guide you, if you be still and listen to Him. It's a still small voice. Once you figure out what it sounds like, you'll never mistake it again. As long as you stay tuned in to it, He won't steer you wrong," she said, and a thought hit her. "Oh crud!" she said, dropping her head back against the wall behind her.

"What?" Liliya asked.

"I now understand what the guys were trying to tell me. I got myself into this mess by not listening to the Spirit. He tried to tell me, but I thought I knew better. You see, sometimes He lets stuff happen to teach us a lesson, sometimes it's a lesson of our own making – such as this case."

"That does not sound very nice," Liliya said, crinkling her nose. "I thought you said He is a loving God."

"Oh! He is! Let me see how to explain this?" Thinking for a few moments, an illustration came to her mind. "Have you ever babysat a little one who was just learning to walk?"

"I lived in orphanage most of my life," Liliya reminded her.

"That's right. Well, when a little one starts to walk, they're going to fall, right?"

"Right. Otherwise they do not know how to get up."

"Well, what would happen if you never let them fall?"

"They will never learn to walk by themselves," Liliya explained.

"Right. So, just like we sometimes let babies take the tumble, God does the same thing. He sees it coming, but watches, encouraging you to make the right choices. Just as we watch babies struggle to get up, as much as we want to help them, they have to do it on their own. God is the same way. He watches, encouraging you. He'll give you direction on how to get out of the situation if you listen, but if He helped you every time, you would never learn."

"Right," Liliya said in understanding.

"But, and don't forget this, while you may fall and struggle to get back up, He is right there beside you."

"I see," Liliya said, processing Angel's words in her mind. After a moment, she said, "Then, I pray He will stay with us, so I do not feel alone."

"You are a child of God's," Angel pointed out. "You are *never* alone. He'll be with you wherever you go," she said, and then took a bite of the oatmeal and shuddered. Struggling to keep it down, she ate another bite. "Yum," she said, tongue-in-cheek.

Elena shook her head with a knowing smile. "It is not good."

"No, but you're right. It *is* food. It will help keep my strength up for when it's time to break out of here."

"How will we get out?" Liliya asked.

"I'm hoping my brother and his friends have ideas already in place, and we just need to wait."

"I pray this is true," Elena said, "or you two may be in worse trouble than you are now. Sergei may sell you, and they may never find you."

"This is true," Angel said, looking at the nine empty mattresses on the floor, that only hours ago had contained girls.

"Angel, I am nervous to go back to my family," Elena admitted.

"Why?"

"Because of what I did here with Sergei."

"You did it to stay alive. You did it so you could live another day. No matter what Sergei did to your body, your heart and soul are now God's. *Nothing* can take that away from you."

"Even though I did what I did?"

"In your prayer, you asked God to forgive you for something you were forced to do."

"Yes. Seeing you and Liliya fight him, makes me wonder what would have happened if I fought him too."

"You would probably be dead, and not a child of the King," Angel pointed out. "You kept yourself alive so you could fight a different way."

"True."

"He knows what you did. You did it to stay alive. Sergei may be able to do stuff to your body, but what he does can never affect your heart or soul. Those are God's. Those are now pure."

"Thank you."

"It's a lot to think about," Angel said. Feeling her heart in her stomach, she set the bowl down. Closing her eyes, she rested her head against the wall in silent prayer, *"Father, I pray for those young girls sold into slavery. I pray that You keep their hearts and souls in Your hands. I pray that You would wrap Your hands of protection around them, giving them opportunities to escape. I pray that You will provide them the strength to take the steps needed to get out and get back home. I pray for You to guard each of their hearts. I pray they trust You and lean on You through this. Please send someone in the direction of those who are not Yours, so they have the opportunity to become one of Your daughters. Father, if Liliya and I end up in that position, I pray that You will protect our hearts as well. I also pray for Elena's heart. I'm sure she has closed it off, except to You. I pray for an opportunity in her future for her to open her heart once again to those who truly love her. I pray all of this per Your will. Amen."*

The last thing she heard before drifting off to sleep was Isaiah 41:10, *"So do not fear, for I am with you; do not be dismayed, for I am your God. I will strengthen you and help you; I will hold you up with My victorious right hand."*

Chapter 12
Run with Perseverance

Around three-thirty in the afternoon, the group was sitting around the room. Jon was reading his Bible, and Katia was reading the Bible from the room, while Josh and Val were reading books, and Sasha was just resting with his eyes closed, meditating in prayer. All of them were plagued with worst-case scenarios going through their minds.

Knowing it was Satan trying to pull them down, Josh finally had enough. Standing, he said, "Stuff this for a game of soldiers! It's been over an hour since the team from London supposedly landed."

"Have faith. They're coming. Your dad's going to be a lot longer, though," Val said to Josh. Then, turning to Jon, he reminded him, "As is *your* dad. He and Derek had an sixteen-hour flight."

"Well, Dad's gotta get Charlie and Danny first. Then they gotta get to Brisbane, before their *twenty-eight*-hour flight," Josh reminded them of how far away his dad was from them.

"This is crazy!" Katia stood and started pacing. "We are here. We are sitting here, while our sestras are in trouble. Why do we wait?"

"Because people *way* wiser than us told us to…including the archangel," Val pointed out.

"Always the voice of reason, eh, Val?" Josh said, as he shook his head with a smile.

"Well, someone's gotta be," Val pointed out. "With you guys being the brawn, *someone's* gotta be the brain."

"More like our conscience," Jon clarified. "You tend to take a step back, look at all angles in the situation, and then pray for guidance before making the final choice. We pray, and go forward, not always with the luxury of taking the time to look at all the angles."

"Having said that, we warned Angel not to do what she did. She ignored us," Josh pointed out. "This is *her* doing. We would only have had to rescue *one* if she listened."

"Look, past is past," Sasha said, trying to refocus everyone. "Cannot change that. We *can* change the future with God's help."

"Good onya! I pray she's learned her lesson this time," Josh said.

"Yeah. Hopefully it won't be too late," Val added.

Hearing a knock on the door, Josh got up to answer it. When he looked out the peephole, he opened the door with a hug for each of those coming in. "Welcome, welcome," he said. When he got to Delaney, he shook her hand and said, "Nice to finally meet you. We've heard nothing but good things about you."

"Ohhh, you must be Josh," she said with a smile. "You may not have Rachel's coloring, but you *definitely* have her accent and charm."

"Yes, ma'am." He grinned. Then he asked, "How's she doing?"

"She'll be better when she's at the Haven resting," Jacob said, sitting down at the table after greeting everyone there.

"And *you*," Delaney said to Jon, "you are *definitely* Jesse's brother." Seeing them standing side-by-side, she shook her head. "Can't believe there are two of you."

"They may be identical twins, but they have completely different personalities. I assure you," Joe pointed out.

"But, their hearts are *always* in the right place," Josh added.

"Thank you!" they said in unison, with a grin.

"It's been a while since we've done that," Jon said with a chuckle.

"Okay, introductions before we get too settled. Guys, this is Delaney Claire," Jesse introduced her. "She's not only a wiz on the computers, but has a couple other hidden talents as well."

"Oh? Pray tell?" Josh asked, crossing his arms as he studied her.

"Well, while it's true I'm a hacker," she admitted. "I also have another talent that Rachel and I have talked about. You see, I'm great at forging documents when needed."

"And, she has the gifts of discernment and *your* gift, Josh," Jacob said.

"Nice!" Josh smiled, pleased.

"Guys, this is Katia Alexandrova. She has the gift of dreams," Val explained. "And, this is Sasha Kazakov. He has Joe's gift of premonitions and Jesse's gift."

"My gift allows me to know when the other side is near. It gets stronger when they're closer, and intense when there is more than one," Jesse explained.

"No kidding," Jon said. "I didn't realize what it actually did to you, until I saw Sasha practically jump out of his skin when Korax and Calliope were close."

"What did it feel like to you?" Jesse asked Sasha, who shuddered as he remembered it. "Yep. That's it."

"Not a good feeling," Sasha explained.

"Guess the Spirit wants to make *sure* we're not mistaken," Jesse pointed out.

"True."

"Well, what other gifts are here?" Delaney asked.

"Mine's languages, as Jacob pointed out," Josh said.

"And, mine's premonitions, as Jon said," Joe added.

"Mine's kind of unique," Jon explained, "I can feel what people are feeling who are near me. Sometimes it's suffocating. Having said that, sometimes it helps, such as in Katia's case."

"Mine?" Katia asked, surprised.

"Yep. You're strong, so at times you're more difficult to read than the others, but I know *exactly* what you're feeling."

"I see," she said, sitting up in her chair. "That is good to know."

"It's not bad. I know it's a self-defense thing," he said, waving her off. "I just used you as an example."

She shrugged. "It is okay."

"I have the gift of Spiritual sight," Val said. "It's kind of an odd one. Like, I can see the dark figures in the Unnaturals, and can almost see in my mind certain things that the Spirit wants me to know."

"Like when you saw I was in the warehouse on a shelf?" Katia asked.

"Exactly."

"Well, I have a couple, but only one is Spiritually given," Jacob explained.

"Pretty sure God made your mind the way He did on purpose," Jesse said as he ruffled Jacob's hair.

While Jacob shoved Jesse's hand away, he explained, "What Jesse's talking about is how I take common household items, and turn them into bombs."

"Like *real* bombs?" Katia asked, wide-eyed.

Jacob shrugged. "I like to blow things up."

"What is the other gift that is yours?" Sasha asked.

"I draw the future," Jacob said. "I don't know how far into the future it is, but I know it'll be a future event, so I start to be on the lookout for it once I draw it."

"That's how they found me," Delaney added.

"Yep. I drew Delaney, Kai, and Cori," Jacob explained.

Josh smiled, pleased. "A well-rounded group."

"I think so," the archangel said, suddenly appearing in the room in a streak of light.

Delaney cocked her head to the side before she touched her forehead with the back of her hand to see if she had a fever. "You all seeing this?"

"Yes, ma'am." Jacob smiled. "Been awhile, sir," he said, going over, shaking his hand.

"Hello, young one," the archangel smiled. Turning to Delaney, he said, "Yes, I am a real angel. I am the archangel, and you are part of my A.N.G.E.L.s. I am given assignments from the Lord, and pass them onto you."

"Interesting," Delaney said, slowly walking around him, looking him up one side and down the other.

Katia giggled as she watched Delaney, remembering her own reaction.

"You have news for us?" Joe asked, not fazed that there was a real, live archangel in the room with them.

"Yes. Some of you are not aware that Korax and Calliope are here, along with several others."

"Really?" Jesse asked, stunned. "We knew there was trouble and it had to do with Angel, but isn't Calliope the one who took out Aden Knight?"

"Yes," the archangel confirmed. "And, Korax is Cassius's second in command."

"I remember that." Jesse nodded. "So, what does this have to do with Angel being in trouble? She's not with…" He stopped short. Catching a glimpse of Jon's face, he shook his head. "Oh no! Don't tell me that! How in *the world* did Angel end up with *them*?"

"Wait! What?" Jacob looked at Jon, stunned. "Who said she was with them?" Seeing Jon stuff his hands in his pockets as he looked down, Jacob shook his head. "Please tell me this isn't true!"

"They do not have her *yet*," the archangel clarified.

"Then, *where* is she?" Jesse demanded.

Looking up at his brother, Jon admitted, "She decided to take matters into her own hands."

"Ignoring us," Val added.

"Yes, she ignored what we told her, and got herself kidnapped," Jon continued. "Now she's smack in the middle of a sex traffic –"

"Stop!" Jesse said, pointing a finger at Jon, cutting him off. Walking over to him, he put his finger in Jon's face. With his face red in anger, he demanded, "How could you let this happen?"

Seeing the two big guys going toe-to-toe, Joe ducked out from next to Jon, and moved over next to Delaney. "Need to give them some space," he said quietly.

"*I* didn't *let anything* happen," Jon said sternly, as he stood there with his arms crossed, doing his best not to react to the anger he felt from Jesse.

"Then, how did she end up in the middle of all of this?" Jesse challenged.

"Have you *met* our sister?"

"What's *that* supposed to mean?"

"'*A gentle answer turns away wrath*,'" the archangel gently reminded them, quoting Proverbs 15:1, "'*but a harsh word stirs up anger.*'"

Putting his hands on his hips, Jesse looked down. Taking a deep, cleansing breath, he took a moment. Looking back up at Jon, who stood there motionless, but with an angry look on his face at the accusations from his brother, Jesse said, "I'm sorry. I just…I just don't understand. There are two rather large guys at her side at all times. How did she get kidnapped?"

"How did Rachel get taken?" Josh shot. "Wasn't she with *you*?"

"We were caught by surprise and drugged," Jesse defended himself.

"Well, Angel got her brumbies in a bunch and stormed outta here," Josh explained. "We couldn't stop her without feeling like we were wrestling a cat into a bathtub. Not sure if you remember her or not, but when she gets something in her mind, she's pretty much unstoppable."

"While this is true," the archangel jumped back into the conversation, "Angel chose her own path. Once she did, she set off a chain of events she could not reverse. You are to be a team. She forgot that. You are a family. She forgot that as well. Having said that, do not ever mistake that you *are* a team, a family, a complete unit." Getting louder with each phrase, he said, "You are to be the light of this world. You are sent as ambassadors for the Lord God Almighty. You were put on this team for a reason. Each of you has value beyond measure. Utilized under the right conditions, these can make great and wonderful things happen. You cannot do that if you are fighting with each other. Brother against brother," he said gesturing toward Jon and Jesse, as his voice softened. "Friend against friend," he said, looking from Josh to Jesse. "You cannot do this if you are arguing with each other. You *need* to operate as *one*. Hebrews reminds you, *'Therefore, since we are surrounded by such a great cloud of witnesses, let us throw off everything that hinders and the sin that so easily entangles. And, let us run with perseverance the race marked out for us.'* You each have a job to do. You were called for a purpose," the archangel reminded them. "God does not do surprises any more than He does mistakes. Do not be mistaken, He knows *exactly* what is going on, and will provide accordingly."

"How did she end up in the middle of a sex trafficking operation, though?" Jesse asked, calmer after the archangel's words.

"She was looking for my *sestra*," Katia said quietly from the table where she was listening intently to the conversation.

Spinning toward Katia, Jesse's face softened at seeing her, with tears brimming Katia's eyes. Stunned, he asked, "*Your* sister is with Angel?"

"Actually, Angel is with her sister, if you want to be technical," Josh clarified. "She wanted to find Liliya on her own, and thought she could do it by herself. Next thing we know, Katia's telling us that she's no longer at the club, and doesn't know where she is."

Sitting on the bed with his head in his hands, shaking, Jesse just shook his head in shock. As the silence hung over the room, Jesse looked up at Jon with tears in his eyes, and asked, "Do Mom and Dad know?"

"They do now," Jon assured him. "Dad's on his way with Derek."

"And my dad's on the way with Danny Hawk and Charlie," Josh added.

"And, once Jerrod gets to Reno and gets Rachel landed, he's pulling a one-eighty to come back here," Val explained.

Taking a deep breath, Jesse turned to the archangel and asked, "So, what now? Do Korax and Calliope know where Angel and Katia's sister are?"

"Her name is Liliya," Katia corrected.

"Tell me," Jesse pleaded with the archangel, "do Korax and Calliope know where Angel and Liliya are?"

"Yes," the archangel said, somberly.

Groaning, he dropped his head back into his hands. Slowly shaking it, Jesse was doing his best not to lose his mind.

Katia got up from her chair and knelt in front of Jesse. When he looked up at her, and their eyes met, the pain they shared was unmistakable.

Feelings overwhelming him, Jon sank down the wall to the ground, holding his stomach. He knew he was partially responsible for Angel, yet he felt as helpless as the rest of them.

Seeing Jon go down, Josh went over to his best friend and put his arm over his shoulder. At the same time, Katia reached up and hugged Jesse. Seeing the reality of the situation around them, the heaviness hit everyone.

The archangel quoted Joshua 1:9. *" 'Be strong and of good courage; do not be afraid, nor be dismayed, for the Lord your God is with you wherever you go.' "*

"What do we do now?" Joe asked.

" 'Wait on the Lord: be of good courage,' " Jacob said, quoting Psalm 27:14, a verse he'd heard many times during the challenger/aggressor game, *" 'and He shall strengthen thine heart: wait, I say, on the Lord.' "*

"Very good, Jacob," the archangel said with a hint of pride. "You have learned so much."

"Well, I had a lot to learn. I still do," he said, appreciatively.

Thinking of the game, Val remembered a verse said to him multiple times. Quoting Psalm 31:24, he said, *"'Be of good courage, and He shall strengthen your heart, all you who hope in the Lord.'"*

"'The Lord is on my side; I will not fear: what can man do unto me?'" Josh said, quoting Psalm 118:6-8. *"'The Lord taketh my part with them that help me: therefore shall I see my desire upon them that hate me. It is better to trust in the Lord than to put confidence in man.'"*

Sniffing, Jesse wiped his face. Looking toward the archangel, he quoted John 16:33. *"'I have told you these things, so that in Me you may have peace. In this world you will have trouble. But take heart! I have overcome the world.'"* Jesse went on, "He *has* overcome the world. What do we have to fear? He wants us to have peace."

The archangel grinned. "There you go, my A.N.G.E.L.s."

"'For God has not given us a spirit of fear, but of power and of love and of sound mind,'" Jacob finished, quoting Second Timothy 1:7.

The archangel rested his arm on his knee as he knelt next to Jesse, Katia, Jon, and Josh, and said, addressing all members of the group, "The training you went through prepared you for this. Whether she is alive here on Earth, or in Heaven with the Lord, Angel's heart and soul are still protected by the Lord God. The blood of Jesus covers her. There is *nothing* Cassius, Korax, Calliope, *or* Lucifer can do to her that will change this fact. The Lord God is omnipotent and omniscient – *nothing* gets by Him, and nothing...*absolutely nothing*...is more powerful than Him. He reminds you of this in Isaiah, when He says, *'Fear not, for I am with you; be not dismayed, for I am your God. I will strengthen you, yes, I will help you, I will uphold you with My righteous right hand.'"* Letting the verse sink in, the archangel went on, "When you do not think you can keep going, know God is there, and He will strengthen you and keep you in His hands. No *one*, and no *thing* can take you out of His hands."

"And, those are some mighty hands," Jacob commented after a moment of heavy silence.

"Yes, my A.N.G.E.L.s, you *are* on the right side. Remember, if something happens to you on this planet, that you will be with Him in the blink of an eye. Hold onto that truth. If you do, then nothing can hurt your spirit. He will *never* leave you. He will protect your hearts and minds, if you stay focused on Him."

"Okay," Katia said, "but, what do we do until the others get here? Liliya and Angel need help. If this Korax and Calliope know where they are, they are in trouble! I *saw* what this Korax did to Stepan! It was horrific! *It* is horrific! This Korax is what I see in nightmares!"

"I know you are afraid, young one," the archangel consoled her, "but have faith. As Jesse reminded you, Jesus has overcome the world."

Hesitantly, Katia asked, "Will sestras be okay?"

"If not here on Earth, they will be sitting with Jesus in Heaven. So, yes, they *will* be okay either way," the archangel assured her.

"I am afraid."

"You need to only put on your armor before you fight, and you will be unstoppable," the archangel said, referring to the armor of God. Working through Ephesians 6:10-17, he continued, "You need to put on the *full* armor of God to fight against the devil's schemes. You do not fight against flesh and blood, but against the powers of this dark world and against spiritual forces of evil. These are not to be underestimated, or it will be the last mistake you will *ever* make in this realm. The enemy knows more about you than you know about yourself. He may be cunning, but he is *not* stronger than the One you serve. My angels will do their best to help you, but they are fighting on two realms as well. You need to do your part. You need to put on your armor, and stand your ground. You are in the Lord's Army. You are His warriors. You are children of the Most High. You are princes and princesses of the King. You have full access to the throne room. You must put on the belt of truth. The devil uses lies to twist the truth. Deception is one of his weapons. Use the truth to combat this. Remember to Whom you belong."

Taking a moment before he continued, he looked at everyone to make sure they were paying attention. "Next, you must use your breastplate of righteousness. The breastplate is used to shield your vital organs from what would be fatal blows. When the things of the past creep into your mind, know whom they are from. Remember that Jesus's righteousness has already covered your past with His blood. And, His blood is pure and clean. Jesus has not only already paid the penalty, but His sacrifice has also ensured your safe place in Heaven. This is *not* something Satan can take away from you."

He paused before going onto the next one. "You need to also make sure to bind your feet with the readiness that comes from the gospel of peace. A warrior can be taken down if his feet become trapped or wounded. You need your feet in order to stand firm. You must advance into Satan's territory in order to reclaim that which belongs to God. In doing so, know that the field of battle has been mined. Be ready, be mindful of this, but have the peace in your heart that only the Spirit can give you. As you fight, you *must* keep your shield of faith at your fingertips. This is your main defense against the arrows of accusations that Satan will try his hardest to propel toward you. Use the words God has given to you in His Word, the Bible. There is a reason you were trained using the Word to fight in the challenger/aggressor game. Use those words to fight against whatever is thrown at you."

Taking another moment for his words to penetrate their hearts and minds, he finished with, "And finally, the helmet of salvation. Your mind is a precious thing. It will guide and direct your thoughts and actions. Your mind is critical to the battle. Do not let Satan use it to tempt you. He knows exactly what can sway you. Use your mind to ensure that you know the difference between spiritual truth and spiritual deception. If you have to lean on the others who have spiritual insight or the gift of discernment, then do so. Use the gifts God has given each of you to win this battle. You are *all* equipped to fight and win. You are all, as a team, perfectly capable of getting Angel, Elena, *and* Liliya out safely. You have the Lord God as your Commander-in-Chief," the archangel said as he stood. "You have Jesus as your Captain, and the Spirit as your guide. We will do our best to help, but you need to do your part as well. Listen to Mark, Derek, Nico, Danny, and Charlie. Lean on their experiences to make it through this. Lean on each other. You were all brought together for a purpose. Together, you are *unstoppable*. You are children of the Lord! Go get your team members!"

"Yes, sir!" the group said in unison.

"Focus on what suggestions and tactics you can until the others arrive. Also, bathe this continuously in prayer. Prayer is your ultimate weapon. Calling on the Lord's power in prayer is the most crucial and most powerful weapon in your arsenal. Run with perseverance this race that is before you. Listen to the cheering from the saints who have gone before you. This assignment will be a marathon, not a sprint. Hold onto the truth that you are *never* alone."

"We will," Josh assured him.

"Be safe. Be well. And, go with God as you protect each other, my A.N.G.E.L.s," he said, and disappeared in a streak of light.

"Well, this will either be an epic failure…" Josh started.

"Or the best thing God put together," Jon finished.

"Either way," Josh said, "it's all in God's hands."

"And for that," Val finished, "I'm grateful."

Chapter 13
The Powers of this Dark World

Sergei woke Angel in the middle of the night. "He says he sell you for good price, and you must get up," Elena translated after he growled at her in Russian.

"What?" Angel moaned, groggy.

"He says he sell you for good price, and you must get up now," Elena repeated.

"I go too," Liliya said, fear evident in her voice. "He sell me too."

"Well, at least we're going together," Angel said in a sigh as she sat up.

Sergei mumbled something that Elena translated as he filled a syringe, "He say he take you two tonight to meet them. They request that *he* be the one to bring you. They pay big money, so he does not say no."

"Interesting," Angel said suspiciously.

"When you wake, you will be in a new place," Elena explained.

"Wait! When I *what*?" Angel spun toward Elena, just as a needle was jammed into her neck, and Sergei emptied it.

"Ohhhhhh," she moaned, as the medicine immediately hit her. "Liliya, you are not alone. Elena, remember, no amount of guilt can change the past. No amount of worry can…can change the future. God is with us," she said before her head fell to the side.

"Now for you," Sergei said to Liliya, who looked at him in wide-eyed horror.

*   *   *

When the entire team finally arrived in St. Petersburg, Mark had everyone sit down as they snacked on the sandwiches and chips that Anastasia brought for them. "Now that we're all here, we all know the situation," Mark said, knowing the team briefed Danny, Charlie, and Nico when they arrived.

"Yeah. What are we gonna do about it?" Nico asked, sitting back in his chair. "Personally, I'd like t' take the bloke out."

"We all would, but our primary focus is getting the girls back. There are three of them. Delaney, were you able to find Sergei Petrenko?"

"I can find all dogs named Bobo in St. Petersburg if you want," she said with a smirk.

Chuckling, Mark asked, "Okay, what have you got?"

"This is where he lives and works," she said, handing him a piece of paper.

"Okay, does anyone have connections into the police, or SVR RF?"

"What's the SVR RF?" Jacob asked. "I've heard of the KGB, but not the SVR RF."

"It stands for the Federal Security Service of the Russian Federation," Mark explained.

"I know someone, but my information is no different than Delaney's. They are gathering information on Sergei, but not able to get enough yet," Anastasia explained.

"My sources say the same," Sasha added.

"Then, *we* need to get enough," Mark said adamantly. "Around eleven tonight, we'll split into three teams. Derek and I will take Jon, Jesse, Josh, and Katia to the house. Anastasia and Charlie will take Sasha, Jacob, Val, and Joe to the authorities. In the morning, if they're not found, Jerrod, Danny, and Nico will go to his work. That leaves Delaney here to man the phones and computer. Agreed?"

"Agreed," the group said in unison.

"Then, until eleven, I believe we need to be organizing, gathering, going out for recon, and most importantly, there are to be multiple people in prayer at all times. Without prayer, we're sunk!"

"Then, I do believe that's where we start," Nico said, and the group gathered together, holding hands, deep in prayer.

The room began to glow as angel after angel appeared around them. With each prayer, the angel's glow got brighter. As they closed in prayer, the archangel suddenly appeared in the center of the group. "The Lord is with you, my A.N.G.E.L.s."

They nodded, as they continued in prayer.

*   *   *

Angel vaguely remembered the familiar pattern of thuds as the sound of train tracks pounded in her mind. Trying to see, she realized she was blindfolded, and her hands were secured behind her back in handcuffs. The medicine was too strong for her to fight, and she went back to sleep, praying in her mind for miraculous intervention.

*   *   *

Groaning, the next thing Angel remembered was a feeling of floating on water. This was quickly followed by another needle jammed into her neck to keep her sedated.

Later, she felt like she was bounding down a road of some kind, as dirt continuously tried to choke her. The road was not smooth at all.

Those were her only memories over a two-day period.

*   *   *

Screams and shrieks echoed in Angel's ears as she struggled to focus quite some time later. Feeling her hands once again in cuffs, now above her head, she lifted her head to see a rough, red, rock cave, with red dirt ground surrounding them. Fires burned throughout the cave system. Stalactites and stalagmites lined the caverns, closing areas that would otherwise be open, crushing her spirit at the possibility for visible escape. The unmistakable cackle of Unnaturals and demons filled the air, echoing all around her, as the brimstone scent offended her senses.

Lifting her head, as the wall was to her left, she looked over to her right to see Liliya and Sergei equally bound. Noticing the sweat dripping from them, she suddenly realized the blistering temperatures of the caves, and the realization as to where they were hit her. They were in Cassius's den. Sergei had sold Liliya and Angel to Cassius!

"Oh, Lord!" Angel cried to God. "Only You can help us! Please do not leave us here."

In her mind, she heard the Lord's response of Joshua 1:9. *"'Have I not commanded you? Be strong and courageous. Do not be terrified; do not be discouraged, for the Lord your God will be with you wherever you go.'"*

"Thank you, Lord. You are our Lord and King. We will need You through this. We will lean on Your strength."

Hearing John 14:27, she felt a peace fill her soul. *"'Peace is what I leave with you; it is My Own peace that I give you. I do not give it as the world does. Do not be worried and upset; do not be afraid.'"*

Feeling His strength, she quoted Psalm 118:6, *"'The Lord is with me; I will not be afraid. What can mere mortals do to me?'"*

*   *   *

After the prayer, with the angels glowing as they surrounded the team, the archangel quoted Philippians 4:6-7, *"'Do not be anxious about anything, but in every situation, by prayer and petition, with thanksgiving, present your requests to God. And the peace which transcends all understanding, will guard your hearts and minds in Christ Jesus.'"* Looking at each of the young warriors, he finished with, "Go now in the strength of the Lord God Almighty. He is with you this night. He will help you, as you remain faithful to Him."

Gathering their things, the first two of the three groups left for the police station and Sergei's house respectively. Not sure what she would see, Katia prayed the entire time for everything to work according to God's will. She also prayed for the strength to accept whatever the outcome. With her nerves on overdrive, she clung to the promise of peace that the archangel had given them before the heavenly angels left. "Your will, not mine," Katia whispered, as they turned down Sergei's street.

Josh reached over and grasped her hand. "God's got this," he encouraged.

"I know. I fear for sestras."

"God's got them," he repeated.

"If He have sestras, who has us?"

"God," Josh simply stated.

"He is more strong than I give Him credit for."

"Give Him a boundary, and He'll blow it every time," Josh said with a smile.

"How are you so calm?"

"I know God has our back."

*   *   *

Reaching the house, Derek, Mark, Jon, Jesse, Josh, and Katia got out of the van. Half went to the front door, while the other half snuck around the back to ensure he wouldn't escape.

Derek was in the front with Josh and Katia. He asked, "Ready?"

Josh shrugged. "Ready when you are."

Checking around the corner of the house to make sure Mark, Jon and Jesse were ready, Derek then went back and knocked on the door. Not hearing an answer, he knocked a little louder, and rang the doorbell. After another moment of silence, he pulled out a packet of tools, which he used to pick the lock.

As they breached the front, Mark and the guys entered through the back door. "You guys get upstairs, we'll take downstairs," Derek told Mark as they met in the living room. Mark only nodded in response before he, Jesse, and Jon headed upstairs.

Heart pounding, Katia followed Derek and Josh down the stairs to a horrific scene. Sickened, she wasn't sure where to look first. The stench of body odor and human waste was overpowering as it sent a tang into her sinuses while she scanned the dimly lit basement. Derek shone his light around the basement, and her heart broke as she saw the filthy mattresses on the floor, along with the chains and cuffs bolted to the wall…her eyes landing on each of the girls occupying the mattresses. A little gasp escaped her when she saw a rat run across the floor. Knowing her sister and Angel were there disgusted her beyond words. The conditions the girls were being kept in was beyond reprehensible!

Running past Derek, Katia shown her flashlight on the face of each girl, searching for Angel and Liliya. When she didn't find either of the girls, she called out, "Elena?"

Hearing her name, Elena said, in Russian, "Over here."

Josh ran over. Using his set of lock picks, Josh released Elena, who gave him a grateful hug. "You're free," he said in Russian. Feeling the relief at finding one of the three they were looking for, he couldn't help the few tears that escaped his own eyes.

"They're down here!" Derek called to the others, who immediately appeared on the stairs of the basement.

"Angel? Liliya?" Jon asked, hopeful from the stairs.

"No." Derek shook his head. "Elena's here, though."

While the others worked feverishly to release the nine girls being held captive in the basement, police lights pierced the darkness.

Josh and Katia spoke with Elena in Russian. "Where are Angel and Liliya?" Katia asked her.

"Sergei," she said. "He took them. He said he sold them for a good price."

"I know you are afraid, but you are now free," Josh said, still speaking in Russian. "The police will help you get back to your family."

"I cannot thank you enough," she said, tears flowing as she hugged Katia. "I am sorry your sister is not here. Angel is with her."

"We are thankful that they are at least together. When did they leave?" Josh asked.

"Yesterday. Sergei was excited to get so much money for them. He said the buyers specifically requested he take them, so he took them himself," Elena explained.

"Can I talk to her privately?" Katia asked Josh.

"Yep. I'll go help the others," Josh said in English as he got up to help Jon and Jesse unlock the other girls.

"Elena, what you have been through is something no one should ever have to go through. Your brother, Erik, has *never* stopped looking for you. He is the one who led me to Sergei through Stepan. He will be very happy to have you back home."

At hearing her brother's name, Elena's tears flowed harder. "He will be embarrassed by me."

"Never."

"You do not know what I did."

Resting her hand on the side of Elena's face, Katia's heart broke for her. "You did what you had to do in order for us to find you. You are now safe. Your brother will be here soon. After you give your statement, you will probably be able to go home. He will be happy. You can start over."

"What is done, is done. I will no longer be able to say I saved myself for my husband."

"We were told you asked Jesus to forgive you of your sins, and to take over your life."

"Yes," Elena said.

"When you asked Jesus to forgive your sins, He wiped your slate clean," Katia said, cupping Elena's face in her hands. "He may have been able to scratch the surface, but he can't touch what's inside. You are a daughter of the King. You are a princess. Hold your head high. You have defeated this nightmare you have been in for two years. You are free. You are strong. You made it out alive. You can now get help to work through this torture you have endured. And, you can turn around and help others."

"But what about Angel and Liliya?"

"Trust me, we *will* find them," she said, reaching for Elena's hand. "We will find Sergei too. And when I do, he will *never* forget what he did to you and these girls. Hopefully they can use Sergei's computer to find some of the other girls."

"Thank you for finding us." Elena hugged her again. When she pulled away, she explained, "We have not eaten all day. Sergei did not come back last night. His people delivered these girls, but he never came back."

Wide-eyed, Katia turned to Josh, who was standing nearby. "Josh, Elena said Sergei did not come back last night after he left with Angel and Liliya," Katia said in Russian.

Looking toward Derek, Josh said in English, "Sergei's been MIA since last night. These girls haven't eaten all day, and they don't know where he is."

Just then, a couple police officers came down the stairs. They wrapped each of the girls in a blanket and helped them upstairs, helping them out of what had been their worst nightmare.

* * *

Trudging into the hotel after finally being released from the police station, the men separated into the three rooms. "We'll meet back here in the morning around ten. Does that sound good?" Mark asked the others, who just mumbled an acknowledgement as they went into their rooms.

"We are going to my apartment," Katia said to Delaney. "Need to pack some and ship some to the Haven. I am going with you, and cannot pay for our apartment too. I have not made final decision, but I need to get my sestra."

"Sounds good. Just give me a minute to pack up," Delaney said, getting up from her chair. Looking at the others, who looked exhausted, she asked, "What happened?"

With his face in the pillow, Jesse explained, "Found Elena. She's with her brother now. Angel and Liliya weren't there. They and Sergei have been MIA since last night."

"Great," she said in a sigh as she put her computer bag on her shoulder. "You guys get some sleep. What time do we need to be back tomorrow?"

"Back at ten," Katia answered, locking and closing the door behind them.

"Do I *want* to know what happened?" Delaney asked, as they walked down the street toward her apartment.

"You do not want to know what it looked like," Katia said with a shudder.

"That bad?" Delaney asked.

"Yes."

"Do we have any idea where Angel and Liliya are now?"

"No," Katia said. "Hoping one of those with dreams will know by morning. Powers of this dark world are strong. I am very scared for them."

"I am too," Delaney admitted. "I'm sorry you had to see that."

"Wish I did not."

"We'll pray for guidance. God won't let us down."

"Wish I had your confidence."

"You'll learn," Delaney said. "Hebrews 14:6 reminds us, *'Let us then with confidence draw near to the throne of grace, that we may receive mercy and find grace to help in our time of need.'* He won't let us down. We will all come boldly to His throne before going to bed tonight. We'll wait for His instruction. He's the One who will guide and direct our steps."

"I know this. This is not the question. My question is: where do we start? We lost both leads."

"God is bigger than anything in this world," Delaney pointed out, as they were in the elevator of Katia's apartment building. "He spoke the world into existence. Pretty sure He can give us directions. Derek explained to me that the archangel blessed this mission. He made sure we all saw this, so we would have the confidence of knowing God is with us in this."

"I know. I guess fear is winning," Katia admitted.

"Fear has multiple meanings."

"What do you mean?"

"The acronym F.E.A.R. either stands for 'forget everything and run', *or* it can stand for 'face everything and rise'. I choose to rise," Delaney said, as Katia unlocked her door. "There is also a third meaning we need to be cautious of."

"What is that?"

"'False evidence appearing real'. Our perceptions may not be accurate. This is why fear is high on Satan's arsenal list. He can use it in a myriad of ways, wreaking havoc and confusion in its wake," Delany said as they walked in.

Taken aback for a moment at the sparseness of the apartment, Delaney realized just how little Katia and Liliya truly had. Understanding that the A.N.G.E.L.s were the best possible outcome for both of them, Delaney encouraged her. "Katia, you should strongly consider the archangel's offer. It will give both of you a better life."

"For Liliya, if she is found, I will consider this. Until then, we need to box the apartment."

"Well, then, let's get started so we can get some sleep. Ten will come a little more early than we'd like with all this work ahead of us."

"I agree," Katia said. "Let us get started. Sooner rather than later."

Chapter 14
To the Ends of the Earth

Walking through the desert lands, Katia could see what was around her, but it was as if she was floating, looking through someone else's eyes. Deeply entrenched in a dream, she saw hillsides covered in green and the pops of color in the form of wildflowers and creatures that mainly stirred at night. The beauty of the high desert scene before her was spectacular. Some wildlife slept, but gently stirred as she passed them, while others were more alert to her presence.

That's when she saw a cave system in the distance. Curiosity got the better of her, so she ventured toward it, fear and trepidation lingering as she thought of her sister inside. Pushing it aside, she remembered Delaney's definitions of fear, and faced it.

Thankfully, she didn't think she was visible to anyone, but was simply a presence. Flowing through the tunnels, she slid between the stalactites and stalagmites with ease.

If it weren't for what she may find, she would have enjoyed this dream. It was almost peaceful…almost. She stopped short when she came upon a group surrounding a fire. At first she thought they were human, until one turned toward her. She froze. It *looked* human, but the eyes were black as night, almost hollow.

"What do we do with them?" one of the demons hissed.

"Whatever Cassius wants," another shrugged as he shoved a burning coal into the fire with a stick, before tossing the stick into the fire.

"I cannot *wait* to get my handsss on that Angel, for what they did to us at Black Rock!" another demon hissed, as it wrung its hands in delight. "I have ssso many ideas!"

"*Only* what Cassius, Korax, and Calliope will allow," the first demon reiterated.

"You are no fun!"

"Are you sure we cannot just play with her for a bit? Would that really be bad?" another Unnatural asked, who was in the form of a woman.

"Yes. Cassius wants her for himself. He specifically said she is off limits," the first demon said sternly.

"What about the others? We could have some fun with them, right?" another demon asked.

"Not until we get instructions. Until then, they stay where they are."

Hearing that her sister and the others were there, Katia flowed down another pathway. Going past multiple other fires with Unnaturals and demons around them, she pushed forward, now on a mission.

Finally finding herself in a cavern, she saw six people – three on one side of the cavern, three on the other – with their hands chained above their heads. The chains were connected to the ceiling. Sweat dripped from each of them. Not recognizing the first three, she went to the other three, and her heart skipped a beat at seeing her sister and Angel!

"They're here!" she whispered, excited.

Raising her head, Angel looked suspiciously around the cavern. "Who's here?" she whispered. "I can feel you."

Wide-eyed, Katia went to stand in front of Angel and studied her face. *Could Angel really feel her? Did she really know Katia was there, or was she faking it?*

"I know you're here. Who are you?" Angel whispered.

After Sergei mumbled something, Liliya translated, "He say to shut up, woman. His words, not mine. He say you are delirious."

"I am *not* delirious. There *is* someone here," Angel insisted.

"There are three others here," Liliya pointed out.

"Nooo," Angel said, looking around. "There's someone else here besides them. Someone who *isn't* a demon *or* an Unnatural."

"Do you think it is an angel?" Liliya asked, hopeful. After Sergei mumbled something, Liliya shot something to him in Russian, before telling Angel, "He still thinks you are crazy. I told him to shut up."

"Thank you," Angel said, still on edge.

"I will be back for you," Katia said, resting her hand on Angel's face.

"Thank you," Angel whispered back.

Taken aback again, Katia took a moment before going over to Liliya. She rested her hand on Liliya's cheek, and whispered to her as well, "I will be back for you too, little one."

"She said she'd be back for you too," Angel said to Liliya.

"Who?"

"I think it's Katia," Angel said, almost surprising herself. "She called you 'little one'."

"Yes!" Liliya said, excited. "She calls me that all the time!"

"I think the Spirit may have granted me this gift," Angel explained. "It's kind of like Val's. I don't know if it's permanent or temporary, but I'll take it for now."

"Is she still here?" Liliya asked.

"Yes."

"Please tell her I love her?"

"She hears you," Angel assured her.

"I love you, sestra," Liliya said aloud.

"I love you too, sestra," Katia said, and turned to leave, but stopped short when a demon suddenly appeared in front of her. Not sure if it knew she was there, she studied it closer.

Terrified, yet fascinated, Katia looked deep into its yellow eyes. She noticed the eyes had slits, much like a snake's eyes. Its blackish-red scales coated its entire body. While Korax's scales were reddish-black, the others seemed to have blackish-red. It was as if Korax was special. Even this demon's wings were blackish-red. The talons on the ends of its fingers were at least an inch and a half long, and extremely sharp. Its teeth could slice through her in a heartbeat, and it hissed when it spoke.

"What isss thisss noissse?" the demon hissed. "Ssstay quiet!"

"Yes, sir," Angel said, and dropped her head. As it walked away, Angel glanced sideways at Katia, and whispered, "Bring the others. We're in the Tanami Desert in central Australia."

Nodding, Katia then took off before she was discovered. Almost to the end of the tunnels, she stopped short when a demon swiped at her and hissed.

Sitting upright in bed, Katia let out a scream, grabbing her arm.

Delaney was to her side in an instant. "What happened?"

"Blood! Get a cloth!" Katia said, trying to stop the bleeding. *The demon scratched her in her dream. How did her arm get scratched in real life? Maybe she was really there?*

"Here, lass," Delaney said, holding a cloth on the wound, while Katia used another to clean her blood covered hand. "How in the world did you cut your arm so badly?"

"I did not do it. A demon did."

Wide-eyed, Delaney asked, "A *what*? Is there a demon in here?"

"No. I…I had a dream. I found them. It was different than other dreams. I was there."

"What do you mean you were there? Found who?"

"I *mean* I was there. I see Angel and Liliya. I touch them," she said, looking at her hand.

"Do you know where they are?"

"Yes. They are in Australia."

"We have to tell the others!"

"Need to empty the apartment," Katia said, frustrated. "Need to ship the rest to the States. But, need to help Angel and Liliya. What do we do?"

"We can do all of it," Delaney said confidently, with her thick Irish brogue. "We need to make a plan, though. There are plenty of men to take care of moving your stuff in the morning. If we can get tickets for the morning too, then we can get to them quicker."

"True," Katia agreed.

The two quickly got a shower and changed before going over to the hotel. Keeping an eye in every direction, it wasn't just the Unnaturals or demons they were worried about at three in the morning…it was the undesirables. Despite only getting an hour's sleep, this was something too important to wait.

*   *   *

Quietly walking down the hall toward the room with Mark, Derek, Jesse, and Jerrod on the beds, and Jacob on the couch, Delaney knocked lightly on the door. When no one answered, she used her phone to call Jacob's phone.

"What?" he groaned, answering the phone.

"Katia and I are outside. Answer the door."

"It's…what time is it?"

"Time for you to answer the door, man," Delaney snapped. "It's three in the morning, and we're two women. It's *not* a good time for you to be arguing with us."

"Yes, ma'am," he grumbled before he hung up the phone.

Grateful to hear the locks click open, Delaney was relieved when Jacob opened the door. "About time," she said, walking in with Katia behind her. Chuckling as she went by Jacob, she mentioned, "Not a morning person, are ya?"

"Not by a long shot," Jacob mumbled, locking the door behind them.

Shaking Jesse's foot, Delaney whispered, "Jesse, you need t' wake up. We got information."

"You…what?" Jesse moaned. "Who? Why? What are you doing here? What time is it?"

"Why are people talking so blasted early in the morning?" Jerrod mumbled before covering his head with his pillow.

"Guys, Katia knows where the others are," Delaney explained. "We need you to wake up."

Propping himself up with his elbows, Mark squinted in the darkness to see who was in the room. "Okay, and *how* did you get in here?"

"Who?" Jerrod asked. Lifting the pillow, he was surprised to see Katia and Delaney standing there with Jacob.

"Called Jacob," Delaney simply said. "Figured he'd be the easier of this crew to wake up. Look, we can go over this twenty times, or you can get the others in here and we can tell you all what we know."

"Good point," Mark said, leaning over, turning the lamp on. "Why don't you call Josh and wake up the room to our right. Then call Derek for the room to our left. By the time you get back here, we'll be a little more awake and dressed."

"Done," Delaney said. Grabbing Katia's hand, she pulled her out of the room.

After they went through pretty much the same thing with the other two rooms, they headed back to the center room to wait. When they walked in, some of the guys were drinking coffee, while a couple others were drinking soda to wake up.

"Weren't you two supposed to pack Katia's apartment?" Jesse asked.

"Oh, we did," Delaney explained. "We finally went to sleep about hour and a half ago."

When Katia took her coat off, Jerrod furrowed his brow. "What happened to you? Want me to take a look at that?" he asked, seeing the blood coming through the cloth.

Katia nodded. "Please."

Sitting down in the chair, Katia watched as he cleaned and dressed the wound, while Delaney told the others what happened.

"Katia woke up about thirty minutes ago with a scream," Delaney explained. "When I went in, she was grabbing her arm, mumbling something about seeing Angel and Liliya. After a few minutes of conversation, I *think* I have an idea of what happened. Since English isn't her first language, I'll take a crack at it first. If I don't quite get it right, she'll correct me where needed." After Katia nodded, Delaney continued, "She had a dream, but it wasn't a normal dream." As the others from the other room came in and settled, Delaney kept on with her story, "She said she was floating, looking as if she were looking through someone else's eyes. She found herself in a desert in Australia."

"Angel say it is the Tanami Desert," Katia added.

"You talked to her?" Jon asked.

"Yes."

"But, you talked to her in your dream?" Jacob asked, making sure he was following the conversation correctly.

"It was not a normal dream. I was like a spirit," Katia said.

"Did anyone else see you?" Josh asked.

"Angel see me. I touch Angel and Liliya," Katia said, looking at her hand, remembering when she touched them.

"So, what happened here?" Jerrod asked, pointing to the scratches on her arm.

"Demon did this," Katia said.

"A demon did *that*?" Derek asked, stunned.

"Yes. In the dream," Katia confirmed.

"Wait," Joe stopped her. "A demon scratched your arm in a dream, and it shows here in the waking world?"

"That actually happened to Casey once," Mark pointed out. "I'm more focused on the Tanami Desert. Where is that?"

"It's southeast of Halls Creek, in the Western Territory," Nico explained. "Northwest of Alice Springs. More people know of Alice Springs than Halls Creek."

"Isn't that about the middle of Australia?" Jerrod asked, wrapping Katia's arm with gauze.

"While it *is* in the middle, it's more toward the north," Nico explained. "That place has rocky terrain and small hills. I would imagine if that's where they are, that they're in the caves there?" Nico asked Katia, who just nodded.

"Now, wait a minute," Val stopped them. "You said you *talked* to Angel…or more that she talked to you? In a dream?"

"She say she had your gift," Katia said to Val. "She could feel me when I touch her, and hear me talk. She tell me where they are."

"I see," Val said, stroking his chin. "This is something new. That's kind of cool to know I could possibly do that too."

"*Anyway*," Nico said, bringing them back to the conversation, "We'll have to get a flight to Alice Springs."

"On it," Delaney said, sitting down at the table, pulling out her laptop.

With Nico looking over her shoulder, he and Delaney worked on finding the best flight. "Here," Nico pointed to one. "We can't go until tonight at eight. This is the least expensive with the shortest time. There is one earlier, but it would cost a lot more. We'll be in flight for thirty-three and a half hours."

"That'll seem like forever," Jacob groaned. "A lot could happen to them in the meantime. Is there no other way?"

"Not without it costing an arm and a leg." Nico shook his head. "There's one for twenty-seven-twenty-eight hours, but that'll cost like forty-four hundred dollars apiece."

Jacob cringed. "Ouch."

"Thirty-three and a half hours at eight o'clock tonight works," Mark said. "Book it. In the meantime, we'll get Katia and Liliya's stuff settled. Delaney, we'll need you to do papers for Liliya. She'll need to get out of Australia and into the U.S., as will Katia and Sasha."

"I have my passport," Sasha said.

"But, do you have a visa?" Delaney asked.

"No."

"You will," Delaney said with a twinkle in her eye. "By the time you are all done with Katia, I'll have the papers."

"I'll help," Derek volunteered. "That's one of my strengths too."

"Great!" Delaney said, excited. "Then we'll definitely get it done in time."

"Can we get some sleep first?" Jacob yawned. "It's going to be a long day tomorrow."

"I don't want them walking around at this time of night any more than they've already done," Mark said, shaking his head.

"We could sleep in shifts," Jesse offered. "There *are* two other rooms. Some could sleep now. Then in the morning, while those who slept are moving Katia, the others can sleep."

"Good idea," Mark agreed. "I'll sleep first, so I can keep everything organized in the morning. That way I can help get her stuff shipped as well."

"We'll sleep first too," Josh said, gesturing toward Jesse and Jon. "You'll need the muscle."

"Delaney and I will work on the papers. Once we're finished, we'll sleep," Derek said.

"I agree," Delaney said, before they returned to working on the tickets.

"I sleep now," Katia said. "Need to be ready in the morning."

"Danny and I'll sleep now," Charlie said. "We can help in the morning."

Danny nodded. "I agree."

"I will sleep now," Sasha announced. "Want to help, an see my home one more time before leaving."

"Jacob and I'll sleep now too," Joe said. "That'll leave Jerrod in case someone needs medical, and Nico can sleep after everyone's gone. We'll need him sharp for Australia."

"I agree," Mark said. "I think that takes care of everyone. Did we miss anyone?" After everyone shook their head, Mark said, "Then, let's divide and conquer. We are heading to the utter ends of the earth to find our missing people. God's got this."

"He is good all the time," Derek said.

"And, all the time, God is good," multiple people said before they separated, while Delaney and Derek worked feverishly on the paperwork for everyone.

* * *

"Okay, sounds good. Love you, Mark," Casey said, before she hung up the phone. Going into the dining room of the Haven in Nevada with the others, Casey sat down at the table, where it was five in the evening. "That was your dad," Casey said to Allie and Callie. "He said he would call when they land in Australia."

"Australia?" Cori said, stunned. "Why are they going to Australia?"

"Seems the Spirit gave Katia a dream, and told them where the girls are."

"I see. Does this happen often?"

"There are many gifts," Casey explained. "You, for instance, have an amazing acuity to sound. Val has an amazing acuity to what the Spirit is trying to show him around him. Joe,

Angel, and apparently Katia too, have dreams and visions, where the Spirit shows them things, or gives them assignments."

"Interesting," Kai said, eating his steak. "How many gifts are there?"

"Oh," Casey chuckled, "We don't limit God around here. He gives whatever and however many gifts He wants."

"We all have one or another," Rachel pointed out. "Even Delaney has the gifts of languages and discernment."

"Really?" Kai asked, surprised. "I didn't know that."

"You tend to not tell people when you have certain gifts until you're more familiar to what they'll accept and what they won't. Me, for example? I have a gift that tells me who is a Christian and who isn't. It also tells me who is an A.N.G.E.L. or who is an Unnatural."

"Really?"

"Yes. The level of brightness differs in them," Rachel explained.

"Wonder what mine is?" Kai said, thinking about it.

"You don't have one?"

"Not that I know of," Kai said, shaking his head.

"What about you?" Rachel asked Cori.

"You're going to think it's ironic," Cori said hesitantly.

"You have one?" Kai asked, surprised. Crossing his arms, he pouted. "All right, now I feel left out."

"No worries. Yours will surface when the Spirit deems it necessary." Rachel then turned to Cori, and asked, "What is your gift?"

"It's actually visions. I saw you guys coming, so I wasn't surprised when Delaney came to me with this story of a young blonde Australian girl coming to her to talk of angels and demons."

"Nice!" Rachel said, pleasantly surprised.

"Do the wonder twins have one?" Kai asked Casey about Allie and Callie.

Casey shook her head. "Not yet. I'm sure they'll surface when the Spirit wants them to."

"I love the feeling of peace around here," Cori commented before taking a bite of her baked potato.

"Need to get used to the dry weather, though," Kai mentioned.

"You will, in time," Rachel encouraged. "You all seem to fit in just fine."

"We're working on it," Kai agreed.

"Um, did ya say they were headed to Australia?" Rachel asked. "Did Mark say where?"

"Tanami Desert?" Casey offered. "He said it was somewhere near Alice Springs."

"Oh! I know where that is. Some from Pete's clan know of others from that area."

"I understand they're being held in a cave system over there."

"Interesting," Rachel said, thinking of the area. "I was only there once, when I was around fifteen. Pretty open area, with rolling hills. This time of year it should start heating up, as the spring is almost done. It should still be green, though. This should help as far as the dirt and water situation."

"Good to know."

"I wish I was there," Rachel said, frustrated.

"Honey, you can't even sit up straight," Casey pointed out. "I think the only reason Jerrod was comfortable enough to leave you here with me was because I used to be a paramedic."

"That, and I am still technically an RN," Rachel reminded her.

"Right, but it's difficult to diagnose yourself," Casey said.

"This is true."

"Speaking of which, it's time for your medicine. How are you feeling?"

"Pain," she said, slightly hunched over, holding her ribs.

"You can't even sit up without holding your ribs. How would you expect to help them in the Outback of Australia?" Kai asked, raising an eyebrow.

"Well…" She pouted. "I don't know."

Resting her hand over Rachel's, Casey said, "Sometimes God has things happen so we can take a break. You are injured. You need to slow down. This will also give the others a chance to bond, while you bond with these two and your sisters."

"We *like* having you home!" Allie smiled.

"Wish we could *keep* you home," Callie added.

"I know, sweeties," Rachel said with a smile. "As soon as I'm healed, I need to join the others, though. I'm a team lead. I can't do that from here."

"We're also a team," Casey reminded her. "And as a team, when one stumbles, the others pick up the slack."

"I only hope it's not at the peril of another," Rachel said, solemnly, as she had a sick feeling in her stomach since hearing about them going to Australia.

"God is in control," Casey reminded her. "We have to trust that He's got this, and has them in His hands. I, for one, am relieved to know that He's watching after them. I also have the confidence that if something *does* happen to them, that they will be with God in an instant. Either way, they will be safe when this is all said and done."

"And for that," Rachel admitted, "I'm grateful."

Chapter 15
Run with Perseverance

Renting four Jeeps, the groups divided up. Making sure to take plenty of food and water, they had otherwise packed light for this trip, and shipped a lot of their belongings back to the Haven.

They bounced down the red dirt road, thanks to the ruts. Katia didn't fully remember the area, but some things looked familiar. Knowing she was so close to getting her sister, it worried her that they may be too late. With the long flight, the drive itself would be another eighteen to twenty hours, depending on how many stops they made. Nico had mentioned that there wouldn't be too many places *to* stop on the drive. They were in the middle of nowhere. They would only be able to drive so far before they had to head in on foot. They would be relying on Katia's memory at that point, or better yet, word from God to one of those who had visions or dreams.

* * *

After three hours, the group decided to take a break. The brutal heat screamed toward ninety degrees Fahrenheit, and no shade was to be found. The transfer from spring to summer was rapidly approaching. Once it hit, the temperatures could reach over a hundred easily.

Stretching as they got out, Katia wiped the sweat off. Coming out of a cool Russian autumn, this was a wicked ricochet to summer. "Hot," she said in a sigh.

"No worries," Josh rested his arm across her shoulders and gave her a gentle squeeze. "Just remember, this brings you that much closer to your sister."

"I know. Just…hot."

"Make sure you drink. We don't want ya to get dehydrated," he said, going over, getting her a water bottle. "We have a long trek ahead of us."

"Why is it so blasted hot out here?" Jacob asked, taking a swig of his water as he sat in the back of the Jeep. "Guess it's appropriate that Cassius's lair is out here in the middle of hell."

"You would *think* with this heat that it's Hell, but it's not," Joe corrected him, with a smirk.

"Are you sure?" Jacob challenged. "Katia said there were demons out here. Pretty sure between that fact, and the blistering heat, that qualifies as Hell."

Chuckling, Joe just shook his head in response.

"Actually, there's a Hell's Hole, Australia," Josh pointed out. "Hell's Hole is in Caveton, and Hell's Hole Creek is in Queensland."

"Seriously?" Joe asked, shaking his head with a chuckle. "Australia's a wild place!"

Josh grinned. "That it is, but there's nothing else like it!"

"Even if it's not hell, it's still blasted hot and dry out here," Jacob pointed out. Then he added, "Of course, now that I think about it, it'll make it easier to blow things up since it's hot and dry."

"This is true. Always thinking of how to blow things up, eh?" Joe smirked. He and Jacob had become close friends, almost like brothers. This was something Joe held dear, because he didn't have any blood siblings.

"Well, you know," Jacob said with a sly smile, "gotta have an exit plan."

"Glad one of us does," Josh said. "Hey, Dad!" he called to Nico.

"Yeah?" Nico answered.

"Do we have a plan when we get there? And, what about an exit plan?"

"Mark, Danny, Charlie, and I are working on it. Katia, can you come over here?" Nico called to Katia. When she got there, he explained, "We have a topographical map. We need your memory. You're the only one who's been in there."

"Okay," she agreed.

While they talked, Jesse walked over to Jon, who was at another Jeep. "Jon, what are you feeling?" he asked.

"A lot. Can you be more specific on who you're wondering about?" Jon asked, pulling him away from the others. "I can see the wheels turning. What are you thinking?"

"Charlie looks anxious, and from what Josh told me, that's abnormal for him," Jesse said.

"Yep," Jon said. "He's as anxious as everyone else out here."

"Can you tell if it's because of where we're going, or if it's something else?"

"It's because we are near Aboriginal territories," they suddenly heard Charlie behind them and jumped.

"Dang! You're quiet!" Jesse said, hand resting on his heart that skipped a few beats.

"Sorry," Charlie said with a grin. "You two looked suspicious. I come see."

"Why is that a concern?" Jon asked.

"They can be territorial. I will do the talking if we stumble onto them. It's a long drive," Charlie explained. "It'll depend on where we stop."

"I see," Jon said, crossing his arms, in thought. "So, are we close to one now?"

He nodded. "We are."

"Do you think they'll give us a problem?" Jesse asked.

"They shouldn't. We're not staying. We're changing out drivers in order not to stop. Just remember, this is a marathon, not a sprint. This is a long trek in a hot area. And, it's only going to get hotter."

"Major adjustments in temperature are something we're going to have to get used to," Jon pointed out. Then he added, "There's a lot we need to get used to. Pretty sure temperatures are the least of our worries. We're headed into a hornet's nest. Last time we did that, we lost two people," Jon reminded them before going back over to where the group was taking a break together.

When Jon was out of earshot, Jesse asked Charlie, "Honest opinion?"

"Always." Charlie nodded. "I know no other way."

"You know this area, right?"

"I know *of* this area. I grew up a little farther south, and to the east."

"Do you know of an area up here that could house what Katia was talking about?"

"Oh yeah! Many places like that deep in the desert. Not many people around. It's easy to hide out here."

"So, do you think we're on the right track?"

"If not, this is a very expensive mistake."

"True," he said, glancing at Mark, Derek, Danny, and Nico, who were still talking with Katia, while the group studied the map. "I trust her," Jesse said, "I also trust the Spirit."

"Then, what's the problem?"

"I just have a bad feeling."

"Probably are the demons and Unnaturals, yeah?"

"Well, yeah," Jesse nodded, "that's part of it. But, I have an extremely uneasy feeling that at least one of us won't be walking out of here, and I *really* don't want to have to paint another name on the rock beside Aden Knight's."

"And, you think there'll be more before we're done here?" Charlie asked.

"We're hiking back into the same thing we walked into in Black Rock. Only this time, they're expecting us."

"Difference is also that we have someone who's already been in there," Charlie pointed out. "And remember, God is bigger than any of this. His angels are with us. The archangel assured us of this."

"Wish I had your confidence."

"You will," Charlie said, resting his hand on Jesse's shoulder. "In time, you will see. God will take care of us. We just need to run our race with perseverance, fixing our eyes on Jesus, who is the Author and Finisher of our faith. We need to concentrate on our own journey, and not on the journey of others."

"Hebrews 12:1&2," Jesse said, nodding his head in agreement. Then a thought hit him. "What do you mean by not concentrating on the journey of others?"

"Many times, we worry about others and their choices, or situations, and take our eyes off our own journey. While we *are* to look out for each other, we are never to lose sight of our own journey, the journey God has planned for each one of us. For example, when we know someone who committed suicide, we focus on them, and what we could have done differently to help them. More times than not, it's them. It's their choice, their lives, and their own journey. When we focus on their choice to take their own life, we look away from our journey and get lost in the emotion. Instead of celebrating their life, and potentially working through the hole left in our hearts because of the life missing, we are focused on what we should have done, or what they could have been. We need to focus our efforts in a more productive way."

"I see," Jesse said. "Good point. So, you're saying I need to focus on my own journey, no matter what happens to Angel?"

Charlie nodded. "Yes."

"Okay. Thanks, man," Jesse said, resting his hand on Charlie's shoulder.

"Anytime, brother," he said, patting his back, before he headed back over to the Jeep to work on the plan.

After another half hour, they split up back into the four Jeeps, and bounced down the road, each lost in their own thoughts. As the dust kicked up around them, they made sure to stay hydrated as they pressed on.

* * *

About six hours into the journey, a tire blew on the second Jeep. This led to the third and fourth Jeeps swerving to miss it. The third Jeep didn't get enough clearance, and hit the second Jeep.

"Everyone okay?" Nico asked, jumping out of the first Jeep as Danny pulled it to the side of the road.

Once Charlie got the fourth Jeep to the side of the road, Josh and Katia jumped out, running for the middle two Jeeps.

"Oh, this isn't good," Nico said, while the others got out of the Jeeps and chaos ensued. Everyone was talking at once. There were moans and groans from the two Jeeps as people made their way out of them.

"We'll have to drive back the six hours to get help," Delaney said, pulling the paperwork out of her computer bag. She was in the first Jeep. "You'll need these."

"Who's going?" Danny asked.

"I need to stay," Charlie said, looking around. "We may be getting company soon as the sun goes down."

"I *wish* the sun would be going down soon," Jacob said, glancing at his watch. "We still have four hours until it goes down. Whoever stays will need to keep out of the sun as much as possible."

"We need enough people to drive the other two Jeeps," Joe pointed out. "We'll also need to leave enough to watch these two."

"Is the second Jeep even drivable?" Jerrod asked.

"Technically they're *both* drivable…for now," Jesse said, as he and Josh changed the tire of the second Jeep.

"With a little rigging, this one would be okay enough to drive too," Jon said, picking the portion of the bumper up that wasn't completely broken, but still hanging by a couple of inches.

"Do we have anything in the backpacks to tie that on in order to hold it up?" Delaney asked. "If so, that should make this Jeep drivable again."

"We cannot go back," Katia said, tears brimming her eyes. "It will take six hours there, and six back, with twelve more to drive. That's too long!"

"She's right," Jesse said, standing, as Josh finished tightening the bolts. "If we can help it, we really shouldn't make it any longer than it already is. Can they make it another twelve?"

"Is anyone injured?" Jerrod asked, looking around.

Mumbles of sore necks, and a few saying they were fine, came from around the group.

Jerrod shrugged. "Doesn't sound like anything serious."

"Can't get this to stay," Jon grumbled, trying to tie the bumper again.

"Little help?" Danny said, looking toward Heaven.

Deciding they needed extra help, Jesse got down on his knees, and prayed. Sasha, Jacob, and Joe quickly followed, as did the others. Some prayed in their own languages, others quietly sung songs of praise as a prayer, while others just soaked in the Spirit.

After a few minutes, Charlie's hair stood up on his neck, and he looked toward the horizon. "Uh-oh," he said, standing. "Back in a tic, mate," he said, and jogged out toward a group of six Aboriginal men heading their way.

While everyone else continued in prayer, Nico and Danny stood to watch Charlie in case he needed help. Both rested their hands on their guns at their waists. With their pasts, their registered guns came in handy in situations like this.

After several minutes, Charlie returned to the group with the six men. The men talked amongst themselves in their own language, as they looked at the two damaged Jeeps.

One of the men climbed under the second Jeep to get a better look near the gas tank to see how close the damage was to it. He called to his friends. One handed him a hammer, while the other handed him duct tape.

Nico had to chuckle as the men made both Jeeps drivable with just a hammer and duct tape. "Unbelievable," he said, shaking his head. "God is amazing! Out here in the middle of nowhere, He provided an amazing blessing!"

"Thank you!" one of the Aboriginal men said with a grin.

"You speak English?" Josh asked, surprised.

"Yes," the man said. "Well, I do," he explained. "I talk for them. We saw the dirt kick up and brakes squeak, and decided we can help."

"We really appreciate it," Nico said, going over, shaking his hand. "Name's Nico. You?"

"Kalti. Charlie said you have friends in trouble?"

"We do, but we're not one hundred percent sure where they are out here. We know it's up near Tanami, off the trek."

"Bad place to get lost," Kalti pointed out.

"Too true," Nico agreed.

"Do you know about where?"

"We have a map. Come here," Nico said, leading Kalti to the first Jeep. Once the maps were pulled out, he explained, "From what we can tell, they're somewhere in here."

"Really?" Kalti said, surprised. "That's part of the never-never out there."

"I know."

"How are they out there? On a walk-a-bout?"

"No. They were taken."

Wide-eyed, Kalti asked, "Police know?"

"No."

"Why not?"

"The police can't help us. These are dangerous folks. Not going to say people, because some are not people."

"They're *not* people?" Kalti asked, raising an eyebrow.

"Demons and what we call Unnaturals," Nico explained. "Unnaturals are people possessed."

"*Possessed*?" Kalti's eyes opened even wider.

"Look, mate, I have quite a few Aboriginal station hands at Serenity Wells Station –"

"*You* own Serenity Wells Station?" Kalti asked, stunned.

"You're kind of walking into the middle of the story here, mate," Nico chuckled, "but yes. Anyway, I'm aware that you blokes know about unnatural things."

"Yes," Kalti said, taking a deep breath. "Almost too much information. Not comforting to know they're in our backyard."

"I know. What's more scary is see that girl over there?" he asked, pointing to Katia.

"Yeah."

"They have her sister. And, see those two? The ones who look identical?"

"The big blokes?"

"Yes. They have their sister as well."

"Oh!"

"Once we figured out where they were, we immediately got on a plane from St. Petersburg, Russia," Nico said. "Now, we've been in Jeeps for a little over six and a half hours. We still have twelve to go until we have to leave the Jeeps and walk the rest of the way in."

"Not true." Kalti shook his head. "You can take them this far," he said, showing Nico a different route through the bush. "Once you reach here, go this way, and then follow this river to here. Once you reach there, then go over here. That's the best way to get back there."

"Thanks, mate!" Nico said, appreciatively. "That'll save us some time."

"If they're with who you say they're with, you *really* need to move it." Turning to his friends, he said something in their language. They looked at him, stunned, as the one under the Jeep bumped his head at hearing what he said. Once Kalti confirmed what he told them, one of the men took off running back into the bush. "He is going to get you a guide," Kalti explained.

"Oh! We can't impose on you like that. This is a dangerous mission," Nico said. "Thanks, mate. We appreciate the offer, but we can't ask you to do that."

"Not asking. We are telling," Kalti insisted. "We have mates at Serenity Wells. If friends of yours are in trouble, we help. Family is family."

"Thank you!" Nico said, excited.

"Without a guide, you could not only get lost, but not get out," Kalti pointed out.

"We'll protect him," Nico assured him. "We'll keep him out of danger."

Kalti shook his head. "Not him. Our best out that way is Amarina. She will get you in and out safe."

Nico shook his head. "I dunno, mate."

"She is the best." Kalti stood firm. "You have girls with you. You are getting girls. This girl," he gestured toward the young lady who looked to be about fifteen, running toward them with the man who had gone to get her, "she is best in that territory. You take her, and bring her back. She will tell you where to let her out."

"Are you sure, mate?"

"Where are we going?" Amarina asked, running up to the pair with a backpack on. Her black sundress with green ivy looked to be from the seventies, but was still in good shape. Walking with bare feet, her hair was in a loose braid, and hung to about the middle of her back.

"Here." Kalti pointed out on the map. "I tell them drive to here, get out here, follow this, and go there."

"Yes," Amarina confirmed. "I will get them there."

"Did Gelar tell you the issues?"

"Yes. Mum said to hot-foot it."

"Good," he said. Resting his hand on her shoulder, he turned to Nico and said, "She will get you there and back."

"We'll take care of her," Nico assured him. "Name's Nico," he said, shaking her hand. "Thank you so much for your help."

"We get the women folk out," Amarina said confidently. "I know what's out there. I see it before. Scary."

"You are very brave. Thank you."

"If girls are there, we need to get them out," Amarina said.

"They are seventeen and twenty-four," Nico explained.

"Still," Amarina said, eyeing the bunch. "You need help. This crew is too big. Need to separate. Make too much noise. They will hear us coming."

Leaning on the front of the Jeep with his arms crossed, Nico was intrigued. "Okay, how would you do it?"

"Need lookouts here and here," she said, pointing to the map. "Have four in each place. Leave four at the Jeeps to protect them. And then three go in."

"If three are going in, you are *not* going to be among them," Nico said sternly. "We need you. You're too valuable."

"I will be with this team here," she pointed to the farthest lookout.

"Can we negotiate that three in?" Nico asked.

"Why?"

"I guarantee those two, and that one," he said pointing to Jesse, Jon, and Katia, "are going to want to go in. Their sisters are the ones in there. We also need a couple experienced to go in with them."

"You, and who?" she asked.

"Him," he said, pointing to Danny. When Danny looked up, Nico gestured him for him to come over.

"Okay," Amarina agreed. "That man is with this team," she said, gesturing to Charlie, and then pointed to the nearest lookout team.

"Jerrod will be with them too. He's medical," Nico insisted.

"Sasha and Josh too," Danny said. "This team needs to be our back-up."

"We'll put Jacob and Mark here," Nico said, pointing to the farther lookout point. "Amarina will be with them. If we need Jacob to blow something, he needs to be close enough to plant it while we go in, yet far enough not to get hurt when he sets it off."

"Too true," Danny agreed. "That'll leave Derek, Joe, and Delaney at the Jeeps to keep a lookout."

"Agreed," Nico said.

"Yes, I think this will work," Amarina agreed as well. "This is good."

"Do I need to know what's going on?" Mark asked.

"Yeah. You and Derek come here," Nico called them over. After he explained the plan to them, the others had finished fixing the Jeeps, so everyone loaded in after saying good-bye, and thanking the Aboriginal strangers who were now friends.

Chapter 16
No Greater Love

Nerves ran high as they bounced down the dirt road. Anxiety pulsed through each member, while they did their best to focus on the mission. Danny, Nico, Mark, and Derek, who were the drivers, passed around the word to the members of their vehicles as to the plan.

While they drove, Jerrod made sure his medical kit was easily accessible and ready to go. At the same time, Jacob had Katia help him make some homemade bombs, and packed them as best he could for the walk in, praying with every muscle in his body that they would go off when needed.

There was a lot riding on this mission. This would probably be as big as Black Rock, or worse. They had been able to catch the other side by surprise at Black Rock. Here, at Tanami, the other side just lay in wait. Who knew what traps they had already set for them?

Praying for continued guidance, the team would rely on God to watch their steps, and help them save their family members. Without God, they were lost.

*   *   *

About an hour from their final destination, a verse came to Jacob's mind. Since he was in Derek's Jeep with Jesse and Katia, he got tired of the silence and anxiety, so he quoted the verse aloud. "Isaiah 26:3 says, *'You will keep peace those whose minds are steadfast, because they trust in You.'*"

"Good one," Jesse said, pleased. "What about Isaiah 41:10? *'So do not fear, for I am with you; do not be dismayed, for I am your God. I will strengthen you and help you; I will uphold you with My righteous hand.'*"

"Good." Derek smiled. "Here's one that was a challenge, but I will never forget it. It's First Peter 5:7-10. *'Cast all your anxiety on Him, because He cares for you. Be alert and sober of mind. Your enemy the devil prowls around like a roaring lion looking for someone to devour. Resist him, standing firm in the faith, because you know the family of believers throughout the world is undergoing the same kind of sufferings. And the God of all grace, who called you to His eternal glory in Christ, after you have suffered for a little while, will Himself restore you and make you strong, firm and steadfast.'*"

"Impressive!" Jesse smiled.

"What about Deuteronomy 31:6?" Katia asked. "That's, *'Be strong and courageous, do not be afraid or tremble at them, for the Lord your God is the One who goes with you. He will not fail or forsake you.'*"

"Good!" Derek said, glad that Katia was able to think of something to add to the group. Up until that point, she had been quiet. "The point is, we are not alone. If you had any questions, they should have been answered when the Jeeps wrecked. God provided us the help we needed with the men, and now with a guide all the way in with Amarina."

"I know it shouldn't, but sometimes His grace and mercy still surprise me," Jesse pointed out. "Just when you think there isn't an answer, He provides it. He knew a long time ago we would need those men and Amarina. He made sure the tires blew at the precise point where they would see it. Now, with a plan, I'm certain we'll be able to get Angel and Liliya out."

"I pray you are right," Katia said nervously, nibbling on her nails. "She is all I have."

"Haven't you figured out by now that she's *not* all you have?" Jacob asked. "You have us, along with an entire family of God. You chose to be with us once you sent your stuff to the Haven. You have a rather large family now. Having said that, there are times where we won't necessarily get along, like any normal family, but we have God in common."

"And with God as our center, we will always find our way," Jesse added.

"True," Katia agreed. "Now to add my sestra to the family. She won't be happy we move from the apartment."

"Oh, trust me," Derek smiled, "she'll have a *much* better life. It'll take a bit of cultural adjustment, but her world is now wide-open. Whatever she wants to do in life, in America, she'll now have that opportunity."

"Really?" Katia asked.

"You have done your best to get her out of the orphanage, and into a school," Jesse explained. "You gave her a shot at a normal life. Having said that, you two were never destined to have a normal life."

"Normal is boring," Jacob added.

"This is true." Jesse grinned. "Katia, you are both destined for a much bigger plan in life. You are going to be an A.N.G.E.L. in God's Army. Liliya can be whatever she wants."

"She loves animals. She wants to be a pet doctor," Katia said.

"She can be a veterinarian if she wants," Derek said. "That's a great profession. If she wants something else, she can have it too."

"We only need to get her out," Katia said, still nervously nibbling on her nails.

"We will," Jacob said confidently. "I've seen stuff I never thought I would since joining this crew. God is amazing! They don't call Him the Lord God Almighty for no reason," he said with a smirk. "He's got this."

Nodding, she turned her attention back to the surrounding terrain. Lost in her mind, imagining the worst-case scenarios, she prayed to God for the protection of everyone there, but especially for Liliya and Angel.

As she prayed, the Spirit gave her Isaiah 40:29-31, " *'He gives strength to the weary and increases the power of the weak. Even youths grow tired and weary, and young men stumble and fall; but those who hope in the Lord will renew their strength. They will soar on wings like eagles; they will run and not grow weary, they will walk and not be faint.'"*

"Thank you, Father," Katia whispered, as she wiped the few tears that escaped down her cheek.

Jesse leaned down near her, and spoke so only she could hear, "We're going in there to get our sisters out. I *promise you* that we will *not* leave without Liliya."

"Thank you," she whispered, as she nodded in acknowledgement, while they turned off the main road, deeper into the bush.

* * *

Pulling up to the point of their driving destination early in the morning, they lined up the Jeeps for a quick escape.

"You three stay here," Mark said to Derek, Joe, and Delaney. "This may not seem crucial, but if the other side takes out our escape route, we're toast. What you guys are doing here is protecting our escape. Derek, I know you know this. I said that for the benefit of Joe and Delaney."

"We know," Joe acknowledged. "Thank you for saying it, though."

"As we learned in Black Rock, when they took the helicopter out, you need to stay vigilant," Nico pointed out as he put his backpack on.

"Yes, sir," Delaney said, holding up one of Jacob's Molotov cocktails. "Jacob's got us covered."

"We'll also be covering you guys in prayer," Derek pointed out. Showing Delaney and Joe the gun resting on his side, he said, "I've also got this."

"I know, man." Mark shook his hand. "Be safe."

When he did, Derek pulled him in for a quick hug. "Be vigilant yourselves. I want you all to come back. Please don't make me tell Casey that something happened to you. You have little ones to raise once again. Those little girls love you like a father. You're the only father they've known."

"I know. We'll bring the others back," he said, and the rest of the group took off for the first lookout point, leaving Delaney, Joe, and Derek to wait, bathing the mission in prayer.

*   *   *

Trudging through the high grass, up and down the rolling hills, the band of A.N.G.E.L.s and Amarina were focused on the mission. After fifteen minutes of hiking, Jacob, Mark, and Amarina reached their appointed position.

"Jacob will set mines while you guys travel on. Amarina and I will stay here. Take this," Mark said, handing Jerrod a radio. "And this is for you," Mark said, handing Nico another one. "Derek has one as well. He will turn it on in another ten minutes, as will we. At that point, you guys will reach the other lookout point. The entrance to the cave system is down between our two points. It's right there," he said, pointing it out to Nico and Danny.

"Right-oh," Danny said in a sigh. "Keep us in prayer, brother."

"Always," Mark said, giving Jon and Jesse each a hug. Shaking Nico and Danny's hands, he said, "May God be with you, and bring you safely and swiftly out of this."

"One way or another, eh, brother," Nico said, with a hint of nervousness in his voice. "Hate to admit that I may be getting a bit too old for this stuff."

"You got this, old man," Josh said, resting his arm over his dad's shoulder. Gesturing toward the open countryside, he reminded him, "This is God's country. Just because Satan and his followers are attempting to lay claim to it, doesn't mean God'll give it to them."

"Too true, son. Just…" he stopped. Turning toward the cave entrance, he said, "It's just that I know what's in there, and they *know* we're coming."

"I'll be with you guys in a bit," Jacob said to Mark and Amarina. "Once I set my charges, I'll get back here as soon as possible."

"Sounds good. You all be careful," Mark warned.

"We will," Jerrod said, before the remaining members continued on.

"God'll protect them," Mark said, more for his benefit than for Amarina's, as the team trudged on.

"There are powerful forces here," Amarina pointed out, "both good *and* bad. *Very* powerful forces."

"That's what I'm afraid of."

*　*　*

Periodically setting charges as they went, Jacob was the last to say good-bye to Jerrod, Charlie, Josh, and Sasha, who positioned themselves around the area in order to provide cover fire if necessary for those going in the rest of the way.

"You're quiet," Jon mentioned to Katia, as they were in the back of the remaining group, with Jesse in the middle, and Danny and Nico in the front.

"I am worried," Katia admitted.

"John 14:27 reminds us, *'Peace I leave with you; My peace I give you. I do not give to you as the world gives. Do not let your hearts be troubled and do not be afraid.'* He's shown us time and time again that He's got our back on this. He's shown us that He'll not let us down. I know you're worried for Liliya. We're concerned for Angel as well, but we know, as do you, that whatever they do to them, in the end, they will be with God," Jon said.

"I only pray they do not suffer."

"That's our prayer as well. The archangel showed us before we left that the Lord gave us His blessing. He placed Amarina in our path to show us the way as confirmation of this," Jon pointed out. "He's shown you that He's here time and time again."

"I know. I only want my sestra," Katia said.

"Trust Him," Jon pleaded.

"I do."

"Katia," Jon said knowingly, "you *do* remember that I feel what those around me are feeling, right?"

She sighed. "Don't care for that gift," she said, tongue-in-cheek.

Chuckling for a moment, Jon then admitted, "Yeah, at times it can be a curse. However, in moments like this, it helps me show the person I'm talking to that they're not fooling me anymore than they're fooling God. They're only fooling themselves."

"True. Okay, I focus," Katia agreed.

"There ya go," Jon said. Putting his arm over her shoulder, he gave her a gentle squeeze.

"This is it," Danny said, and crouched down, as the others with him crouched as well.

"Shhh," Nico hushed them. Seeing the mouth of the cave not more than ten feet to their right, Nico pointed to Jesse and Jon, and gestured for them to get to the other side. Then he gestured for Katia to follow he and Danny to the opening.

As Jon and Jesse maneuvered around into position, Nico, Danny, and Katia flattened themselves against the wall of the cave, right next to the opening. When they were in position and had a clear view of the opening, Jon and Jesse nodded that the way was clear.

"Here we go, folks," Nico whispered, as he was first in line.

Sandwiched between Nico and Danny, Katia said, "God be with us."

"He will," Danny said confidently. "He hasn't let us down yet."

With that, the trio breached the opening. Jon followed them in, leaving Jesse to watch the opening of the cave. Pistol aimed at the doorway, Jesse stayed in his position, stomach flat on the ground, praying for his family, both figuratively and literally, for safety.

*   *   *

"Okay," Derek said, turning on his radio. "Time to get this started." Into the radio, he said, "This is the nest. Anyone out there?"

"Eagle one is on," Mark said into the radio.

"Eagle two on," Jerrod said into his radio.

"Eagle three on," Jesse said into his radio. "Team en route."

"Copy," came from the other two radios.

Watching from his position, Jesse saw Jacob set a charge on either side of the cave opening before he headed back up the hill for the closer lookout. From that point, he would make his way back to Mark and Amarina, and wait to set them off when needed.

Jacob knew it wouldn't be a matter of *if* they would be needed, but when…and he had to be ready.

*   *   *

Katia lightly ran her fingers on the stone walls as they made their way down the tunnel, conscious of the fact that Danny was marking the walls with arrows made of chalk, showing their passage in. Nico was on high alert as point. Meanwhile, Jon periodically set a glow stick on the ground, against the wall. If the caves became smoke-filled, they could break the glow sticks. The glow sticks were also set five feet apart, in case they got lost. It was a backup mapping mechanism.

300

Tapping his right shoulder, Katia let Nico know the direction in which she'd gone in her dream. She would either tap his left or his right for directions. Periodically, the group would have to crouch out of sight when they would come up to a fire with Cassius's minions around it.

Keeping to the outer edges of the caves, the group of four silently crept behind as many rocks as possible, moving slowly and stealthily in the shadows.

Suddenly, one of the creatures perked up. "There are A.N.G.E.L.s here," he announced.

"Of course they are, Azazel," another one said. "We have Angel in the back."

"No. There are more," Azazel said, looking around.

"How close?" another one asked.

"Close."

"Ravana, go tell Cassius and Calliope that they're here," one ordered, as the others stood. He had blonde hair, and yellow eyes. Firm in his physique, his heart was another story.

"Yes, Korax," an Unnatural female said, and took off down one of the tunnels.

While Korax searched the shadows, looking for movement, Nico made a fist with his hand, and everyone in their group froze. "I know you're in here," Korax called out. "You can't help them."

Nico gestured for the group to slowly follow him through an opening in the stalactites and stalagmites, getting them out of the main chamber.

"Where are they?" they heard Cassius demand from Korax as they made their way away from the fire.

Korax explained, "Azazel said they were close."

"*Where?*" Cassius shouted.

"I-I can't tell direction, sir," Azazel stammered. "I can only tell they're close."

"*Where?*" Cassius growled in Azazel's face.

"D-don't know, sssir."

At that point, the group heard Azazel shriek for only a moment prior to an abrupt silence. Indistinct shouting was all they heard as they straightened up and ran down the tunnel, continuing to follow the path in Katia's dream.

"There," Katia whispered, patting Nico's right arm.

Seeing a red glow down the cave tunnel, Nico made a beeline for the opening. The four stumbled into an opening, where they found a chamber with six people chained to the ceiling. Their feet barely touched the ground, while sweat and dirt dripped from each of them.

"Need to get you all out of here," Nico said, running up to Angel.

"No. Get the others first," Angel ordered. "They won't hurt me. They need me. Get them out first."

"We're going to get *all* of you out," Nico whispered.

"There are four of you. Get the others first," Angel insisted.

"Right oh," Nico said, going over to Sergei, while Jon and Danny worked on two from the other side of the cave, and Katia got Liliya.

As soon as she released Liliya, Katia hugged her sister like she never wanted to let her go. "We have to get you out, sestra," Katia said, pulling away. "Need to get Angel too."

Just as Danny and Jon released the captives they were working on, and Nico got Sergei released, a demon appeared in the doorway. "Where do you *think* you are going with Cassius'ssss prizzze?" it hissed as it crossed its arms, blocking the tunnel entrance.

"Get them out," Danny ordered, pulling out his gun.

"Angel and the other one?" Nico asked, shoving everyone else out the other end of the cavern.

"Go!" Danny shouted, before opening fire.

Ducking at the sound of gunfire going off, Nico tucked his gun into Danny's waist so he had another when his ran out. Hearing a couple of bullets ricochet off the wall, one narrowly missed Nico's head before he turned to leave. As the cavern filled with a mixture gunpowder and dirt from the ground and walls, he took one last look at his friend before running down the tunnel.

Hearing the shrieks of the demons, and not knowing how close they were to Danny, Jon turned to Nico as Nico caught up to him, and said, "I can't leave him."

"You *can* and you *will*! Now, come on!" Nico shouted, grabbing Jon's arm.

"No! Get Katia and the others out of here! I'm going back for Danny!"

As the others continued to escape, Jon ran back to the cavern. Positioning himself in the doorway, he watched Danny and the demon wrestling. The demon was hit, but still alive and fighting Danny. As they wrestled, Jon pulled out his gun and aimed at the demon. Fear filled every portion of his being at the thought of hitting Danny on accident. "Lord, guide my hands," Jon prayed, before firing the gun at the pair wrestling on the ground.

The demon screamed a high-pitched, shrill scream, as yellowish-green blood oozed down the side of its face. Taking one last swipe at Danny with the little fight it had left in it, the demon's talons dug deep into Danny's abdomen. Pulling its blood covered hand out of Danny, it rolled over and, in a moment, burst into flames.

Staring at Danny for only a moment, Jon was taken by surprise when two more demons appeared at the entrance to the cavern.

"Jon! Get Danny out of here!" Angel shouted, bringing Jon back into focus.

Glancing down at the blood pouring out of Danny's abdomen, Jon quickly looked toward the cavern entrance to see the two demons glaring at him. He fired two bullets, and they landed square in the forehead of one demon. With yellowish green blood oozing from its head, it dropped backward onto the ground in a heap. As it hit the ground, it balled up and burst into flames.

When Jon fired his gun at the second demon, the gun clicked. Wide-eyed for only moment, he threw the gun on the ground and whipped the knife off his belt.

"Quit messing around! Get out of here!" Angel shouted. "Jon! Go!"

"Not without Danny!" he yelled, as he ran for the other demon.

The demon slashed its claw at Jon, but missed. In that instant, Jon lunged forward and jammed the knife into its neck. Quickly pulling it out, he slashed its throat, and then dragged the knife across its body in a zig-zag pattern. As it dropped to the ground, Jon looked up at Angel.

"No!" Angel said sternly. "Get Danny and go!"

"I can't leave you!"

"There are more coming! Just go!" she said, as they heard the yelling in the distance getting closer. "Get him out of here! NOW!"

"I love you!" he said, scooping Danny off the ground.

"I love you too. Now, get out of here! They're coming!" Angel insisted.

Throwing Danny over his shoulder in a fireman's carry, he heard Danny groan in pain. Taking only one more moment to look at Angel, who shook her head, Jon ran from the cavern…leaving Angel and another young man still in chains.

Knowing he would have some serious explaining to do to his brother and father for leaving Angel, Jon sprinted with Danny, his adrenaline carrying both of them. Sudden streaks of light shone around him, and angels positioned themselves between Jon and the incoming hoard of demons.

"That way," an angel pointed to one of the three openings before Jon. "That way to safety. Go!"

Tears streaming down his cheeks, he knew he was leaving his sister in the hands of evil, but he pressed on. Danny needed help. He'd sacrificed himself to get the others out.

Running into the bright sunshine, he was met by Jesse, who took Danny. Stumbling up the hillside, Jon and Jesse made their way to the first lookout.

As soon as they were clear, they heard Jacob's explosions. Turning in the direction of the explosion, Jon watched as portions of the cave entrance landed on a demon, crushing it, sealing the entrance of the cave. Relieved to see it burst into flames, hoping nothing else would be able to follow, Jon ran after the others.

When they hit the first lookout point, they joined the others and headed for Mark, Amarina, and Jacob at full sprint. As they left certain points, Jacob set off his bombs, making it extremely difficult for someone to follow them.

Making it to the Jeeps twice as fast as when they headed in, Jesse flipped Danny in the back of one, with Danny's head on Charlie's lap. "Are they following?" Jesse asked, out of breath.

"Don't know, but you're covered in blood!" Delaney said, stunned. "Is that all yours?"

"No, it's his," he gestured toward Danny, as Jon sank to the ground, holding his stomach, nausea taking over at the amount of emotion flying around, on top of having to deal with his own emotions.

"I had to leave her," Jon said, tears streaming down his face as him body trembled. "I didn't have a choice!"

Mark knelt down in front of his son and grabbed his face. Making sure Jon could see him through his tears, he said, "Nico told us she made you leave her. It wasn't your fault."

"I know, but Mom –"

"Will understand. Come here," he said, and held Jon while he cried.

Jesse stood with his arms crossed, watching the scene before him, as Charlie brushed the hair out of his friend's face. "I'm here," Charlie whispered to Danny. "You're safe now, my friend."

"Hurts," Danny groaned, holding his mid-section.

Jesse wasn't sure how Danny was still alive, but he was grateful Jon didn't leave him. There was no telling what they would have done with his body. His thoughts were now flooded with what they would do to Angel and the other one left behind.

"It is okay, my friend. You have served the Lord well. *'His Lord said to him, Well done thou good and faithful servant: thou hast been faithful over a few things, I will make thee ruler over many things: enter thou into the joy of the Lord.'"* Charlie said, quoting Matthew 25:21. "Your fight is over, my friend. You have been a good and faithful servant of the Lord. Go now into the joy of the Lord," he said, and closed Danny's eyes as Danny took his last breath.

"Oh, God," Jesse said, dropping to his knees. "Why?" he shouted, looking to the Heavens, beside himself.

Katia hugged her sister, while Sasha went over to Jesse to console him. "You are safe, little one," Katia whispered to Liliya. Then her attention suddenly turned toward Sergei, and her eyes narrowed. Whipping out the knife on her side, she released Liliya, and stormed over to where Derek was talking to those rescued. Slamming her arm against his throat, she backed Sergei into the Jeep, pinning him to the hood of the Jeep. Tightening the grip on the knife she had in her hand, fire flashed through her eyes as she growled at him in Russian.

"What's going on?" Nico asked Josh.

"She's threatened to kill him. She said he hurt innocents, and now people died," Josh said, as he ran over to Katia. He pulled the arm with the knife off Sergei's throat, but couldn't quite get her to let go.

Val ran over, resting his hand on Katia's back. Everyone froze, engrossed in the scene, as he said, "Katia, this isn't our way. If you kill him, then you are no better than those in the caves."

"He got A.N.G.E.L. Danny killed! He could still get Angel killed!" she snapped, not taking her eyes off Sergei. "Because of him, Liliya and Angel could have been sliced like

A.N.G.E.L. Danny! I will *not* let him kill anymore! I will *not* let him sell daughters anymore!"

"We need to let the authorities take care of him. He *will* face justice," Val said, still not taking his hand off Katia. While he spoke, he prayed for the Spirit of peace to pass from him into her. "He has been through a lot. He now knows what it feels like to be a prisoner. I don't think he will do it anymore. And, when he gets back to Russia, he will *not* be a free man. Elena will testify and get him sent to Siberia. In the meantime, the Russian authorities are tracking down the other girls by using his computer. When they find those girls, they will also testify against him."

Turning back to Sergei, she got in his face again and shouted at him in Russian, making sure Sergei heard every word.

"Uh, do we *want* to know?" Joe asked, raising an eyebrow.

Delaney translated, "She said, 'I know who you are! I saw what you did! I saw it with my own eyes! I have been waiting for this moment to tell you that you are a filthy wretched soul who is not worthy! What you did to my sister, and to those other girls, is not human! I never want to see or hear from you again!' Pretty sure she means it," Delaney added.

Sergei pleaded with her for a moment before Josh translated, "He said she would never hear from him again. He promised. Then he begged her to let him go."

Katia stared at him for a moment before she responded, and Delaney translated, "Katia asked if he learned his lesson."

Sergei answered, with his hands in the air. "He said he has," Josh explained. "And then he asked her to let him go. How about it, Katia? Wanna send him back to Russia…with love from the A.N.G.E.L.s?"

An evil smile crossed over Katia's face as she looked over her shoulder at Josh. "He will find out what they do to his type in prison."

"That's right," Josh agreed, still holding her arm with the knife still in it.

Standing, Katia pulled her arm back from Josh. In Russian, she told Sergei to not bother trying to run away, that she would watch his every step until he was taken into custody.

Once Katia gave up the fight, Derek went over to Jesse, who was still on the ground next to the Jeep with Danny and Charlie in it. "Danny is with Jesus now. He now only knows peace, the peace of a warrior who fought a good fight," Derek reminded Jesse.

"I don't want to paint his name." Jesse shook his head, agony churning within him as he held his stomach and shook his head, beside himself. "Doing memorial services for our A.N.G.E.L.s is bad enough, but having to paint their memory onto the boulder as well, is –"

"A privilege," Derek cut him off. "You have the honor of creating a permanent memory of them, so they will *never* be forgotten. Their work will live on in the lives of not only those they saved, but those who worked with them. John 15:13 reminds us, *'Greater love has no one than this: to lay down one's life for his friends.'* Danny knew what he was doing when he ordered them to leave. He knew he wouldn't make it out, but he wanted to make sure the rest of you did. Jon went back for him, and got him out of there so he could go in the arms of friends and family. Remember, the body is a shell. His soul is with the Lord. He is now with the Colonel, Jack, and Keith. He's with Victoria and Shawn. He is with the others who have gone before us. The best part is that he is with Jesus, helping to prepare the way for the rest of us, who will also someday go to join them. The archangel called us all for a purpose. We have a divine legacy we have sworn to protect. To that end, we know the consequences of this legacy. We don't fight against flesh and blood. As an A.N.G.E.L, we know our lives will potentially be cut short."

Jesse nodded. Looking toward where Charlie was still stroking the hair of his best friend, whispering prayers to the Lord. Jesse's heart broke once again. Shaking his head, he admitted, "I don't know how much more of this I can take."

"You are strong," Derek encouraged, taking him by the shoulders. "You have been trained for this purpose. We still have to get Angel and the other one out. She *needs* you to be strong. While they take the others back, we'll hang back, preparing for another shot at it. We're going to need a foolproof plan in order to pull this off…and we'll need God to do it. Angel is counting on us. She knew when she told them to get the others that we wouldn't stop until we got her too."

"Okay," Jesse said, wiping his face from the tears. Slowly standing, he said, "Okay, what do you need us to do?"

"Focus," Derek said. "I need to go help those rescued. I *need* you to focus."

"Got it."

"Go get cleaned up as well," Derek mentioned. Jesse just nodded in response.

"He fought a good fight," Charlie said in the silence. As everyone turned their attention to him, Jon and Mark got off the ground as well, with Mark keeping his arm around his son. "He finished the race that was set before him," Charlie said. "God will honor this. Safe travels, my friend."

Chapter 17
God is the Strength of My Heart

After dropping Amarina off where she requested, Jon, Jerrod, and Nico drove three of the Jeeps back to Alice Springs. They had Danny's body, Charlie, Katia, Liliya, Sergei, and the two others rescued from the caves.

Charlie accompanied Danny's body to the morgue. Afterward, he would take Danny's ashes to the Haven for a memorial service, and then let his ashes join the Colonel's around the boulder with the A.N.G.E.L.'s names painted on it who had since passed. In the meantime, Katia and Liliya would go with Charlie, so he could take them back to the Haven as well. Katia wanted to stay and help, but Liliya needed her more.

Sergei was taken into custody, waiting in jail until the day of his extradition. St. Petersburg police were anxious to get their hands on him after what they'd found in the basement and on his computer. His future looked pretty bleak, much to Katia's delight. She knew it wasn't good to have those feelings, so that was one thing she would work on with Casey at the Haven.

*　*　*

"Oh, dear Lord!" Casey said into the phone, color drained from her face, as she talked in the living room at the Haven in Nevada. "Are Charlie and the others okay?"

"Yes. We're sending Charlie your direction, along with Katia and Liliya," Nico explained. "All three need the Spirit to touch their hearts. I don't think it's sunk in for Charlie yet, Liliya's been held captive, and Katia just about killed Sergei on sight. You got your work cut out for you over there. I'm thinking of checking with Kit to see if she wouldn't mind coming over to help you guys."

"That would be great! If she can't, it's nothing we can't handle. If she can, that would be a huge help. How is Mark? How are Jon and Jesse? I can't imagine what they must be feeling for having to leave Angel. I'm sick just thinking about it. I pray every spare moment for her safety."

"I'm sure. As her mum, I would expect no less. She is a brave warrior for Christ, though," Nico reminded her. "She yelled at me, and wouldn't let me release her until the others were released. I'm really sorry we weren't able to get back to her. We left another as well. The other two we rescued said he is a pastor."

"Wow. What are they doing?" Casey said, shaking her head as flashbacks of what Jackie had done to her shot through her mind. "I pray she doesn't have to face what I did at their hands."

"She's strong, Casey. You and Mark did a phenomenal job raising her for the Lord. Without that foundation, I doubt she would have survived this long."

"While I appreciate it, it doesn't really help," Casey pointed out. "Until she's out of there, I'll be worried sick. The twins have constantly been in prayer as well. We even stop homeschooling sometimes when they feel the Spirit leading them to pray. I'll never discourage that."

"Don't. That'll be their strength," Nico said.

"I know," she said, glancing at the girls, who were doing their homework at the table in the kitchen, while she spoke on the phone in the living room. "I only wish I could tell them their sister's okay, and that they're all on the way home. When I tell them I have to go to the airport to get Charlie, Katia, and Liliya, there are going to be some major questions. I also have to tell the other three before I even begin to attempt to explain it to Allie and Callie."

"I don't envy you. Next time I talk to you, I pray I have better news. Again, I'm sorry for the loss of Danny Hawk."

"I felt it. I just didn't know who it was," Casey admitted. "I pray the Lord protects the rest of you, so we don't have to process any more loss. Keep an eye on Jon. I'm sure this is bringing up memories of the Colonel."

"Will do. I need to call Kit before we take off for Tanami again. I'll have her call you if she's going to be coming your way, so you can pick her up at the airport too. The group from here takes off around one today, and should land in a little over twenty-seven hours from then," he said, looking at his watch. He then shook his head at his silliness, knowing there was no way for her to see his watch.

"What time is it there now?" Casey asked.

"Around eleven in the morning. We told the authorities an animal attacked him. With Danny's injuries, there is no reason to doubt the story. They started the cremation a couple of hours ago, so they should be almost done. Once his remains are in the urn, they should be on their way to the airport. They're not going to seal it, so they can be spread around the boulder there at the Haven."

"I should expect A.N.G.E.L.s to start coming in then?" Casey asked.

"I would. They tend to know. Hopefully we can be there before the service."

"We'll hold off until you guys *are* here," Casey insisted. "This is going to be hard enough to process. Those with you will need closure."

"I agree. Thanks, Casey!"

"God be with you all, and keep you safe."

"You all as well," he said and hung up.

"Well," Casey said, phone still in her hand, "not sure how to tell them *this* one."

"What's wrong, Mommy?" Allie asked. "You look sad."

"Just trying to hold it together," Casey admitted, walking into the kitchen.

"Do we need to pray?" Callie asked.

"We do, but I need to talk to the others first...mainly Rachel. Why don't you two pray however the Spirit leads you, while I go talk to Rachel. She will probably need some of your hugs when I'm done talking with her."

"What happened?" Callie asked.

"She lost someone close to her, and I have to tell her."

"Mommy," Allie asked, "who is Danny?"

"Where do you know that name?" Casey asked, confused.

"God told me."

"Oh!" Casey said, stunned. "Not sure why that surprises me, but it does. Anyway, that's Daddy, Derek, and Charlie's friend."

"Why is he with God?" Callie asked. "Wasn't he with Daddy?"

Wide-eyed, Casey's heart raced. "What do you mean?"

"God told us that Danny's with Him, and that Rachel will be sad," Allie explained. "When you told us it was Rachel's friend, we knew."

"When did you know this?"

"Around ten-thirty last night," Callie said. "We both woke from the dream, and I looked at the clock."

"That was when he died," Casey admitted after doing some quick math. "Looks like you guys have your first spiritual gift."

"Dreams?" Callie asked. "How is *that* a gift?"

"That is one way the Lord speaks to us. It's a gift, because He can show you things through your dreams. You two are also strangely connected," Casey observed. "You finish each other's sentences a lot, and now you share a dream."

"Cool!" Allie giggled, as Callie smiled proudly.

"Now," Casey stood, "I need to go speak with Rachel. Please go ahead and pray, and then keep doing your homework. We'll head into Math as soon as I finish talking to Cori and Kai in the cyber cave as well," she said, referring to the basement portion that was sectioned off for support. They'd nicknamed it the cyber cave initially as a joke, but it stuck.

"Knock, knock," Casey said, poking her head into Rachel's room as she lightly knocked. "Got a minute?"

"Got nothing but," Rachel said, holding her ribs. "I'm obviously not gonna sleep with this pain."

"I'll give you more in a bit," Casey said, looking at her watch. "You still have an hour."

"Great," Rachel sighed. Then she got a good look at Casey. "What happened?" she asked, heart racing as she struggled to sit up.

"How do you know something happened?"

"The look on your face. You may be able to hide it from some, but you won't from me. Are Josh and my dad okay? Is the team okay? What about Angel and Liliya?"

"I just got off the phone with Nico."

"Not Mark?" Rachel asked, confused.

"Mark was with the others still in the Tanami Desert," Casey explained.

"Where did my dad call you from? Why didn't he talk to me when he called?"

"Well, he called from Alice Springs, because they brought part of the team back, along with two they rescued."

"Wait. What? Why? What happened? They wouldn't come out and leave the others there if everything went okay. Why did Dad leave the others and go to Alice without them? What's going on?"

"Calm down," Casey said, sitting on the side of the bed. When Casey took her hand, Rachel looked from her hand to Casey nervously. Casey knew she would have to tread carefully for this one. "Lord help me," she whispered, looking to Heaven.

"What is it? Please talk to me, Casey?" Rachel asked, holding her breath.

Psalm 34:18 came to Casey's mind, so she quoted it, "'*The Lord is close to the broken hearted and saves those who are crushed in spirit.*'"

"No." Rachel shook her head in understanding. "Who was it?"

"I'm afraid Danny…" As soon as Casey said his name, Rachel felt like a knife slashed through her gut. Grabbing her stomach, she felt as if she would throw up at the loss of one of her mentors. Casey continued, "…is no longer with us. Charlie's bringing him home, along with Katia and Liliya. They'll be here tomorrow afternoon. I'm so sorry, Rachel."

"He-he was one of the ones who trained us," Rachel said in shock. No tears, no thoughts or feelings. Complete shock. "Does Mum know?"

"Your dad was calling her next. He wanted to give me a head's up before the other three got on the plane, and he knew it would be a long conversation with Kit."

"How did it happen?" she asked, looking back up to Casey.

"Nico said they were trying to get the six out they found in the caves. Angel and Liliya were with them. They were able to get everyone but Angel and one other man."

"*They still have Angel*?" Rachel asked, wide-eyed, heart racing as she tried to process. "How did this happen?"

"Angel insisted that they free the others before her. And, you know Angel." Casey sighed, shaking her head. "Once she gets something in her mind, that's it."

"Right." Rachel nodded, still trying to focus as her world spun around her.

"Well, when they were almost done freeing those they first went to, and went to get Angel and the other guy, a demon caught them. Danny insisted that they get the others out, that he would hold them back. The demon got him. Jon ran back for him so they wouldn't have the satisfaction of having his body, and carried him out. A group headed back to Alice Springs, but left part of the team behind to keep an eye on the situation. If the other side moved Angel, they wanted to know about it. In the meantime, a portion of them got those rescued to safety. Charlie took Danny to the morgue, for Danny to be cremated and brought back here. Then they got plane tickets for Katia, Liliya, and Charlie to come here. The remaining should be heading back to the others in the desert soon. Hopefully the others will already have a plan formed so they can get the last two out quickly."

"Was anyone else hurt?"

"Not that I know of."

"I don't know how to process this," Rachel admitted.

"Just give it time and a lot of prayer. When Katia and Liliya get here, I will need to do some heart work with them. You and Charlie can work together through this. It's a lot for both of you, and you may both be able to carry each other through."

"*'He heals the broken hearted and binds up their wounds,'*" Rachel said, quoting Psalm 147:3.

"Exactly," Casey said giving her a hug. "*'Blessed are those who mourn, for they shall be comforted,'*" she quoted Matthew 5:4.

As a tear crawled down her cheek, Rachel added, "And, He gives us each other for such a time as this."

Just then, Casey's phone rang.

"Go ahead," Rachel said. "With the team out, it's best not to wait."

"Well, it's from Australia, so," she said, and answered the phone on speaker, "Hello?"

"G'day, Casey! It's Kit."

"Mum?" Rachel said, as her heart skipped a beat. "Mum, is that you?"

"Yes, love. How are you feeling?"

"Pain."

"I understand. Pete's making a couple bags of herbs and spices together for you, so when I come –"

"You're coming?" Rachel asked, excited. "Are you really coming here?"

"Yes. I heard that I may be needed. Willow and Caleb have a good handle on the station. So, if there's room, Casey?"

"Definitely!" Casey said, relieved. "Between homeschooling the twins, the support crew setting up the cyber cave, and now what all went on in Australia…I could honestly use the help. We're also about to get invaded here shortly by A.N.G.E.L.s coming in for Danny's celebration of life service. When we lost the Colonel, we didn't have to tell anyone, they just showed up. It's as if there's some sort of radar instilled in all of us to know when one is taken to the Lord."

"Completely understand," Kit said. "Okay, I have a two-hour flight to Brisbane, where I'll catch a flight to Reno. I should be there in about a day and a half. I'll email you my itinerary."

"Thank you, Kit," Casey said, relieved.

"Would you mind if I talked to Mum?" Rachel asked Casey.

"Of course. Since it's the phone number Mark and Nico have, if it tries to beep through, please answer it."

"Sure. Thank you," Rachel said, grateful.

"Thank you, Casey," Kit said.

"No, thank *you* for coming," Casey said.

"It's a multipurpose trip," Kit admitted. She still had a hint of her southern accent, but it intermixed with her Australian accent she garnered since living in Australia for over twenty years. "I get to see my kids, and see y'all. I can also be there to help you when you get invaded, and I'll be there for Danny's memorial service."

"Either way, I appreciate it," Casey said, and left the room.

"Mum," she heard Rachel say, as she closed the door. After that she was out of earshot.

"Thank you for the help, Father," Casey said to the Lord before heading down to the cyber cave to talk with Kai and Cori.

*   *   *

After they got everyone where they needed to be in Alice Springs, and stocked up on supplies as well as what Jacob had asked for, Nico, Jerrod, and Jon headed the eighteen hours back to the others, who were tucked away safely with the other Jeep, deep in the Tanami Desert.

*   *   *

"How are you doing?" Sasha asked, sitting next to Jesse, who was propped on a log next to their fire, watching the sun say its last good-bye for the evening.

"Honestly?" Jesse asked.

"Always."

"Not good." Jesse shook his head. "My sister's still there amongst the evil. There's no telling what they'll do to her…or *are doing* to her right now."

"She is strong. I met her before she was taken," Sasha pointed out. "She is a good woman. God is strong with her."

"That's true," he said, looking toward where he knew Angel to be.

"What if they move her before we get there?" Sasha asked.

"They won't. Jacob sealed them in. They're actually sealed in with angels of God. There's no telling what's going on in there right now."

Sasha couldn't help the chuckle that escaped him. "Cannot imagine that is good for them, yeah?"

"Yeah," Jesse said, finally cracking a smile.

"You *do* smile," Sasha said, impressed. "I was wondering."

"Just worried about Angel," Jesse admitted.

"You tell Katia not to worry. Why are you allowed?" Sasha asked.

With a smile once again, Jesse said, "You two have an amazing way of cracking us up…in a good way of course."

"Good. That is not a bad thing."

"Thank you for staying and helping us."

"This is my team now too. Wild horsies could not keep me away."

"Think that's wild horses couldn't drag me away," Jesse corrected with a chuckle.

Sasha shrugged. "Same thing, yes?"

"Close enough, my friend. Close enough," he said, patting Sasha's back.

Meanwhile, Delaney made her way over to Joe, who was sitting on the hood of the Jeep, watching the moon rise as the sun finally set. "You look deep in thought. What's going on in there?" she asked, leaning on the hood of the Jeep next to Joe.

"You sure you want to know?"

"I wouldn't have asked if I didn't wanna know," she pointed out.

"God's creation amazes me time after time," Joe said. "In the midst of all of this chaos, God is consistently keeping the world spinning. While we think it should stop due to the pressing matters around us, He reminds us that He's got it all under control."

After a moment, Delaney observed, "I love the way you look at things. I've watched you. You're laid back, but serious when you need to be. You always seem to find God in the most desperate situations. When we were waiting for the others, hearing those bombs go off, you stayed focused on prayer, never ceasing. When we saw Jesse carrying Danny, I could see that your heart broke, but you headed straight for those who were rescued. I could tell that you wanted to go to the others, but you did what you knew to be right. You went to the ones who needed you most, complete strangers, even though you wanted to go to your friends."

"It's what God would want me to do," Joe said with a shrug. "He doesn't want us to always do what we want to do. He wants us to do what's right. It's better when those two things are in line. However, if there's doubt, do what He wants, and you'll always be in the right."

"Galatians 6:9 tells us, *'Let us not lose heart in doing good, for in due time we will reap if we do not grow weary.'* Staying focused on the good is exactly what He wants."

"Yep. *'My flesh and my heart may fail, but God is the strength of my heart and my portion forever.'* He is where my strength is, so that's what I stay focused on," Joe said, quoting Psalm 73:26. "That way when I can't think straight, that verse is never far from my thoughts, and I can stay focused on Him until I can think straight again."

"I just pray Angel remembers that verse," Delaney said, as a shooting star shot across the night sky. "If I had one wish, it would be that the rest of us get through this safely."

"From your lips to God's ears," Joe said, still staring at the moon.

A short distance from camp, Jacob and Josh were perched on a rock, keeping lookout. "Why did Danny have to die?" Jacob asked.

"That's a question for God," Josh said. "Danny's been around since before I was even thought of. While he was my mentor growing up, he was helping people, doing things for the Lord for pretty much forever. He was actually in charge of those who helped rescue my mum. Our lives were connected long before any of us kids were born."

"Really?"

"Yep. Mark and Casey were captured. Danny's team saved them. Mark was the one who helped my mum later, when she was in trouble in the States. If he wasn't there, I don't know who would have been," he pointed out. "Then it came back around full circle when he, Charlie, and Ethan trained me, my brother, and my sisters, passing down what they learned to the next generation. It all works together in God's Kingdom."

"That's cool! I didn't know that." Then a thought struck Jacob. "That's pretty heavy when you think about it. Are you okay?"

"No. Not really," Josh admitted. "I'll have time to mourn when the time is right. At this moment, though, I need to guard everyone here until the others return. Then afterward, we need to get Angel and the other one out before I can even *think* of mourning."

"That's the idea," Derek said, as he and Mark walked up to the pair. "While we're waiting, we need to work on a plan. We're now four short with Charlie, Katia, and Danny going to the Haven, and Amarina back with her people."

"No, I am not," Amarina said, climbing onto a rock next to Josh and Jacob.

Jacob jumped. "Where'd you come from?"

"I came from home," she said adjusting in her seat to a more comfortable position. "I check with elders. They say I can help again."

"Amarina, we can't ask you to help. It's way too dangerous," Mark said, shaking his head. "We've already lost Danny, and possibly Angel. We don't want to lose you too. You're too valuable."

"I talk to the elders. They say it is my path. They knew you were coming. They knew you would need me," Amarina insisted.

"I know they have their ways, but did you tell them we lost one of the A.N.G.E.L.s?" Josh asked. "Do they understand what they're sending you in to?"

"Yes," she said firmly. "It is my choice. I see them. I feel them. I *know* what they are. I have known for a long time. They are evil. I will *not* leave innocent people in there. I want to help get them out…even if it may cost me my life. If I was in there, I would want others to not leave me. I will help."

"We could use as much help as we can get," Mark said, kicking the idea around in his head. "*If* we let you stay to help, you are not to go any closer than you did before. I *do not* want you going in. I don't want to lose you. We could use your help with backup, though."

"Agreed!" she grinned. "I help! Let's plan! Need t' get those bloke's sister outta there!"

*   *   *

Nico drove around Jerrod and Josh's Jeep and spun around to the side. Both Jeeps slammed on their breaks, and swerved to avoid hitting Nico's Jeep. "What in blazes are you doing?" Jerrod snapped, getting out of his Jeep, closely followed by Jon from his.

"We need to take a break. We've been awake and driving for more than twenty-four hours. Those energy drinks won't keep us alert enough to get in and out safely. We're not doing Angel any favors by going in beyond exhausted," Nico explained.

"All right. Pull off to the side of the road," Jerrod grumbled. "A little warning next time would be appreciated, though. Having said that, we *should* take a break. You're right. We'll do something stupid if we're exhausted. The others are okay where they are."

After they pulled over, Jon made a fire, while Nico and Jerrod got MREs and water. After they were settled and eating, Jon asked, "Jerrod, want to share some of that?"

"I hate your gift," Jerrod griped.

"What's going on, mate?" Nico asked.

"Nothing." He shook his head, feeling sick to his stomach.

"Spill it," Jon snapped. "The anger, anxiety, fear, and hopelessness are overwhelming. You need to get rid of it or it'll swallow you whole."

"I'll deal with it when we get back to the Haven," Jerrod said.

"You need to deal now if you're gonna focus. If it's strong enough to send Jon into a fit, than it's pretty big," Nico pointed out.

"It's just…" he shook his head. "I thought I had wrestled those demons and won. Seeing Danny die in Charlie's arms brought so many…" He shook his head again.

"Any in particular?" Nico pressed. "I've had a few of those type of demons to battle myself."

"It was one of those middle of the night wake-ups for a casualty evacuation. When we got there, it was a hot zone, when it wasn't supposed to be. We couldn't leave them there, though. The Marines did their best to fight them off while the choppers laid cover fire and we landed. They loaded up the two injured. I was in one chopper with this young kid." Jerrod shook his head. "They kept getting younger and younger every year. Kids. They were just kids outta high school. They were still a glint in their momma's eyes, and now here they were, lying in front of me fighting for their lives, miles away from their families. Their lives were in my hands." He looked at his hands, seeing the faint bloodstains. "He fought with everything in him. He said he felt like he was on fire…which he practically was. He was near an IED when it blew. He had severe burns over eighty percent of his body, including his face. His entire left arm was missing, and he had shrapnel in his thigh. It cut the femoral artery. He didn't have a chance."

"Wow," Jon said, feeling everything Jerrod did as he told the story. Feeling like he was going to throw up from the emotions Jerrod was emitting, he asked, "How did you manage?"

Shaking his head, Jerrod went on, "At first he was somewhat cognizant enough to know I was the one helping him. After a few minutes, he was shouting for his mom." He shook his head, wiping away the tears that escaped. "It broke my heart. I knew I wasn't supposed to have a heart out there. I knew I should shut it off in the field. But I couldn't." As tears welled in Jerrod's eyes, he refused to let any more fall. "That kid fought for as long as he could. He finally said, '*Mom, I need to go. Jesus is standing there waiting for me. I'll save you a seat next to me at the great banquet when Jesus comes back.*' With that, he was gone." He shook his head again. "There was nothing I could do."

"I'm not going to comfort you with some malarkey," Nico said. "There's no way to comfort someone after they watch people die right in front of them. Watching Danny die in Charlie's arms today, I didn't know what to wish for. He was a great man, and a terrific friend. I didn't want to watch him suffer, but I also didn't want him to leave. I know we'll see each other again in the ever after, but it doesn't make it hurt any less."

"It doesn't," Jerrod agreed.

"While we generally only have to process the actual life that passed, those of us who served in various parts of EMS, military, or civil service, fully understand what it's like to watch someone die right in front of you," Nico pointed out.

"Exactly. You really don't know *what* to wish for," Jerrod said. "And, serving in the capacity we served, you only wish to not see them in pain. Most of the time, you don't know what they were like before. You don't know their families. Being in the military, you *may* know their spouse or kids, but not always. Yet, there they are, right in front of you, with their lives in your hands. You do your best, but in this case, your best isn't good enough."

"We've had this conversation before, mate," Nico reminded him. "You're not God. He is the only One who truly has their lives in His hands. You can do your best, and your best *is always* good enough, but you're not the One who determines who actually lives or dies."

"I understand that here," Jerrod said, pointing to his head. Then he pointed to his heart and said, "It's here I have a hard time processing that. My heart wants to save them all. It's not for my glory. It's more so I don't have contact the CO who would have to write the memorial letters to their families. I know what it's like to see that black SUV drive down the road. You see them coming, praying they're not coming to your house, but you know. When I lost my dad, I saw them coming. He was deployed. We knew as soon as we saw the vehicle pull over in front of the house. Mom grabbed my shoulders and told me to stand strong, but…" Shaking his head again, he did his best to process. "It's not something you get over."

"You never get over a loss," Nico pointed out. "You only learn to live with the hole left in your heart by that person. Look, mate, we all have suffered loss. Danny was a great mate. It *is* a struggle between the head and the heart. It's one you'll have to battle more than most in what you did."

"Definitely," Jerrod agreed.

"*'Therefore, they are before the throne of God and serve Him day and night in His Temple; and He who sits on the throne will shelter them with His presence. Never again will they hunger; never again will they thirst. The sun will not beat down on them, nor any scorching heat. For the Lamb at the center of the throne will be their Shepherd; He will lead them to the springs of living water. And God will wipe away every tear from their eye,'"* Jon said, quoting Revelation 7:15-17.

"That's one of my true sources of comfort," Jerrod said. "My only fear is that the nightmares will ramp back up, just when I was starting to get them under control."

"You have nightmares because your mind doesn't think you're finished with something. Unfortunately for combat veterans and warriors, there is no 'finishing it.' It's as done as it will get. There's no going back and fixing what your mind can't comprehend," Nico pointed out. "This is something you and God will have to wrestle with through. You may be able to find solace, but only in Him."

"How?" Jerrod asked, desperation in his voice. "Where can I find an escape from hell on earth? Seeing their faces. Remembering their deaths." He shook his head. "I remember every one of them."

"Honestly, couldn't tell ya, mate. It's different for every person. You have to find your own path. I would love to help, but I think this is something you and God are gonna have to figure out together."

Jerrod sighed, shaking his head.

"Wish I could ease your pain," Jon said. "While I can feel it, I wish this gift had the benefit of being able to take it away if I could."

"That would be nice, but I wouldn't want to wish this on you. It's a lot to process as an older person," Jerrod said. "You're too young to carry this kind of weight."

"I've already lost the Colonel, and now Danny," Jon pointed out.

"Wait until it's someone even closer, younger, and you don't have any control over it. Not that I want this to happen, but imagine if it were Angel. You know in your head that she would be with Jesus, but you can't call her when you're excited. You can't be frustrated with her when she doesn't listen. You can't fight with her when she tries to take matters into her own hands. And, you can't be proud of her when she has you rescue everyone else over her, even when you're standing in front of her with the keys to her freedom," Jerrod said, glancing at Nico, who cringed. "I know, man. I get it."

"She demanded I let the others out first," Nico explained. "She said they needed her, and wouldn't kill her. When I went to try to release her again, she yelled at me."

Chuckling, Jon said, "That's our Angel."

"Now imagine she's suddenly gone," Jerrod said, and Jon immediately sobered up. "*That* is the feeling I'm fighting. The kids I worked on were even younger than Angel. Some were only a year or two older than Liliya."

"I don't know how you did it, mate." Nico shook his head. "In the FBI, when we lost someone they weren't anywhere near as young."

"Some are young and stupid, but their hearts are in the right place. They wanted to serve their country, and they did. They made the ultimate sacrifice," Jerrod said. "These military boys and girls are fighting for our way of life. Then there are some who disrespect them, and I completely lose my cool. There's no calming me down when I reach that level."

"I can see that," Jon said, "…or rather, I can feel it."

"I just pray I can get the sleep I need in order to do what we need to do to get Angel and that other guy out," Jerrod said.

"We'll sleep in shifts," Nico decided. "I want us to each have at *least* four to six hours sleep."

"Agreed," Jon said. "We need at least that to focus."

"Glad you agree, because *you* have the first lookout," Nico said to Jon. "I'll take second. I want Jerrod to have as close to solid sleep as possible."

"Why?" Jerrod argued.

"Because you're our only medic. We need you sharp."

"Fair enough," he agreed.

"Good. Sun's down, so get to it. Jon, keep your weapon in your hand and set your watch for three hours. When it goes off, wake me up," Nico instructed. "We'll sleep in the vehicles we drove in, so we won't wake the person in the other vehicle."

"Sounds good," Jerrod said, as they cleaned up their dinner.

Settling in, Jon set his watch, before humming praise songs to stay awake. He never once stopped looking in every direction.

* * *

"You are a pretty, young thing," Calliope said, tossing a portion of her long brown hair back over her shoulder, as she stood in front of Angel. Leaning down, her yellow eyes looked deep into Angel's green eyes. "If we were in a different time and place, I am sure we could be a good team."

"We could *never* be on the same team," Angel shot. "You have an evil within you that anyone with an inkling of humanity can see from a mile away."

"Oh," she countered, "I have led many a man into battle or their ruin. Men are putty in my hands…much like Korax and Cassius."

"The A.N.G.E.L.s see you for what you *truly* are."

"Nice try, young one," Calliope said, condescendence evident in her tone. "You see, it is in a man's nature to fall to beauty."

"Our guys see below the surface."

"We will see, young one. We will see," she said, tipping Angel's chin up so she would look at her. "In the meantime, Cassius would like to have a gentle conversation with you in a little while."

"Oh, I don't think so," Angel said, shaking her head. "I *highly* doubt *anything* he does is gentle."

Calliope cackled as she left the cave.

"Angel, why do you antagonize them?" the young man left behind with her snapped. "All it does is make them angrier."

"Doesn't bother me either way." Angel shrugged. "Think about it, Allen. If they kill me, I'll be in Heaven with Jesus in a heartbeat. There's nothing they can do to me to hurt my soul."

"Why don't you just do what they want? Maybe then they'll leave you alone. The more you antagonize them, the more they'll want to torture you."

"Because they want me to disavow the Trinity. They want me to deny that Jesus Christ is my Lord and Savior…and I won't do it."

"That name is *not* to be spoken in this place!" Korax snarled, his yellow eyes boring into Angel as he walked into the cavern in his human form, followed by four demons and Calliope.

"Jesus Christ *is* my Lord *and* my Savior!" Angel snapped. "There is absolutely *nothing* you can say or do to change that! I am covered by His blood. I am a daughter of the Lord God Almighty! The Holy Spirit is my guide. Jesus is my Savior. And, God is my Father."

"Ha!" Korax laughed. "You say this, but where are They? You got left behind, much like *this* strapping young man," he said, turning his attention to Allen. "Now, young man, are *you* one of Jesus's followers?"

"Yes," Allen said, determined to stand as strong as Angel.

"*I am here, young Angel,*" an angel whispered to Angel. Angel could feel its presence behind her, and drew strength from it, knowing God did not leave her alone.

"Is that the best you have?" Calliope skirted past Korax to stand in front of Allen. Lifting his chin so he would look into her eyes, she hummed a soft song, down near his ear for a moment. Then she asked Allen, "Whom do you follow?"

"Jesus Christ," he said resolutely.

"Deny Jesus, denounce the Trinity, and join us," she said, and hummed a mesmerizing, ethereal song down next to his ear.

After a moment, shaking his head to clear it, he stammered, "N-n-no, I –"

"Jesus is *nothing*. He was just some man. The world should have told you that a long time ago," Calliope said. "You are nothing but a speck in time, barely a blemish. The Spirit is *supposed* to be your guide. Where was He when you were taken? Hmm? As for God? Again, *you* are here, and *He* is not. *I,* however, *am* here. I can give you *whatever* you want. You want power? *I* can give you power. You want success? *I* can give you success. You want fame? *I* can give you fame. All the world will know of Allen Wilson. All you have to do, in turn, is deny the Trinity. You can do this. Just say the Trinity means nothing to you. Just disavow the Trinity, and you and I can be together…forever."

"Jesus is –"

"Stop! They mean *everything*!" Angel yelled.

Shaking his head to clear it, Allen looked to Angel. "You're right, Angel. You're right. They *are* everything!"

Glaring at Angel, as Angel smirked at her, Calliope then turned back to Allen and said, "No, she is *not* right. If she were, then neither of you would be here right now. You would have been rescued with the others. But, look around," she gestured around the cavern, "they left you behind…all alone. They only left this bloodstain of your fellow A.N.G.E.L. who was killed trying to rescue you. They're not coming back. They won't risk losing another of those precious A.N.G.E.L.s." Breathing lightly on his neck, Calliope said, "I'm here for you, though. You *want* me to be here. Don't you?" As her perfume enveloped Allen's senses, she said in a soothing voice, "You are *nothing* to the Spirit, Jesus, *or* God. You are *everything* to me."

"You are *everything* to the Trinity!" Angel yelled, getting angry. She would do her best to help fight with Allen. "The Father gave His only Son for you! Jesus gave His life for you! The Spirit guides and directs you every day! He sends His angels to be with you! You are *not* alone, Allen! Listen for that still, small voice! *He is here*!"

"Shut her up!" Calliope snarled. When she glared at Angel, her eyes flashed red before changing back to yellow.

"*Fight for him,*" the angel whispered behind Angel. "*There is an angel with him as well. He is trying, but Calliope is winning. She is strong.*"

"You cannot shut me up!" Angel said sternly. "I will stand up for Jesus every chance I get. Fight them, Allen! You are strong! Fight them with everything you have! An angel is trying to help you. You only need to listen to hear the encouragement."

Korax nodded to one of the demons, who backhanded Angel, scratching her face as its talons raked across her cheek. "If you want more, keep it up!" Korax growled.

"I will not only *never* deny that Jesus Christ is the Son of the Living God. I will defend Them with every fiber of my being. The Trinity is everything. Without them, we are nothing," Angel shouted. "Oh," she said, calming her tone, as a smile crossed her face, "and, guess *what*?"

"Good, Angel! Stay strong!" the angel encouraged Angel. *"'But resist him, firm in your faith, knowing that the same experiences of suffering are being accomplished by your brethren who are in the world.'"* the angel quoted First Peter 5:9 to Angel.

Nodding, Angel stood her ground.

"What?" the demon hissed, getting in Angel's face.

"In the end…we win," Angel said with a satisfied smile. "By the way, I've read the Revelations. Do you want to know *your* fate?"

A low growl started deep within the demon, as the other three hissed. The demon in front of her flexed its talons in front of her face. They reflected in the firelight of the caverns, truly showing their razor sharpness. Running a talon lightly down her cheek, the demon asked, "May I, sssir? Jussst a little?"

"Have at her, only do not kill her," Korax warned.

"She will only wishhh she was dead, but shhhe will not die," it promised, as Allen watched in wide-eyed horror.

"'My flesh and my heart may fail, but God is the strength of my heart and my portion forever,'" the angel said, quoting Psalm 73:26, knowing what the demon was about to do to Angel.

Starting with her wrists, it ran its talons from her wrists, down to her shoulders. A shrill scream was heard from Angel as the demon left small slices up and down her arms, making sure not to press too hard. Twisting and turning in agony as she continued to scream, Angel pleaded in her head for God to make it stop. She wasn't sure how much more she could take.

Its talons felt like tiny razor blades everywhere they touched, cutting just deep enough to draw blood, but avoiding hitting any vital veins or arteries. When the demon finished, it asked, "Will you disavow Them now, pitiful Angel?"

"*'Blessed is the one who perseveres under trial because, having stood the test, that person will receive the crown of life that the Lord has promised to those who love Him,'*" the angel whispered James 1:2 to Angel.

Taking a moment to get her pain under control, Angel hardened her face as tears of pain still streaked down her cheeks. Narrowing her eyes, she said, "Never! I will *never* deny the Trinity! Jesus is my Lord and –"

Since she was still wearing the dress she wore to the club so long ago, the demon cut her off when it used its talons to put small slices in her legs. Screaming in agony, she squirmed in an attempt to get away from it, but it continued to slice into her legs, scratching and clawing. The demon took immense delight in its torture of her.

"Now?" the demon asked, getting into her face when he finished.

With more determination than ever, she screamed through her tears and gritted teeth, "*Never!*"

"The sweat will drip into thessse cutsss long after I leave thisss area. Once it doesss, thessse will sssting worssse than any hornet *ever* could. You will have pain beyond imagination. And, I can do worssse. Thisss was jussst a tasssste, little Angel," it hissed, slightly spitting in Angel's face, "of what you can faccce if you do *not* disavow Them. Go ahead, disavow the Trinity. *I dare you!*"

"Never!" Angel growled, and then twisted in pain as the sweat continued its descent down her body, dripping into the cuts. Feeling as if salt were being rubbed into the cuts, she squirmed and groaned in an attempt to escape…to no avail.

"Can I get the whip?" another demon pleaded. "*I* can get her to shut up!"

"Not yet." Korax shook his head. "Cassius may want to toy with her a bit himself. I want him to have a good time so he does not take it out on us."

"Awww." A demon in front of Angel crossed its arms as it pouted.

As Angel went to open her mouth again, the demon reached up and roughly covered her mouth so she couldn't talk. Holding tightly, the demon put continuous pressure on her jaw while she struggled to get free.

Angel was in so many different levels of pain, it was excruciating. Behind her, she heard the angel whisper Deuteronomy 31:6. "*'Be strong and courageous. Do not be afraid or terrified because of them, for the Lord your God goes with you; He will never leave you nor forsake you.'*" Angel took solace in those words, and held onto them as she fought through the pain and agony of the slices all over her body. While she writhed in pain, the demon held onto her mouth to keep her quiet.

Knowing holding her mouth wouldn't keep Angel quiet for long, the demon went behind her and wrapped its other arm around her torso, making sure to hold tightly, putting pressure on four different ribs. Once it had her secured, the demon nodded to Calliope to continue.

"Now, where were we?" Calliope asked, nuzzling up to Allen. "I believe we were having a conversation. What is it you like about me?"

"Your beauty. And, that…that perfume," Allen said, taking in a deep inhale of the perfume. Suddenly realizing what she was doing, he snapped out of it. "No! I can't do this! You are evil! Get away from me!"

"Awww, Allen," Calliope pouted as she lay her head on his shoulder. Running her fingers gently up and down his arms, she said, "That was *such* a mean thing to say to me. I thought you wanted to be with me. I thought you wanted to enjoy a fresh-made feast just for you. That's not to mention the ice-cold water, and anything else you want to drink. I'll bet it will feel good against your parched lips," she said, rubbing her finger on his lips. "You only need to ask, Allen, and it is yours."

"I can't do it." He shook his head, steadying his resolve. "I *won't* do it!"

"Oh, I'll bet you can. It's easy. You only need to ask."

"No," Allen said firmly. "No, I won't."

Snuggling closer to Allen, Calliope began to hum again. For a few moments, she let Allen soak in the perfume and sound of her voice singing the ethereal tune that penetrated deep inside him. Once she felt him start to melt, she made another attempt. "Allen, I want to be with you every day. Do you not want that?"

"That would be…" Allen's resolve was diminishing. "That would be nice," he said, taking in another inhale of her perfume. "But, I don't know if I can."

"Sure you can."

"I don't know if I…" Allen's voice trailed, as he began to fall under her spell.

"No!" Angel shouted under the demon's hand, seeing him falter. The demon tightened its grip on her. Groaning in pain, she did the only thing she could at that moment, and that was to pray for him.

Lightly breathing near his ear, Calliope said in a low voice, "I want to as well, Allen, but the only way I can do that is if you denounce the Trinity, and follow Cassius for the rest of your life." Running her fingers down his chest to his waist, she asked, "Who is Jesus to you?"

"Who?" He asked, mesmerized by Calliope's overpowering presence.

"Jesus. Who is he to you? The Spirit? Or God? You *know* you are *nothing* to Them, right?"

"I-I don't –"

Screaming and squirming under the demon's grip, Angel did her best to make noise to bring Allen's attention to her. The more she wiggled, though, the stronger and tighter the demon held. Feeling a rib crack under the pressure, she screamed. Seeing stars, she desperately tried to get a breath of air. Fighting the black cloud that threatened to take over, she knew she had to fight for Allen. The pain, however, was horrific!

"They're *nothing*," Calliope continued. "Just denounce Them, deny Them, and follow Cassius. Only then can we be together. You want that, don't you?"

He shook his head only a moment before he nodded, giving in to his desires, "Yes. Yes, I want to be with you."

"Then all you have to do is deny Jesus, and follow Cassius. Fourteen little words stand between us being together forever," she said, lightly running her fingers on his chest. "Jesus Christ is *not* my Lord and Savior, and I choose to follow Cassius. That's all you have to say. They're just words. Just say them, and I can set you free. We can go together and enjoy that feast. You can eat and drink to your heart's content. And *then,* we can discuss what power and prestige you want for your life. You can have it all. All you have to do is say that Jesus is not your Lord and Savior, and that you choose to follow Cassius. You say that, and we can leave here *together*...right now."

"I don't want to," he groaned.

"Why not? They're just words."

"You don't understand."

"Help me to understand, Allen. Help me to understand why saying fourteen little words causes such distress?"

"Th-that's an...an unforgivable sin," Allen stammered.

"I do not think there is such a thing. They are fourteen words that do not mean anything, yet they are the only things standing between us. Can you not do that...for *me*? I am willing to give you *everything*. Just curse the Spirit. Disavow God. Say that Jesus is not your Lord and Savior, and that you choose to follow Cassius," she said, cuddling closer to him.

Wrapping her arms around him, she coaxed, "Just repeat after me…Jesus is not my Lord or Savior."

"Jesus is…He is…" Looking to Angel, he saw her shake her head. "No. In Matthew 12:31 and 32, and in-in Mark," he took a deep breath, doing his best to concentrate as Calliope snuggled even closer. "It's in Mark 3:28-30. I cannot blaspheme against the Holy Spirit."

"Look," Calliope said, inches from his face as she lightly ran her fingers down his arms, "the Spirit is nothing. Jesus was just a man. As for God? Well, I promise He won't do anything. All you have to do is renounce them all."

Seeing the pain Angel was in, he didn't think he would survive, so he relented, "Jesus is not my Lord or Savior."

"And finish with…I choose to follow Cassius for the rest of my life. Come on, Allen, you are almost done. Once you finish, I get to be with you forever!"

"He is not my Lord and Savior, and I-I choose to follow," he stopped for a moment. Seeing the tears in Angel's eyes as she shook her head, he knew he had already broken the Spirit's heart, so he finished with, "And, I choose to follow Cassius for the rest of my life."

"Wonderful!" Calliope said, delighted. "So, you would like to join us then?"

"I…" He shook his head, distraught.

"You get to be with me. I want you to come wholeheartedly."

"I…" He looked to Angel, who dropped her head as she shook it. Knowing he had already done it, he sighed before he said, "Yes. I want to be with you forever."

Humming near his ear again for a moment to calm him, Calliope then looked him right in the eyes as she said, "You are mine. Right?"

When he shook his head, Calliope started her song again. As the song took over his will, her perfume enveloped his senses. After a few moments, she mesmerized Allen.

"Now, are you mine?" she asked again.

He slowly nodded. Lost in her eyes, he whispered, "Yes. I am yours."

Angel narrowed her eyes at Calliope. *What had she done to him?*

"Yes, my dear," Calliope said with a pleased smile.

The other demons danced in joy, while the demon who had held Angel let go, and immediately freed Allen. "Do you want to eat?" the demon hissed.

"Yes, please," Allen said, as his wrists were released. While he rubbed his wrists, he looked toward Angel.

"*'The fear of man bringeth a snare: but whoso putteth his trust in the Lord shall be safe,'*" Angel said, quoting Proverbs 29:25.

Looking to Angel, his shook his head. Turning her face from him, Angel still prayed for his soul.

"Come with me," the demon said to Allen, leading him out of the cavern by one hand, as Calliope had the other.

On the way out, Calliope stopped in front of Angel. "He was a *pastor*. You may *think* your A.N.G.E.L.s are strong, but they are *still men*."

"They will see you for what you *really* are," Angel challenged.

"We'll see," she said, and laughed as she left the cavern, Allen in hand, following her like a lost puppy.

When there was only Korax and another demon left, Korax went over to Angel. Almost nose-to-nose, he transformed from his human form to the demon form with reddish-black scales. "You will have more chancesss to deny Him," Korax hissed. "I'm *sssure* we can come up with a way to convinccce you."

"That will *never* happen! You might as well kill me," Angel snapped.

"Ohhh, I'm sssure I can find sssomething more creative," Korax said with an evil smile. "Perhapsss I will get one of your other preciousss A.N.G.E.L.sss in here. If you do not deny Him, I will torture him in front of you until you do."

"As an A.N.G.E.L., we know the risks. I promise you that *none* of our men will *ever* deny Jesus Christ."

Slapping her where the demon already cut her, the slap drew more blood on her cheek, as well as in her mouth. Korax then got in her face, and warned, "Do *not* sssay that name!"

"Which one? Jesus Christ, or The Lord God Almighty?" she asked, and then spit blood out of her mouth.

"Neither one!" Korax snarled, his face contorted in anger. With each of Angel's words that followed, Korax became more enraged.

"He is the Alpha and Omega…the First and the Last. He is the Great I Am. He is King of all. He is the Lord God. He is known as the Lion of Judah and the Lamb of God. Oh! And, there's Adonai, Yaweh, El Shaddai, Jehovah, and the Shepherd. I can keep going with the many various names of my King as you want. Jesus Christ is my Lord and Savior, and I will *never* deny Him! I am covered by the blood of Jesus Christ and there is *nothing* you can *ever* do to change that!"

Anger started as a low growl, before Korax let out a yell and punched Angel in the rib Korax knew was broken. Delighted to see her scream in pain, Korax laughed. "That isss enough for now. Feed her and then leave her to her own thoughtsss, alone, isssolated from everything shhhe has *ever* known," Korax said. As the demon form went to leave the cavern, with each step, Korax transformed back into the human form.

Once Korax was out of hearing distance, the demon with Angel attempted to feed her. It said, "You *will* bend, or he *will* kill you."

Spitting out the food she was fed all over the demon, she snapped, "That will *never* happen."

Looking up at her, he punched her midsection before it snapped, "Fine then! Starve!"

Groaning in pain, she twisted to get a breath of air.

"Sssee how you like being in complete isssolation," it growled, and left her alone.

As soon as the demon was out of earshot, the angel who had been speaking with Angel the entire time walked in front of her. As he stood there, he was translucent, so he could disappear at a moment's notice if the demons returned.

Lifting Angel's chin so she would look at him, the angel whispered Joshua 1:9 to her, *" 'Have I not commanded you? Be strong and courageous. Do not be afraid; do not be discouraged, for the Lord your God will be with you wherever you go.'"*

As the angel rested his hand on Angel's cheek, Angel nodded in understanding. She looked toward Heaven. "Lord, I needed You today, and You sent someone for me. I am grateful for all that You are and all that You do for me, Your servant," she said, and groaned, twisting in pain. "Lord, I cry out to You, and I feel You near me. I will hold tight to all I know of You. I know I am never alone, despite what it may look like. Although I can't see You, I am reassured that You are here. I am trusting You with all of my heart, body, mind, and soul." Squirming in pain, she took a moment before she continued, "I know my pride got me into this mess. I'm sorry for that. I will follow You and Your instructions in whatever happens here. My soul is Yours. Please protect it, and hold me close to You. While he fought, Allen fell today. Lord, please give me Your strength! You are my source of strength. You are the strength of my heart. G-give me the endurance to," she stopped to catch her breath from the piercing agony she was in. "Give me the endurance to make it through this, or please bring me home to You. Please do not let me fall. I do not want to let You down. You *are* my Lord and Savior. Without You, I am nothing. I commit my soul and this situation to You. Your will, not mine."

Psalm 118:6 *"The Lord is with me; I will not be afraid. What can mere mortals do to me?"*

Epilogue
Hearts United

With the loss of Danny Hawk fresh in their minds, the team focuses on trying to get to Angel without losing anyone else. In the meantime, Angel is doing her best to fight Cassius, Calliope, and Korax in complete isolation, with only God's strength to pull her through. Already tortured, how much more can she endure?

In the meantime, Jerrod's battles with the ghosts of his past become overwhelming. Will he be able to see past them to find his future?

As the A.N.G.E.L.s converge for yet another memorial service, Jesse struggles with feelings of anger and resentment. Knowing Angel's choice triggered this loss; he fights within to reconcile his feelings.

With emotions at an all-time high, ricocheting all over the place, the team is more divided than ever. Will they be able to focus on God enough to center themselves and carry on their legacy? Will they continue to be divided or will they become **Hearts United.** (Book 3 of the **Divine Legacy Series**.)

Proverbs 4:20-23 *"My son, pay attention to what I say; turn your ear to my words. Do not let them out of your sight, keep them within your heart; for they are life to those who find them and health to one's whole body. Above all else, guard your heart, for everything you do flows from it."*

The books in the Divine Legacy Series –

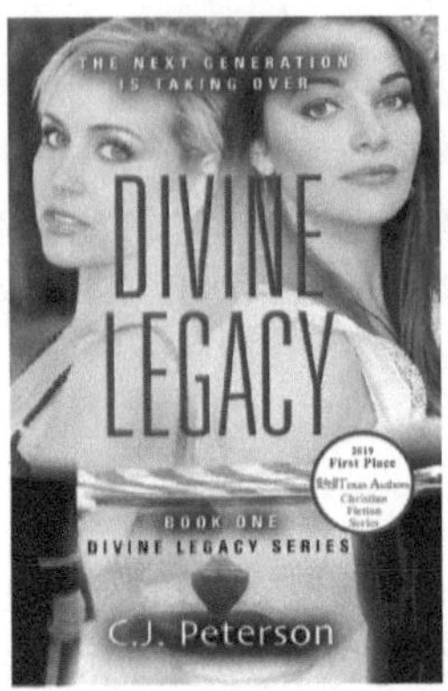
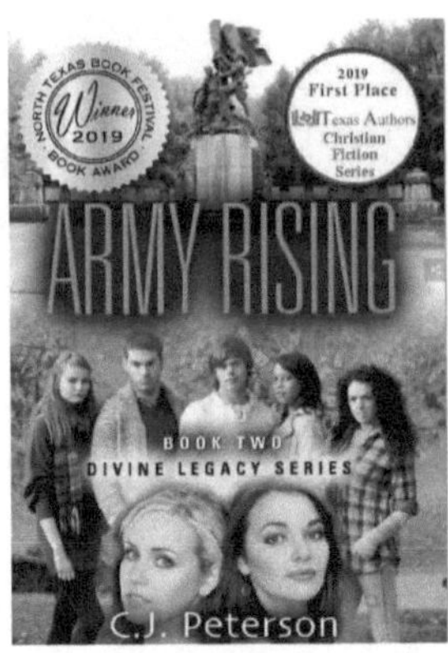

Connect with CJ – _CJPetersonWrites.com_

Meet the previous generation of A.N.G.E.L.s -

Grace Restored Series

Book 1

Book 2

Book 3

Book 4

Book 5

Katie MacKenna experienced one storm after another in her life. When Leukemia stole her mother from her and her father, Katie was only seven-years-old, and her father didn't know how to cope after such a catastrophic loss. His response was to shut down and become abusive. The overwhelming devastation which surrounded Katie throughout her journey in life forced her to shut down just to survive as well.

Trust is a difficult thing for many people, but for Katie it's virtually impossible. Every life has Seasons of Change. Will those seasons open Katie to new opportunities or will they forever isolate her in survival mode? Will she be able to overcome the storms that have surrounded her to answer a call for help?

Meet the previous generation of A.N.G.E.L.s -

The Holy Flame Trilogy.

Book 1

Book 2

Book 3

Summary

Courageous. Brave. Fearless. Valiant. These synonyms are often used to describe firefighters/paramedics, police officers, and military personnel. They face danger and lay their lives on the line when they leave for work. What are their struggles? Could that hinder their job proficiency? Who is taking care of those who are taking care of the citizens of this country?

Casey Carter is a 'newbie' to the firefighting family of Engine Company 15. Not only does she have to prove herself as a probationary firefighter, but she also has to battle misconceptions of females within her newly chosen profession. As situations begin to arise, can she count on the firefighter brotherhood to have her back? Will she be able to pass the tests placed before her, or are there aspects that she was not even aware existed?

Often in life there are two realms in play. There is the physical realm - what is right before you; the other is the spiritual realm - what is unseen. Each can directly affect you, whether you believe they exist or not. Can Casey keep them in balance when she is not exactly sure what she is fighting? Can a group of men help her see what cannot be readily seen, hear what cannot be readily heard, and be able to overcome what she never knew existed? Will they be able to show Casey her true Call To Duty?

9 781952 041150